ISLAND of the WINDS

ISLAND of the WINDS

A Historical Novel by

ATHENA G. DALLAS-DAMIS

EFSTATHIADIS GROUP S.A.
14, Valtetsiou Str.
106 80 Athens
Tel: (01) 5154650, 6450113
Fax: (01) 5154657
GREECE

ISBN 960 226 515 9

First published in the U.S. by
Caratzas Bros., N.Y. .... 1976, two printings
Signet/NAL, N.Y. .... 1978, five printings

Printed and bound in Greece, 1995, 1996, 2000

To my husband, George Damis,
who nurtured this book and me.

ABOUT THE AUTHOR

Author, journalist, translator **Athena Dallas-Damis** was born in Baltimore, Md. of immigrant parents who came from the Aegean island of Chios. She grew up in Weirton, W.va. where she began writing as a child, and moved on to a professional career in New York City until 1985 when she relocated to Greece.

Island of the Winds is her first novel, published originally in the U.S. in 1976 and 1978. Its sequel, **Windswept**, followed in 1981. The last of the trilogy, **Follow the Wind**, is currently in progress.

Ms. Dallas-Damis has been writing newspaper columns since 1957; her *Greek Diary* currently appears in the Greek American Weekly of New York. Her English translations include five works by Nikos Kazantzakis -his last novel, *The Fratricides; Three Plays: Melissa, Kouros, Christopher Columbus;* and a collaboration with Kimon Friar, *Buddha*, published in New York; as well as numerous volumes on Chios history and art, published in Greece.

Among her citations are the Nikos Kazantzakis Award for Literature (N.J.); The Haleem Rasheed Award for Achievement in Letters (N.Y.); The Greek World Award (N.Y.); the Julia Iatridis Translation Award (Athens) and the key to the City of Savannah, Ga.

The author now resides in Chios with her husband, George Damis.

AUTHOR'S NOTES

Although ISLAND OF THE WINDS is a work of fiction, the events in this book are true, and the historical figures appear in their original settings. Only the main characters are fictitious, woven from people of today and yesterday.

My research into the period of the early 1800's began in Thymiana, the village of my parents, and continued throughout the island. During the Summer and Fall of 1972 and 1973, I lived with the villagers of Chios, most of them descendants of the survivors of the great massacre of 1822. I walked the same streets as my ancestors, visited the monasteries where signs of that infamous period still exist.I pored over numerous old volumes in the Koraes Library, spent many hours in the museum, talked with scholars and peasants alike. Through all this I uncovered a wealth of information, an insight into the lives of these people. It was a moving, unforgettable experience, this return to my roots, this retracing of events of long ago. And those days on the still somewhat primitive island, a strange thing happened. Chios seemed to stir, to come fiercely alive . . . as though to help me see what she once was . . . to guide me in writing this story. Old ghosts seemed to have awakened—friendly ghosts—who followed me in my wanderings, in my studies. ISLAND OF THE WINDS is a memorial to those ghosts . . . and to my parents James Gianakas and Angeliki Andreadis.

I would like to express my deep gratitude to those who inspired and guided me along the way—to Christos Stratakis, Esq., Panos Makrias, Paul Grivas and my son, Peter Dallas of New York; to Kostas Haviaras and Professor Stephanos Kavadas of Chios. Special thanks are due George Xenophon Andreadis, the then-president of Thymiana, whose Knowledge of the history, social and sociological aspects of Chios proved invaluable to my research and writing, and to my husband, George Damis, without whose encouragement this book would not have been written.

CHIOS
Kardamylla
Anavatos
Vrondados
Nea Moni
Chora
Kontari
Thymiana
Kalimasia
St. Menas
OTTOMAN EMPIRE
ca. 1800
THRACE
Constantinople
THASOS
SAMOTHRACE
Pera
Dardanelles
ASIA
MINOR
LIMNOS
Zagora
GREECE
LESBOS
SKYROS
ROUMELI
CHIOS
Smyrna
St. Laura
Tsesme
(Athens)
MOREA
ANDROS
IKARIA
Tripolitsa
HYDRA
TINOS
SAMOS
SPETSAI
NAXOS
AEGEAN SEA
SANTORINI
N
CRETE

PROLOGUE

I walk the narrow streets of Chios, the barren hills once covered with green, past fields of olives, orchards of almonds and lemons, down to the shore of Megas Limionas. The sun nears its peak, gleaming on white pebbles, sparkling over a sea of diamonds in the horizon. Crystal clear water . . . cool, calm water . . . what stories it whispers when the moon is high and the waves pull into shore . . . stories only the islanders understand.

Peace dwells in strange places. It clothes the past, hiding ferocity and pain with tenderness. While softly, the winds bring the sound of voices long stilled . . . of swords clashing, blood flowing, women weeping . . . and of Jason, whispering, pleading. Oh, my beloved son, how often I relive those bittersweet days, those short-lived years of love and hate, of passion and bloodshed. My gentle, beloved Jason . . . your youth was a blossoming almond tree cut down before its prime. Perhaps it was how you wished it . . . your chance for immortality.

. . . Helena Andreadis
Thymiana, Chios
August 15, 1825

PART I

I

Helena walked quickly up the winding path, pushing aside the thick brush and low-hanging pines. A thousand tiny hammers pounded inside her head, and her heart was heavy, choked from the burden she had carried all these years. Jason had had that dream again. Just before dawn he awoke sobbing . . . that same nightmare that disrupted his sleep too frequently the last few months. Helena knew the time had come to talk to her son, to reveal the secret she had guarded so carefully.

She reached the top of the hill and stood beside the chapel of the Prophet Elias. From here she could see the entire valley—the villages of Kalimasia to the south, Thymiana in the center, and Kambos to the north. The blue waters of the Aegean stretched out in breathtaking beauty. To the west the hills were rolling mounds of green bordered by taller ones of granite and pine. Her heart skipped a moment as she drank in the sight for the thousandth time. She could never get enough of it or get used to this wonder. But then she looked to the east, across the straits, and her smile froze. Tears came to her eyes as she fixed her gaze on the white hills that stretched on the other side of the waters. Somewhere out there in that land of minarets and harems and barbarians, was a part of her . . . a part of her son Jason. It was a wound that lay open, festering, never healing.

A human moan broke the stillness. Helena had unthinkingly approached the cholera pits to the south of the chapel . . . two large, deep holes looking down on the horrible fate that awaited incurable victims of the dread disease. Thrown inside in the ignorant hope of saving others from contamination, they were left to die. Why must all this be, she thought. Why can't people die simply, quietly, with dignity? She could not understand the ways of God, nor, for that matter, the ways of man. This disturbed her but she kept it to herself. For she knew that young Jason had the same doubts and misgivings, the same intensities and yearnings as his mother. And because he was young, they seemed more urgent, more dangerous. Jason, she thought, my gentle Jason . . . tomorrow he will be twenty-one . . . he must learn the truth.

She walked into the chapel, lit a candle, made the sign of the cross and, not being able to look into the piercing eyes of the Prophet who stared down at her from the iconostas, walked quickly outside. The sun rose higher . . . the winds blew stronger . . . the moans stopped. Poor devil, he must be out of his misery, she half-whispered. The wind was soothing. She sat down on a rock to spend a few moments alone with her thoughts.

It was August and the *meltemi** swept briskly through the valley, caressing the olive trees that glistened like silver in the light. Cypress trees, Nature's monuments to God, towered here and there among the pines, while man's monument, the church of Saint Efstratios, stood humbly to the side. Inside the walls, the town awakened. Children whimpered, a donkey brayed, and the roosters which had crowed sporadically a short while ago, were content in their places. The villagers rose to begin their daily tasks. They were hard, sun-burned people, these Chiotes, who had worked under the protective yokes of foreign conquerors so long they'd almost forgotten the meaning of freedom. First the Genoese, then the Turks . . . nearly 400 years now. And though they enjoyed special favors, that feeling still stirred within them, and a voice cried out: Some day . . . some day, the Greek banner will rise over the island of Chios, on all of Greece, and that vile crescent of the Ottomans will be gone forever.

The iron gate creaked open and the villagers stepped outside the fortress wall with their sheep and goats, heading for pasture. Some went to the quarries to cut the coveted Thymiana stone used in building throughout the island. Others set out to work in the orchards and fields that spread throughout Kambos. Here the nobility, wealthy Chiotes and Turkish overlords, lived in majestic estates deep within orange and lemon groves, among the olives and grapes.

**meltemi—the summer winds that blow northeasterly in the Mediterranean*

Helena gazed over all this splendor that August morning of 1820. And her thoughts went back . . . twenty-two years . . . was it centuries or moments?

* * *

She was eighteen. He was twenty-eight. Barely recovered from the death of her mother two years ago, she turned to this handsome sea captain who peddled romantic dreams to naive girls. The afternoon his ship docked at the harbor of Chios was one Helena thought she would always cherish. Tall, self-assured, experienced in the ways of life and love, Stratis conveyed his strong attraction to her the moment they were introduced. She noticed the spark in his eyes, the look of discovery on his face . . . and her heart went out to him. She had felt so lonely since her mother's death. They had shared everything—books, their garden, the intricate embroidery they spent hours perfecting. It seemed she had lost her best friend. And her father, in his grief, could offer little companionship. The world took on a new light as Helena felt the throes of first love.

Within three days Stratis sent a proposal of marriage to her father. By the end of the week he visited their home to ask formally for her hand. It was romantic to be swept away by this dashing Greek god, and she gloried in the feeling. There was a lightning courtship, and a hurried wedding in the chapel, for Stratis' ship was to sail. Helena was going with him . . . Stratis was anxious to show his bride to his widowed mother. And the girl was thrilled at her first sea voyage, at the thought of seeing the Greek mainland and Stratis' home. There were tearful farewells with promises to return soon. Stratis assured her father they would make their home with him. After all, Helena was an only child, the large house was empty, and the elderly widower was alone.

Helena was born late in her parents' life. Sheltered and loved, yet firmly disciplined, she had never been a demanding child. Her mother, a strong, intelligent woman, had instilled in her daughter a love of life and a strength to overcome its obstacles. She had seen to it that Helena learned to appreciate the finer things. For she was not the typical village woman, as she proved when it came to naming her daughter. Disliking Eleni, *which was her mother-in-law's name and according to custom must be given the son's first female child, she named her* Helena, *which was more dignified. It seemed tragic that she did not live to see Helena married.*

Helena's father watched his daughter go with apprehension. He had been reluctant to give his consent to the marriage. But Stratis was young, personable, with good references. And Helena was persuasive. When he saw the happiness on his daughter's face, he could not refuse. After all, the young captain seemed capable and sincere, was well spoken of by the few Chiotes who knew him, and he obviously loved Helena. The dowry seemed of little concern to him, although it was substantial. All this impressed the older man . . . he brushed his misgivings aside and gave his blessing.

Life on the Greek mainland was a nightmare. The village of Zagora was not like Chios which lived peacefully with the conqueror. There were no considerations here . . . no allowances. Helena was shocked at the humiliation these Greeks suffered. Considered inferiors, they were deprived of human liberties. Life, property were without security. Travel was strictly limited, taxes were exorbitant. Every possible method was used to break their spirit. Forbidden to ride horses, they either walked or went by mule. Upon meeting a Moslem rider, they were obliged to dismount and prostrate themselves before them. Red, Islam's national color, was not to be used in their dress or decoration. Studying their language was punishable by death. From time to time these unbearable conditions erupted in desperate revolts. On such occasions the most inhuman acts were perpetrated in reprisal by the Turkish overlords. The barbaric instinct inherited from their Steppe ancestors exploded into fiery, bloody violence.

Helena cringed at the stories she heard—one freedom fighter from Zagora was skinned alive by Janissaries. His carcass was tossed in the field, his skin stuffed with straw and strung up in the village square as example to others who considered further revolt. One rebel leader was impaled and left under a tree where townspeople could witness his slow, agonized death. Another Greek was carefully pounded with mallets, joint by joint, until every bone in his body was broken—an excruciating process that was begun at his outer extremities and worked inward. Helena had heard, while in Chios, of the frequent rape and abduction of women, the pillaging of homes on the mainland, but these other atrocities were beyond imagination. A hatred for the conqueror rooted itself within her and grew.

Helena could not wait to return to her home. But as the months passed, Stratis said nothing. She noticed a decided change in her husband. He became restless. He began to drink heavily, to stay away nights. She could not understand it. He had shown such love, such devotion when they were first married. When she questioned him about their plans, he avoided her eyes and casually announced he was not returning to sea or to Chios. His mother had convinced him it was better to remain in Zagora, and had offered her fields and her home as enticement.

Helena knew, from their first meeting, that her mother-in-law disliked her, and with the days, she watched the old woman's resentment grow to unreasonable lengths. Her son's love for this "wretched Chiote girl," as she called Helena when they were alone, was a weakness she was determined to cure. She could not forgive Stratis for denying her the selection of his wife and she would make Helena pay for this disappointment.

"Stratis should have married one of his own kind," she would tell the girl at every chance, "you don't know how to make him happy."

And when she was alone with him, she would goad her son, "Men don't fawn all over a woman, my boy. She's going to take your manhood away from you."

She encouraged him to drink, to stay out with his friends, to reign sternly in his household. Helena could not believe the weakness in her husband. Where was the strong, self-assured young man she had met in Chios? How could a mother do this? Helena could not understand the woman, and prayed to God Stratis would stand up to her. But his attitude only worsened. He listened to his mother's ideas on everything, particularly on how to run their lives. The old woman was clever, feeding her son advice while she fed him raki, *for at those moments he was most gullible. The more Stratis drank, the more he was a puppet in his mother's hands. And the more fault he found with his wife. He began to resent married life and the ties it held. Helena was stunned at the destruction this woman sowed. And so, within the prison of their house, Helena busied herself with daily chores and her intricate embroideries, always under the watchful eye of her mother-in-law, dreading each day, fearful of the nights Stratis made drunken love to her. In the mornings, when he was sober, remorse overcame him and he would cry and beg forgiveness. Helena pitied him then, but she had lost all respect. Soon her love was gone, too. Stratis could not seem to fight the demon inside him, the demon that was nurtured by his mother. And Helena was powerless to help. She sensed an evil in the woman the villagers had discovered long ago, for they avoided her at every opportunity. She often watched her mother-in-law lighting her oil candle and making the sign of the cross beside the icons. Helena cringed at the hypocrisy that lay hidden inside that black-clothed figure. She knew everyone in the village feared her, but only later heard the rumors that told of her wild youth in Smyrna, her turbulent marriage in Zagora, her familiarities with Turkish soldiers, and the unexpected death of her young husband. Many claimed she dabbled in witchcraft. Helena believed the woman was capable of anything. She found herself caught between two fears—Stratis and his mother on one side, the Turkish yoke on the other.*

When she learned she was pregnant, she was crushed. Now she had little hope of escaping. But somehow, she gathered courage. Roses thrive on dung, she told herself, remembering the phrase from some book of her mother's. She would have this child and no evil would ever touch it. Later she would find a way out.

It seemed a miracle when, nine months later, she held the two small bodies in her arms. She lay in her bed, spent, tired, glancing from one tiny head to the other . . . and her despair eased. The twins were dark and resembled her. She prayed they did not inherit their father's weakness.

At first Stratis showed pride in the boys. A flicker of ambition appeared, only to be squelched by his mother's constant reminder of how little the boys resembled him. Stratis tried to ignore his mother's remarks. He made honest attempts to take on his new responsibilities, and talked again about going back to sea. Helena prayed he would succeed. But the devil often overpowers the saints. Stratis' feeble efforts dissipated when his mother gave him a bagful of gold coins saved for such an emergency. She would keep her son with her at all costs. After all, he was her only child . . . and she had more than enough for all of them. Stratis was won over . . . and Helena felt more trapped than ever. Stratis returned to his old drinking habits . . . and to sleeping with every available woman in the area. He became vulgar and abusive. Soon Helena could not bear his touch.

The twins were a year old when he said to her, one morning, "I'm restless . . . I can't stand this place anymore. I want to go back to sea."

To her silence he added, "I'll take you and the children to Chios when I come back from my first trip."

She knew he was lying and she did not care if he

never returned. He left that night, taking Besma, a young Turkish prostitute, with him.

Two days later the old woman was dead. Her heart could not stand the shock. She had torn Stratis away from Helena only to lose him to a whore.

In her numbness, Helena was glad. She silently thanked God her mother-in-law's evil would never touch her sons.

* * *

The news spread quickly through Zagora. The Turks are coming . . . the Turks are coming for our children! It had been five years since the faithless ones had set foot on this rocky village in northern Greece. Five years since Greek children had been gathered to be sold as slaves, to be adopted by wealthy Turks, or, worst of all, to be trained as Janissaries. The town was in an uproar as women quickly rounded up their children, bolted their doors and turned to their icons to pray. Mothers wept, fathers paced the floor, families gathered together to discuss the one alternative to this disaster—gold. Those fortunate enough could buy their children's freedom. But who were these? In the entire village, only Simeon Petrilakos had the gold pieces to save his son. Heartrending, mournful cries filled the air. The August sun, hot, piercing, beat down mercilessly on the hapless people of Zagora that day in 1805.

The villagers knew about the abduction of male children throughout Greece. The boys would be taken to Constantinople to be scrutinized and selected for various duties. They would be bathed, dressed in fineries and brought before the Sultan for the final selection. Some would be trained to care for the fabulous gardens in the palace with their exotic flowers and plants. Some would be castrated for service as eunuchs in the harems. Others would be designated for the Sultan's personal service . . . to serve his raki, *his fruit, to help him bathe and dress, to sleep with him. The more fortunate grew up as playmates of the Sultan's children. And when the young Turks came of age and took their places as princes of the palace, they would grant titles to their Greek friends who had by now renounced their faith and taken on Islam.*

There were also those sold as slaves to the highest bidder—each with his own destiny, each falling into unknown hands.

Those on whom Fate smiled, the most favored Greeks of the Sultan, were made pashas and viziers and enjoyed lives of luxury and abundant wealth. And finally, there were the select few, the strong, healthy Greek boys who were destined for training in the Janissaries, the cruelest, most cold-blooded regiment of the Turkish army. Raised to hate Christianity, they would eventually be sent back to the Christian provinces to slaughter their countrymen. The indoctrination was so thorough, so successful, that the mere mention of the word giaour* *made these soldiers itch for the sword and for blood.*

The thought of all these disasters awaiting their children made the Greeks of Zagora shudder. In every home that contained a boy, terror lurked that fateful afternoon. Soon, any moment now, the call would

**giaour - Turkish usage for "infidel," Christian subject peoples*

come.

The village was still. It was two hours after noon and only the children were taking their naps.

Yiannis Petropoulos looked at his two sleeping boys and at his wife who sat by softly weeping. He motioned her to the next room.

"Maro," he said in a choked voice, "you know they won't take an only child."

Maro gasped. She knew what her husband meant and tremors wracked her body. Yiannis fought back the sobs that struggled to emerge, and embraced his wife crudely, affectionately, as best as his peasant upbringing allowed. They stood there together, softly weeping. Then they turned and went back to the sleeping children. Quickly, before he could change his mind, Yiannis placed his hands around the throat of his eldest, the heathy ten-year-old, and tightened his grip. The young body spurted in its bed, trying vainly to cry out. The boy's hands struggled frantically with his father's . . . his eyes rolled . . . but only for a moment. Then he lay limp under the sheet.

The youngest turned on his side, fast asleep. Maro lit the oil candle beside the icon of the Virgin Mary. Two bent, forlorn figures made the sign of the cross.

Throughout the village similar incidents were taking place. One father cut off his son's ear, another removed his boy's eye, another broke his child's leg . . . all in the knowledge that the Turks did not take crippled children.

The town crier brought the message to every narrow street and corner of the village. The people were ordered to gather in the Governor's courtyard, bringing all male children aged five to twelve. The Kadi, *the Turks' religious judge who ruled over the area, arrived with the list of names. He handed it to the Turkish ruler as the crowd began to appear. Six soldiers, followed by three Janissaries resplendent in silken uniforms, gathered at the designated area, ready to execute orders.*

Yusbasi Hassan, the leader of the group, stepped out into the terrace and motioned to them. He was tall, very dark, with sharp features . . . an ugly man with sensuous black eyes. He turned to the Kadi.

"How many male children are there?"

"Sixty." The Kadi *did not enjoy this task. Why must Allah, praise him, frown upon my particular jurisdiction, he wondered in dismay. These* giaours *cause no trouble . . . why couldn't it be some other village? But it was. Every village in the area was facing a similar doom.*

"Let's begin," Hassan growled, "I'll take twenty."

"You'll take twelve," the Kadi *replied curtly. And, seeing the frown on the other Turk's face, he added, "According to law, you're entitled to one out of five male children. You'll take twelve."*

Hassan was silent. The Kadi *was sly. He knew the extra children were to be sold privately . . . gold for Hassan's own pocket.*

"Curse him!" Hassan mumbled softly, and motioned to one of the Janissaries who walked up and stood at his side.

Helena had washed and dressed the twins. She was certain fate was with her that day. The Turks wanted the strongest, handsomest specimens. And her boys were thin, dark, hungry-looking. Thank God, today she was grateful for this. No, they would not take her children. They had all suffered enough.

The courtyard was filled with people. It seemed the whole town had gathered to witness the event. Children screamed. Women wept. Some fainted, others prayed. Some simply stood there, numb with grief. Even the Turkish families looked on solemnly . . . they, too, had children and felt the pain of the Greeks. It was a sad day for Zagora, one that would never be forgotten.

The Turkish soldiers who stood guard throughout the village watched Helena with lust as she walked slowly towards the courtyard, holding tightly to the twins walking on either side of her. She was a striking woman . . . tall, stately, with long, black hair that lay in a bun at the nape of her neck. Every man in the village longed, at one time or another, to possess her. For she was unpossessable, unreachable, a warm, lovely woman whose tears had turned her heart to stone.

The twins knew something was wrong. They watched their mother's face anxiously. Her dark eyes were deep, brooding, but tearless. Helena had stopped crying long ago . . . since Stratis left. Stratis, she thought bitterly, what a waste.

They reached the Governor's house and Helena caught sight of Costas' anxious face in the crowd. Her heart softened as it always did when he was near. Costas loved them as Stratis never had. He drew in his breath when he saw them now. Fear and concern clouded his eyes. His dark features made him stand out among the blondness of these northern Greeks. He, too, was a "foreigner" like Helena.

Costas was from Skiros, an island halfway between Zagora and Chios, in the Aegean Sea. He had arrived with his fishing boat shortly after Stratis left. Helena had asked him to take her back with him, hoping from there to find a way back to Chios. But Costas could not help her. No Greeks were allowed to leave the mainland . . . and the Turks watched Zagora closely. They were everywhere. Helena was torn with grief and frustration. Costas' heart went out to her. He admired this courageous woman who stood alone in the chaos with two small children to protect. And when the boys' small arms encircled his neck, Costas knew he wanted to stay. He fished in the waters below this mountain village and worked hard, managing to make as good a living as possible under the Turkish yoke. He was always close by . . . always there when Helena and the children needed him . . . yet careful to keep his place for the sake of her reputation. And the usually narrow-minded villagers, stirred by his unselfishness, opened their hearts to him. For they loved and respected Helena. They had been glad for her when the old woman was finally laid in the ground. In fact, it was then that they offered their friendship.

Helena wished Fate had been different, that she had married Costas instead of Stratis. Her boys adored him . . . he was the kind of father they should have. These past three years Helena realized he was the only man she could trust, though she also knew she would never go to a man again. Even if she wanted to, she was still Stratis' wife.

Helena took her place with the other parents just as Hassan turned to the crowd. His gaze fell on her and halted there. What a woman, he thought, all fire and beauty . . . a rare jewel. Yusbasi Hassan had an eye for women, and took great pleasure as well as care in selecting them for his harem. The thought of taking

Helena back to Constantinople was shattered by the somber look of the Kadi *who guessed what he was thinking.*

Hassan had no desire to tangle with this man of the law. Curse him a thousand times, he thought, he acts more like a giaour *than one of us. He turned to his task.*

"Andreopoulos! Antonopoulos! Botaropoulos!" The Turkish lieutenant went down the list in a forced voice. One by one, the parents came up the steps to the terrace, trembling. Yiannis brought forth his six-year-old.

"My oldest died last night, effendi,*" he muttered, "this one is all we have now. As you can see, he's very thin, and he's sickly."*

Hassan smiled cruelly and his bony face became uglier.

"Never you mind, giaour, *I'll take him anyway."*

Maro fainted. Yiannis Petropoulos stood there numb, stark terror rending him motionless. My God, he thought remembering the limp figure on the bed, oh my God!

Helena ran to the prostrate woman. Hassan watched her for a moment, then turned to the Kadi. *He pointed to the twins.*

"What's the name there?"

Helena turned pale. She stood up, walked hurriedly to her children and clutched them tightly. The Kadi *was silent. He looked first at her then at Hassan.*

"Delipetros," he finally answered. Then, as an afterthought, "Weak children . . . spend most of the winter in bed."

Hassan ignored the remark. They're worthless to us, he thought, but the woman . . . He ordered a

Janissary to bring them to him. Helena looked up at the tall, scrawny Turk, at his deep-set eyes and crooked nose. Her gaze was all hate, obstinacy and steel. Hassan was shaken momentarily. His look of desire turned to one of calculation. He smiled again.

"It's a shame to separate twins . . . I'll take them both."

Helena thought she was going to faint, but she managed to keep her composure. Fear flashed so quickly on her face that Hassan was not quite sure it had been there. He turned to the Kadi *and added in a condescending tone.*

"Wait! Mark down just one for now . . . " he pointed to Joseph, "that one. I'll decide about the other later."

He smiled slyly at Helena and his eyes squinted.

"My men and I will spend the night here. I have a matter to settle."

Helena guessed what he was thinking and felt all her strength leaving her. I'm tired, she thought, I'm so tired. How am I going fight this? Oh God, give me strength.

Hassan could not read her face. Strength rushed back to her. She bit her lip and with a stern, unbending look, handed Joseph to the Janissary. Her heart turned over inside. The boy began to cry and clutched his mother's dress. Jason, too, began to whimper, and reached out to Joseph. As the Janissary took the child away, he stretched out his hands towards his mother, then towards his twin.

"Mo . . . ther! . . . Ja . . . son . . . ! " They were heartrending cries.

"You see?" Hassan did not let a thing escape him. "They should not be separated."

Then, seeing Helena catch her breath, he added, "But we'll decide tomorrow."

"Go light a candle to your saint, woman," he laughed, nodding towards the hilltop where the chapel of the Prophet Elias nested, "maybe he'll help you."

He came closer and his tone was gruff.

"Tonight, when the moon is high," he half-whispered.

His eyes squinted . . . he licked his lips. His body was so close to hers she could feel the dagger inside his sash. She drew back quickly, looked into his eyes for a brief moment, and tossed her head up angrily. Then she turned without a word and walked away with Jason.

I'll be there, dog, she said to herself, I'll be there. She'd lost one son, she was not going to lose the other.

The moon was at its peak as Helena hurried up the path to the chapel. She was trembling with anxiety . . . how could she beg Hassan to spare her sons, knowing what it involved? She despised the Turks. But Joseph is in their hands now, she thought with agony, and soon Jason, too.

She paused for breath when she reached the top of the hill, and walked slowly into the tiny chapel. Lighting a candle before the icon of the Prophet, she gazed upon the elongated face, the holy countenance, the piercing eyes.

"Oh, Prophet Elias," she whispered, "help me!" Then with a choked voice she added, "Forgive me. . ."

She felt a penetrating gaze and turned quickly around. Hassan stood menacingly in the doorway staring at her with those cruel eyes. The smell of raki *reached her nostrils and she placed her hand on the candle-stand to steady herself. Mustering all her courage, she walked out to him.*

They were both silent and she could hear his heavy breathing. If I plead with him—she weakened for a moment—he will give me back Joseph. She knew she had the power to save both her children and a battle raged within her. In moments her maternal instinct cowered before her honor.

She walked to the edge of the courtyard with Hassan following silently behind. There she paused and looked down at the valley. It was peaceful . . . as though there were no Turks, no slavery, no snatching of children. The sky was dotted with myriads of stars. Beauty and despair, she thought, what a strange combination.

Hassan's silence confused her. She turned to him, her heart pounding. In the light of the moon he saw her eyes flashing. He smiled . . . perhaps it would not be too difficult after all. He might let her keep the child . . . both children . . . he would take her to Constantinople. Thoughts whirled in his mind . . . her naked body against his, smooth and olive-skinned . . . he knew she would fight like a tigress but he would have her.

He pulled her to him and was surprised that she made no move to resist. Not used to being gentle with women, he clumsily caressed her face, fumbled as he undid the bun on her neck. Her black hair spilled over her shoulders. The thought of pleasing a woman was new to him . . . and irrational. He was angry at this sudden weakness. Helena, too, was unprepared for his gentleness . . . Turks were not known for this virtue. She let him kiss her neck and hesitantly put her arms around him. The smell of rose-water blended with the raki *on his breath. Hassan could not believe his good fortune. Her hand caressed the back of his head. She pulled away for a moment, looked into his eyes and kissed him harshly on the lips. Allah be praised, he thought as stars whirled above him, I am in paradise with this rare flower. He reeled with ecstasy.*

The blood gushed from his stomach before he realized what had happened. He fell at Helena's feet, a half-smile frozen on his face. She stood there stunned, her eyes fixed on the dagger imbedded in Hassan's body. She stared at the jewels on the handle, at the blood oozing around it and began to tremble. She could not believe what she had done. Nausea swept over her.

"God, what am I going to do?" she whispered in her terror. But she quickly rallied . . . she knew she must get away.

The thought of what might happen to the villagers if Hassan were found made her stop. There would surely be reprisals. She could not do this to people who had been so good to her. She must dispose of the body . . . she looked around frantically. She would throw it over the cliff . . . but they would find him in the morning. Her eyes stopped at the chapel shadowed in the moon's light. Greek churches did not have cellars, but many of the chapels had trapdoors leading to underground rooms where secret meetings were held. The Turks would never find the body there. With great effort she dragged it across the way. Poor Hassan, she thought in her desperation, you are in your paradise now. A tinge of remorse surfaced only to disappear at the thought of the alternative to this killing. One death, three lives . . . the scales were tipped. God would understand.

She was in the doorway of the chapel when she heard a sound in the bushes. Her heart stopped as the pines parted and Costas stepped forward. She breathed a sigh of relief . . . Costas was always there when she needed him. She should have gone to him first, but she was not quite sure of her plans when she set out to meet Hassan. The thought of what might have happened with the Turk made her shudder. Death was the only alternative to such degradation. And Fate had chosen Hassan's death over Helena's.

The escape was something she would not forget as long as she lived. Like hunted animals they leaped over bushes and ravines . . . she and Costas and little Jason. As they ran in the darkness Helena turned quickly for one last look at the village. Joseph, Joseph, she sobbed. She was giving up one son to save the other. But better one than none at all. Perhaps one day, somehow, she would see Joseph again. A chill ran through her as she remembered what he could become in the hands of the Turks. Costas hurried her on . . . they must get a headstart before morning when they would surely be missed. Two days and two nights they travelled, stopping only long enough to rest and steal fruit for their hunger. They finally reached the harbor where the ship was secretly docked, waiting for people like them, desperate escapees from the cruelty of the Turks. Costas had the gold that was necessary to carry them off.

There was no moon . . . it was the right time to sail. Quickly the three refugees hurried to the rowboat. Costas helped them in, paid the man at the oars and turned to Helena.

"I'm going to leave you now." His voice was sad. His eyes looked at her with pain and tenderness.

Helena could not speak . . . she was stunned by his sudden decision.

"I must go back . . . for Joseph's sake . . . for yours."

Hope sprang in her heart. Perhaps Costas could save her other son, too. She smiled sadly at him, gratefully. This man had given them so much and asked nothing in return, ever. Now he was risking his life to save them. He put his arms around her and held her for a moment. They were friendly arms, loving . . . she did not withdraw.

"How can I . . . how can we . . . repay you, Costas?"

"By taking care of yourself, and of Jason."

He bent and picked up the child. Jason began to whimper.

"Don't cry, Jason. I'm going to find Joseph and bring him to you. You take care of your mother now, alright? I promise I won't be long."

The boy hugged him tightly, refusing to let go when his mother tried to take him. As though he knew he would not see Costas again . . . as though he wanted to show him he loved him.

Costas jumped out of the rowboat and pushed it out to sea. He did not hear the two Turks creeping behind him. The man in the boat let out a cry and rowed as fast as he could. Costas turned as one of the Turks lifted his sword. He rammed into the soldier, knocking him to the ground as the other leaped upon him. Helena watched the shadows, terrified, as the sprawling Turk rose and aimed his pistol at the rowboat. She froze . . . they would not make it to Chios after all . . . they would all be killed. But she did not know the strength of Costas, the fury with which he protected those he loved. She saw him now, kicking the pistol from the Turk's hand as the other held his arms and twisted him away. The refugees neared the ship as Costas' body fell to the ground. The Turks stood over him a moment, wiped their swords and walked away. This would be the last Greek escaping from this spot.

Helena could not see in the darkness, but a shudder went through her . . . she knew Costas was dead. A sob escaped her and she held onto her child desperately.

"Hurry!" It was the voice of the captain on board. "Hurry ma'am, we're sailing."

The man in the rowboat knew it was useless to return to shore. They would have to find another quay for future runs. As he quickly followed Helena up the rope ladder, he thought of the fate that awaited others who would be arriving at this spot tonight. The ship set sail . . . they leaned on the railing and looked towards shore for the last time. Costas' body lay on the sand waiting for the tide to carry it to its grave.

How much pain can a heart stand, she wondered? How much loss can a person feel? There was nothing for her, no one. Then she looked down at Jason, at his small hands tugging her skirts. She had this child, she must be strong for him.

"Mother, where are we going?"

She picked Jason up and kissed him.

"We're going home, son . . . to Chios . . . to your grandfather . . . "

She was never to forget the agony of that night. To know she had left a part of her behind, in the hands of barbarians, was almost unbearable. The pain became more intense as she thought of Costas, the only man who had befriended them and loved them.

"God," she whispered in the darkness, "why do you keep punishing me like this? What have I done?"

The North Star shone brightly . . . the thousands of smaller stars gazed down upon them as though nothing mattered. As though it were any ordinary night, any ordinary ship cutting through the waves. The further they went, the more her pain grew until she thought her heart would burst. She looked down at her sleeping son . . .

"Poor Jason, a part of you too, is gone," she spoke softly and caressed his hair, "you will never be the same again." Jason was orphaned in many ways . . . father, brother, friend.

They sailed all night. Dawn came and the sun seemed to bring new hope. They were nearing Chios but the island was still not in sight. They should be there by nightfall. How will it be, she wondered . . . what will I find? She had heard nothing all these years and had no way of contacting her father. The thought of seeing her home and him again gave her new hope. To see Chios once more . . . to climb the green hills and walk among the orange groves . . . to smell the lemon blossoms . . . her heart beat in eager anticipation.

Their welcome was a sad one. Her home was empty . . . her father lay buried in the small cemetery of St. John. Once again Helena felt that fate was working against her. Everywhere she turned there was disaster.

All her grief erupted as she stood in the cemetery the next morning, watching her father's remains being dug from the earth. She hugged the coffin and cried . . . the sobs wracking her body for a long while. Then she composed herself—she was drained of tears, she would not cry again, ever. And then she began the obligatory task . . . she washed her father's bones in the blessed wine, according to custom, and placed them carefully in the small wooden box that was to be his final resting place. She did not cringe, was not afraid during the ritual. She looked tenderly at the bones of his hand, that large, manly hand that had cupped her childish one as she skipped alongside of him. She remembered his tall, heavy frame as he walked up the hill to their house . . . and how she ran down to greet him. He would pick her up and swing her high . . . then he would kiss her and put her down. She remembered those childhood days with tenderness.

Memorial services were held the next day. They brought her father's box into church and placed it beside the table that held the tray of boiled wheat. A box of bones, this is our fate, she thought as the priest chanted the memorial hymns. A life of suffering and then some bones, and a priest chanting over you. She sighed. Jason looked up at his mother and smiled sadly, trying to be a grown-up, hoping to comfort her.

"Don't feel bad, mother," he whispered, "we have each other." And he kissed her hand.

She stared down at the little man and smiled . . . somehow the pain became bearable.

Helena had a great deal of work ahead of her. The house was much too large for them and she closed off part of it. She busied herself making it livable once more, setting off one room as a workshop, for teaching embroidery and handcrafts. She was fortunate to have that talent to fall back on. The fields and orchards would be leased out, for she could not keep them up herself. With this income and the gold pieces her father had left her, Helena would manage.

She was home at last . . . this is what mattered, and she would make a new life for herself. For Jason's sake, she must forget Joseph and the pain of his loss. She knew that Jason would need her more than ever.

The years passed quickly on, softening Helena's pain, cultivating her mind and her role as a mother. She tried to be both parents to Jason, to fill the void in his life. It was a difficult task, but it was made easier by the many relatives that filled their lives as only a family can. The Andreadis family was large and respected in the village . . . the men were all stonecutters and merchants. Her uncles and aunts were always there to offer guidance and companionship with their love. It made the burden lighter, and Helena was grateful. Xenophon Andreadis, her father's youngest brother, became their new protector. Though only ten years her senior, he felt a deep responsibility for his niece. He was always there to help her every need. Jason loved Xenophon, too, but he was shy and withdrawn, seldom turning to anyone for advice or comfort. He was afraid, it seemed, of close relationships, afraid of losing yet another person he loved—as he'd lost his brother, his father, Costas. Xenophon studied him carefully, sensing his unhappiness, feeling helpless.

Jason grew into an intelligent, serious young man. But he was sensitive, an introvert, showing little joy or love of life. He was an adult in his thoughts, and in his ways he was often like an old man. This disturbed Helena . . . her heart cried for the boyhood Jason never knew. She wept inwardly, too, for the boyhood her other son was not to know. And for the manhood, too, that would surely be twisted. The thought was so painful that she had steeled her heart and tried to pretend Joseph was dead. It was her only hope of survival. She could not bear the agony of wondering where he was. Yet in spite of herself, she often wondered . . . was he a Janissary? Could he have been adopted by a Bey instead, and now enjoyed a life of luxury? She hated the Turks so much she preferred Joseph dead to the other alternatives. Yet there were Greeks who accepted such fates, who enjoyed the luxuries of family life with the wealthy overlords. Some gave up their faith and accepted Islam without complaint—a welcome alternative to Turkish cruelty. Helena could never accept this in her son . . . her sense of pride and honor were too deeply instilled in her.

* * *

The sound of rustling leaves brought Helena back to the present. She looked around and saw Jason walking towards her. A warm feeling crept over her. All the past tragedies disappeared when she looked at this tall, thin, ascetic-looking son of hers. He was dark, with large black eyes—slanted, olive eyes—under drooping lids that gave him a melancholy look. And a kindness, a gentleness in his countenance endeared him to everyone. Jason could not hurt a living thing. He would not even hunt, to the consternation of his friends, for he hated the thought of taking an innocent life. But the villagers loved him in spite of his strangeness, and often admired him for not bending to the whims of others. Yet, from all this gentleness, a fierçe side of him emerged in his struggle to help the cause, to win freedom from the Turks. Jason was the first of the young people to join the Revolution movement in Chios. He had been involved in it for years, since he was fourteen, and was successful in rounding up others his age. Now he was the leader of his group, and reported periodically to the adult committee at every secret meeting. Helena smiled as Jason bent to kiss her.

"I knew I'd find you here . . . you're always sneaking off like this," he teased her. He was suddenly serious. "You love the Prophet Elias, don't you?"

He knew she did, for she spent many moments here. Jason loved it too. Every chance he could get, he climbed the hill to this spot where he sat for hours, meditating on life and the future, and staring across the sea to those white cliffs in the east.

"I remember back in Zagora . . . very faintly, though . . . there was a chapel of the Prophet too, wasn't there?"

A shudder went through Helena at the thought of that chapel . . . and that ghastly night. She tried to hide her turmoil from Jason. He sensed something was wrong and changed the subject.

"Do you know the legend of why the Prophet's chapels are located on hilltops?"

"No son, I don't. Tell me." Of course she knew . . . she had told him the story when he was a child. But Jason loved to tell stories, to talk on end—he was a born teacher—so she let him go on.

"Well, it seems that before the Prophet Elias was a Prophet, he was a seaman who'd spent a good many years at sea. He finally became so tired of it that he decided to get as far away from the water as possible. So he set out for unknown places on land, carrying an oar across each shoulder. He stopped at the first village he came to and asked them to tell him what he was carrying. They did. This was not the place for him. He went further on. He climbed a high mountain, stopping at every village along the way to ask the same question. They all recognized the oars. At last, after much travelling, he reached the top, deep in the mountains, and asked the villagers there to identify the objects on his shoulders. They could not, they had never seen them before. 'Aha,' he exclaimed, 'this is the place for me. Here I will build my chapel and spend the rest of my days.' And he did. He built a little church and settled there until his death. Since then, all the chapels of the Prophet Elias are found on hilltops, far away from the sea."

"I'm proud of you," Helena smiled sadly, "you would have made a fine teacher."

She wanted to cry. She had dreamed of his going to Paris to the university there, and returning to teach in Chios. It was his dream too, but he had given it up to stay and work for the Revolution. He found solace, however, in his job at the Koraes Library, whose valuable manuscripts made it renowned throughout the world. Helena was grateful.

Jason had never known hate until he learned of the Turkish cruelty on the mainland. The fact that he had never experienced it personally was of no consequence. He could not get it out of his mind that his countrymen must hide in dark basements to teach the Greek language to their children. Hounded like animals, fearful of their lives, in order to educate themselves, to keep alive their heritage and traditions. How can man dehumanize his brother so vehemently? No, Jason could not bring himself to go to Paris. He was glad he had decided to stay here and fight.

"It bothers me . . . infuriates me . . . " his face was

crimson . . . Helena could see the blood pounding in his temples. Her heart burst with pride. What did it matter about higher education? Her son was a man of conscience, of principle. Thank God he was nothing like his father.

Helena felt guilty too, at the favors her island enjoyed from the Turks. But it would do no good if they suffered, too. At least this way, the Chiotes who were amassing wealth and power in trade and in the sea, would be in an ideal position to help their fellow Greeks when the time came. Some had already begun to secretly transport guns and ammunition.

The Chiotes knew well that if it were not for the mastic bush, they would have had the same fate as the others. Chios grew the only mastic in the world. The white, clear liquid its bark secreted hardened into a delicate aromatic gum that delighted the Sultan's harem who chewed hours on end. The gum was also used to make the powerful *raki,* a liqueur that kept the Turkish troops in a state of happy stupor when they were not fighting. The Sultan's pleasure was boundless and he showed it in many ways. He could not do enough for the Chiotes, whom he called his "favorite children." He spared them from the stern laws and humiliations suffered by the others. There was no rounding up of children, no taxes (except for mastic taken in place of gold), no subjugation or tortures. Thus the Chiotes concentrated on education and on becoming great merchant seamen, on controlling business and trade in the Middle East. Jason knew all this but could not condone it. He prayed that in the Chiotes' hearts the flame of freedom burnt no less bright than in their brothers' elsewhere. He knew that the people of his village, and many others, hoped one day to be completely free men. A loose yoke is still a yoke . . . and still degradation to those who love freedom. And Greeks were meant to be free . . . Jason believed this fervently. He lived for the day he would take part in the glorious Revolution they had been planning for years. Soon, very soon, Jason's wish would come true.

"We've called a meeting for tonight. The young people will gather at sundown. Fatouros will be there."

It would be in the church. While Father Stelios chanted vespers, the committee would hold their meeting, in a corner, near the candlestand. The church was the safest place for Greeks to congregate, for Turkish law forbade Turks from entering. Peaceful in the thought the *giaours* were praying to their God, the Turks paid little heed to the enthusiasm with which the men gathered at the church, even during weekdays. On Sundays there was more discussion and planning . . . the priests had managed to stretch the liturgy for hours, giving the Greeks ample time to themselves . . . away from Turkish eyes. But often the Turks waited outside the church to take the Greeks along for various chores. Soon the liturgy grew to such lengths the Turks tired of waiting and went their ways. And the liturgy hours lengthened with the years. And the Greeks became holier by the day. It was no wonder then, that the Revolution began in the churches, with the clergy as their leaders.

"Jason, you're twenty-one today, son." Helena's love shone in her eyes but pain clouded them. "I think it's time we talked about Joseph."

"What about Joseph?" He rememberd, faintly, the outstretched arms and the voice crying his name. His mother had told him that Joseph died after that day in Zagora, and he had never questioned it.

Now he felt a strange turmoil. Bewildered, he looked at his mother, then across the sea towards the east. So many times he had stood here, gazing with hatred and often with longing at that land of the barbarians. He could never explain these mixed feelings. For though he hated that shore, there was something that drew him to it, an urgency that made him want to cry out.

"What about him, mother?" he asked anxiously, then nodding towards the white cliffs across the sea, he added, "does that have anything to do with Joseph?"

Helena told him the whole story. All except the stabbing of Hassan . . . she could not bear to speak of that. She watched Jason's face as he learned that his brother, his twin, was alive somewhere in that country he despised . . . that his own flesh and blood was a part of the yoke that strangled the Christians. Now he understood his confused emotions—it was the other part of him calling across the straits . . . drawing him close. Helena watched Jason's eyes flash, become sad, then fierce. She felt the pain in his heart, and the agony she had experienced all these years almost burst within her. She controlled herself for Jason . . . he would need her strength.

"What are we going to do?" he murmured, almost to himself, "we've got to find him."

"What *can* we do?"

They both knew that even if they found him, Joseph would not want to come back. Trained fanatically since childhood to hate the Christians, he would never accept such a family as his own.

Jason looked across the sea to the Asian shore and a chill went through him. He vowed to find his brother and convince him to return.

He suddenly remembered the meeting and set his own feelings aside. Always in control, like his mother. It would be an important meeting . . . word had arrived that the Revolution was set for the following Spring. They would determine how Chios would participate. The sun's rays became warmer as the two figures descended the hill. Jason's arm was around his mother's shoulders. He was such a comfort to Helena . . . she felt a joy, a security in his presence. But that ache for Joseph never left her. As though reading her thoughts, the tall youth leaned over and kissed his mother on the forehead.

"I love you mother," he said simply, "I love you for both Joseph and me."

II

Captain Petros stood in the courtyard and watched the *mangano* bringing up the water. It's wearing out, he thought as he watched the huge wheel, I must have it taken care of. He noticed the grape arbor above it . . . it needed strengthening. All these years of neglect . . . the wood was almost rotted. Everything rots without care, he thought . . . love, too. There was a lot of work to be done before Maria and Joanna arrived. He wanted his wife and daughter to find his ancestral home as he'd left it . . . to see the place of his childhood. He never realized, until now, how much he missed Kambos . . . and how deep were his roots here. But it was not too late. He was going to try to fit the pieces together. In this atmosphere, within these walls that enclosed the majestic estate, he hoped to rekindle the love he and Maria once felt . . . a love that had cooled somehow, that had become tolerance and habit. A man needs love, he thought, he needs affection no matter how old he is. Now, at forty-two, Petros felt this need more than ever . . . and a strange emptiness. He had travelled the world and had seen all there was to see. But he felt unfulfilled. These past few years, something had urged him to return to Chios, as though here at last he would find all he needed in life. He felt, too, that Chios needed him as much as he needed it. So he gave up the sea, made plans to close his house in Constantinople, and returned to Kambos. His ship would be run by a capable man, his cousin Captain Demetris. Petros would oversee his interests from his island home, among his family and friends. Yes, it might be different when Maria arrived. He felt a deep, unexplainable yearning. As the smell of jasmine drifted in the wind, he turned and stared at the bush against the house. He loved jasmine. Maria had loved it too. That was so long ago . . . ages. Perhaps now they would enjoy that delicate fragrance together. He looked out across the orchards. His estate was large, like most in Kambos. Acres of orchards and grapevines bordered by cypresses on three sides, and the wall . . . the tall, protective stone wall of Kambos, on the other. It was all the tangible security man could hope for. And yet without love it was nothing. Soon he would know if he could recapture that too. He was going to try. First he must go to Thymiana and find workers. He must also find some diversion for his daughter . . . and decided she would take lessons in cooking and embroidery, the right thing for proper young ladies of the day. Petros was pleasantly surprised to discover that Helena was the finest teacher of needlework in the area. The thought of finally meeting her excited him. He had seen her from a distance many times in the past, and he never forgot the afternoon they played together as children. Suddenly Maria and picking up the pieces of their life together were not as urgent. What a strange feeling, he thought. He could not understand it.

As Helena and Jason approached the village, they spied several carriages outside the fortress walls. It must be noblemen from Kambos, Helena thought. One of the neighborhood children ran up to her.

"There's someone to see you, *Kyra** Helena, a gentleman!"

Jason wondered who it could be, but he was anxious to leave. The news of his brother Joseph had stunned him . . . he wanted to go somewhere alone, to think. Helena tried to discourage him.

"Come and lie down a while, son, I'll make you some tea."

She was afraid, knowing how sensitive he was. She realized the shock he experienced. Should she have told him sooner, from the very beginning?

"No, please,"Jason replied, "I'll be all right. I think I'll go back up to the chapel."

And he was gone.

Helena arrived at her house and found Petros waiting in the courtyard. He smiled and offered his hand.

"Good morning. I'm Captain Petros Sofronis. I was told to see you about embroidery lessons for my daughter."

She smiled at his friendliness. There was something

**Kyra - Madame*

clean and warm about him . . . she invited him in.

"I just returned to Kambos after twenty years at sea . . . too many years," he smiled wistfully. "My wife and daughter will be arriving from Constantinople in a few months. We're closing our house there. I want to come back to my roots."

The look on his face made Helena sad . . . she sensed an urgency, a longing in the man. This is what absence and the sea do to them, she thought. What fools they are, to give up their lives, to deny themselves a home and loved ones. But Helena also knew that everyone could not make a living on land, that the sea was a chance at a good livelihood.

Petros was a tall man with broad shoulders, a face weathered by winds. It was a good face, not handsome, but strong, belying the softness within. His eyes are bloodshot, she noted to herself . . . as though he's been drinking, or crying, or not sleeping. But their look was honest and straightforward. She was surprised at herself for surmising all this in so short a time. They discussed the hours and cost of the lessons. He was more than generous, offering her twice what she asked. Without hesitation, he invited her to visit his estate, to see the house, where she would be spending her time. He hoped Helena would befriend his wife. Maria would be lonely after the social life in Constantinople. Kambos would be a difficult change for her. Helena could help her adjust.

"She may feel imprisoned within our huge walls," he said. "Luxuries don't always drive away loneliness."

He was anxious for Maria to be happy here. He felt guilty at having left her alone so many years while he gloried in his life at sea. To command the winds and oceans was a joy unsurpassed by any woman's love, he thought once. Now he had realized it was only half the joy of life. He looked at Helena and felt a mild sensation. He had seen her several times, when his ship docked at the harbor of Chios to load cargo. And he had kept the image of her in his mind all these years. Like a beautiful picture one sees for a moment and remembers always. Once she was hurrying by, with a boy of about ten at her side. The next year he saw her buying fish at the dock. She had not seen him but he watched her as she bent over the baskets and bargained with the fisherman. She was so serious, so untouchable and so lovely. He had not thought more of the scene. A few years later he saw her again . . . at Saint Hermione's festival where she sat with some older people. A young man had asked her to dance and she politely refused. Then the priest said something and his wife prodded her. She relented and her escort led her to the small area near the orchestra. They danced a *syrto*, holding a handkerchief between them. Petros watched them go around the dance floor to the sound of the lively island music. Her somberness clashed with the spirit of the evening. When the dance was over she promptly returned to her group. Petros had leaned against the wall and observed all this from aside. He remembered thinking what a strange woman she must be.

Helena stood before him with a tray in her hands and Petros returned to the present. She was serving him rose petal jam on a spoon and a cup of water. He noticed her hands holding the tray, and the small doily in it. She had probably made it herself . . . it was delicate. The water was cool and refreshing . . . from the stone jug in the corner. The room was spotless . . .

it would be.

"To your health," he said, and his voice caught. He was annoyed with himself.

It was early afternoon when Petros returned from Thymiana. He was beginning to feel better. Things did not look quite so dark. There was a new optimism in his heart, an anticipation that was not there before. It did him good to talk with Helena. She was soothing . . . a beautiful person who spread warmth around her. He looked forward to her visit the following week.

Jason stopped, out of breath, at the top of the hill. He had run all the way up, as though he were being pursued. Perching himself on a rock, he looked down at the sea in the east. He could not believe that Joseph was alive . . . and somewhere with those barbarians. The thought set him on fire. Where was he? Would he find him? Had he been sold to slavery? Had he been taken for the Janissaries? The questions stumbled over one another in his mind. Fear gripped him at the thought of the Janissaries. What if his brother had been trained, all these years, to slaughter the Greeks? Everyone knew the cruelty of this regiment—they hated Christians with a passion. Jason felt trapped, not knowing where to turn. Joseph . . . Joseph . . . they had been inseparable as children. When they took him away a part of Jason went with his twin. All these years he thought Joseph was dead. And now . . .

"Alive . . . he's alive," Jason whispered, "and I'm going to find him."

But his thoughts returned to the Revolution . . . it was more important than anything else . . . he could not give up his part in it. Somehow he would find a way. His heart pounded at the thought of independence drawing near. He promised himself it must come above personal interests. Word had arrived from the mainland that the Greeks would rise again. How many times in the past they had tried, but the fierce Turkish troops, outnumbering the *giaours,* had cut them down. Now there were new plans. The Greeks had re-organized carefully, more precisely this time. They were gathering greater strength, more ammunition, better leaders, stronger fighters. Help was coming from Europe. The forming of the Friendly Societies, known as the *Philike Hetaireia,* in Europe and America had awakened the world, and financial help began to trickle in from phil-Hellenes everywhere. This time they would not fail. These hundreds of years of slavery could go no further. The mainland Greeks had suffered the depths of degradation at the hands of the Turks, who ran rampant through the villages, taking Greek women as they pleased, often raping them in the presence of their men. Jason had heard how they confiscated Greek homes, rounded up women and children to take back to Turkey. He cringed at the knowledge of his countrymen's being robbed not only of their possessions but of their pride and dignity. The Greeks had had enough . . . death was preferable to such a life. It was only a matter of time now . . . of months. The seed Rhegas Pheraios had planted in the minds of the Greeks less than fifty years ago had taken root. They would never rest until the Turk was thrown from Greek shores forever.

Jason suddenly thought of his father and wondered where he might be. Surely if he were alive he would have been in touch with them. What kind of man was he? Helena spoke rarely of him to Jason, and when she did, it was only to say that his work had taken him away. She could not bring herself to condemn him to her son. And, knowing Jason was tormented with doubts, she could not bear to tell him the truth about his father.

But the child, in his man's wisdom, knew something was wrong. His heart ached when he thought of his father. Often, when he was alone, he prayed for Stratis to return. And he dreamed a child's dreams of him—his father would surprise them and suddenly arrive one morning, laden with gifts. Jason would run to him and throw his arms around his neck, hold his father tight and never let him go. And they would live together always. Jason would go fishing with his father, and sailing in the schooner. They would till the soil together and climb the hills. But as the years went by and Stratis failed to appear, Jason realized his father was not coming home. His father did not care to see him again. It was a pain that gnawed at the boy constantly. And though later, it lessened with the excitement of planning the Revolution, the pain never quite went away.

Jason looked up at the sky and realized it was noon. He pushed aside the dark thoughts as he remembered the work that must be done. Jason had his mother's fighting spirit and sense of survival. It will all work out, he thought optimistically, as he hurried down the hill.

III

Petros rose with the sun. He sat for hours on the huge terrace sipping coffee and staring silently ahead. The workers had begun the many repairs, and the field-hands had gone to the orchards. He went over various papers on shipments he was expecting and carefully put them away. The hours refused to go by . . . it seemed the moment would never come. He smiled to himself, thinking of all the women he'd known throughout the world in his twenty years at sea. He had never waited with such anticipation for any of them. Even for Maria. Love, infatuation, whatever it had been with her, it did not have this urgency. It's nerves, he thought . . . loneliness, remorse, nothing more. He thought of his wife and daughter and reprimanded himself severely. There had been others in his life as a world traveller—but he did not think of Helena in these terms. She was more than just a beautiful woman to be desired. There was dignity and courage, warmth and strength in the woman.

The sound of the carriage interrupted his thoughts. He ran down the steps to the courtyard. The driver had helped Helena down and she was standing at the gate when he opened it. She was dressed in white linen with a black sash around her waist. A white scarf embroidered with tiny flowers covered her head. He noticed the black hair that peeked out in front . . . it glistened in the sun. Her eyes were fresh and clear . . . he felt a surge of excitement as he gave her his hand.

"Welcome," he said, "welcome to the Sofronis estate."

Her smile was friendly but austere. Her seriousness becomes her, he thought. She was cautious and he did not blame her. Many men must have made overtures.

He led her through the gate to the courtyard inside.

"This is my home," he said with pride, "this is where I was born. I know every stone and every inch of this ground. It's as though I never left."

Together they went from building to building. He showed her the wine-press, the huge baking oven that supplied bread for the estate, the *mangano* that pumped water to the vast citrus orchards, the olive trees and grapevines. All this . . . land, houses, workers' buildings . . . were Petros'. He looked at her and suddenly, foolishly, wanted to say, Share this with me . . . it's all I have and all I ever hope to have. He tried to say something else, anything to express his feelings, but her sternness made him mute. He could do nothing, after all, for she belonged to another . . . and yet to no man. He had heard about Stratis, how he'd possessed her briefly and managed to destroy her for anyone else. A wave of sadness engulfed him, and then shame, that a grown man with serious ambitions—his family's survival, his homeland's verge on Revolution—would act like a schoolboy. His mind wandered to his schooldays and an incident in his past leaped out. They were children when he had visited Thymiana. Helena was among the group playing outside his aunt's house. He'd pulled her hair and she ran away crying. She never came out to play when he visited again. Soon after, when he was twelve, he left Chios to live with an uncle in Constantinople, where he attended school. From there he went to sea, to Maria and to marriage.

Now thirty years later he came home to stay. But it was too late. She was tied to a ghost. The best years of her womanhood were sifting through the hourglass. What a waste, my lovely Helena, he thought. He felt almost ridiculous. He had possessed many women, and married one, but he had never felt this way before. Now, at life's half-span, he had come home to be born again. He smiled at the irony of fate, and caught Helena watching him curiously . . . as though she were trying to read his mind . . . as though she had succeeded.

She knows, Petros thought. He put out his hand to touch her but she turned away.

"Let me show you the house."

"I can't stay," she was cool, distant. "Why don't I see it when your wife arrives?"

He was embarrassed and did not want to press her.

"The servants are making coffee . . . and they baked a delicious *baklava.* Please have some with me. I won't keep you long."

She gave in, smiling sternly. It annoyed him that she

was so cautious, but a sudden realization came to him. She feels it, too, he thought, she feels it and she's afraid.

They chatted casually over cups of thick, rich coffee. She told him about Jason, careful not to mention his involvement in the Revolution, or the Revolution itself. She was not certain about Petros' feelings on the subject. After all, he had lived in Constantinople, and all Greeks who did, felt a certain loyalty to the Turks. Most of these Greeks were wealthy merchants and landowners who lived comfortable, luxurious lives in Asia Minor. Why should they risk losing all that? Yet Petros did not strike her as a man who placed material things above honor.

Helena noticed the sun nearing its peak . . . she got up to leave.

"I didn't realize it was so late . . . how the time went."

Idle talk . . . she could not think of anything else to say. Petros wished she would never leave.

"I know Maria will be happy to have you as her friend. And I look forward to meeting your son. Please bring him by one day."

Helena smiled as he helped her onto the carriage. She was going to like this work. Petros was a good man—she sensed it—there was no evil in him. She wondered if his daughter was like him. And what about his wife? He did not give the impression of being a happily-married man. But that was no concern of hers. Helena turned her thoughts elsewhere. She wondered where Jason was. She was worried about his reaction to the news of Joseph. Thank God he was kept busy with the movement . . . all week he had been planning the youth meeting. My gentle Jason a rebel, she thought . . . it does not suit him. But she knew that the fire of freedom often burns brightest in the most gentle, most peace-loving hearts.

IV

September moved into October. Pomegranates ripened. The *meltemi* blew across the island more fiercely than ever. And the rains came. The orchards drank in the water gratefully after the dryness of summer. Snails crept out from their hiding places and the villagers hurried to gather the large, succulent bits of life. In every house a pot boiled . . . onion and tomato simmered in olive oil, to be added to the snails, while eager mouths waited to enjoy the feast. The island was rich, Nature's gifts to it were abundant.

Captain Petros left Kambos early that morning. He drove his carriage carefully through the mud of the narrow road that led to the main thoroughfare to the harbor. Maria's ship would be arriving, and he was anxious to see his wife and daughter. Work on the house was completed . . . he knew they would be pleased with the results. Soon, too, Helena would begin coming to the house regularly . . . his heart leaped at the thought. She would be in his home, a part of his life. That strange feeling engulfed him again; he still could not explain it.

Maria stood sadly on the ship's deck and looked at the harbor ahead. The wind-swept rain clouded the air. It was a cold, unfriendly welcome. How she hated coming to Chios! If only she had persuaded her husband to remain in Constantinople. Things were ideal there. But Petros' mind was set . . . and she did not have the heart to disillusion their daughter who had an obsessive love for her father. Poor Joanna, she thought, at sixteen she was just beginning to know him. Maria tried to hide her feelings. She stepped down into the rowboat that would take them to shore and felt that she was going to her doom.

"Father, *kale mou patera,*" Joanna ran to Petros and threw her arms around him. "At last . . . at last, we're going to be together . . . the three of us."

Petros turned to Maria and smiled. She went to him and they kissed politely on the cheek.

"Oh father, kiss her for heaven's sake," Joanna pushed her parents together. Petros hesitated, smiling embarrassedly. Maria turned abruptly away.

"Really now, Joanna, what will these islanders think of us?" Her voice was ice.

Petros felt ill-at-ease. It was not a very good start, but he would be patient.

Joanna caught her breath as the gate swung open. She looked at the mosaic courtyard, the water wheel, the grape arbor, the huge house. Like all the homes in Kambos it was high, with many terraces overlooking the orchards. The long stairs led to the living quarters on the second level. It was majestic, and Joanna was impressed. Their comfortable home in Constantinople was not as large as this. She squealed with delight. Maria remained silent. A light rain began to fall.

"Father, I never dreamed you had anything so beautiful . . . so large . . . and so elegant!"

"Wait til you see the rest of it." There was pride in Petros' voice. "But let's go in, out of the rain."

He had never felt so close to his roots as now. Soon Joanna, too, would feel it. She was a part of him, a part of his past. I'll make it up to her, he thought, I'll be the best father a girl ever had.

* * *

Jason watched as they unloaded the ship's cargo. He looked at the crates marked BOOKS and stood over to the side as they piled them on the dock. They were addressed to the schoolmaster, who now hurried to join the young man.

"How many do we have?" His voice was anxious, careful.

"Ten. I'm going to open one for the customs man. Not that they questioned us . . . but it's better to be safe."

"Fine. Which one is it?"

"Here. The one with the notch on the corner."

Jason went up to the Turk at the other side of the dock, spoke briefly to him, and together they returned. He broke open a crate and showed the Turk the books piled inside. The man nodded his head absentmindedly and waved approval as he walked away.

The Turks were at peace where the Chiotes were concerned. There had never been the least trouble on the island. The Turks knew the Chiotes were no fools . . . they realized they were better off than any other Greeks. They had nothing to fear, for the Turks' presence in Chios was only a matter of routine. It was a great concession to the islanders to be able to govern themselves and to run their affairs as they saw fit.

The schoolmaster's carriage pulled up. Two boys, strapping youths, leaped down and hurriedly loaded the wooden crates onto it.

"That's it, boys." Jason was in command as he counted out the crates and jumped on the carriage after them.

The schoolmaster watched him with satisfaction. Jason's an asset to us, he thought, he's a real leader . . . one would never guess it to look at him. For inside this calm, sensitive youth was a ferocity few could see.

Jason wondered where Joseph might be now. He looked behind him as the carriage started off, past the dock, to the cliffs across the sea. Joseph was somewhere out there. Soon, soon, the time would come . . . he was sure they would meet.

Suddenly, a Turk stepped in front of the carriage, his arms outstretched. It was the man from the customs house.

"Wait—you there!"

Their breaths caught.

"You're going past Kambos aren't you? Sofronis left a suitcase behind . . . can you drop it off?"

They sighed in relief as they took the package aboard. Then, not wasting further time, they hurried off. Jason would drive straight to Thymiana, unload the crates where they would be safe, then return to Kambos to deliver Sofronis' suitcase. They could not take any chances.

The crates were carried inside the schoolhouse, down to the secret room beneath the trapdoor. One crate, the one with the notch on the corner, remained in the schoolroom, open, with the books piled neatly inside. The others were unloaded below. Underneath the top row of bibles were the rifles they had been expecting . . . and the ammunition. Things were going well . . . no one suspected. Jason counted the rifles and marked the numbers on his list. He would give this report to Fatouros who would be coming soon. Jason's heart leaped with excitement. The time was approaching. A few more months . . . November . . . December . . . and soon . . . March, and the fateful day of the Annunciation, when the Greek banner would rise above the Ottoman's crescent. Perhaps Joseph, too, might rise from the chaos. It was all Jason could hope for.

* * *

Jason knocked on the iron gate of the Sofronis estate.

"I have something for Captain Sofronis—may I see him?" he asked the servant who appeared.

It was noon and the sun was out after the morning rain. Jason's gaze fell across the courtyard to the orange grove that stretched as far as the eye could see. He noticed the drops of water still clinging to the leaves. Then he saw the young girl on the terrace. Joanna stood there smiling. She hurried down the steps.

"Good morning. I'm Joanna, Captain Petros' daughter."

She's forward, Jason thought, not at all like the coy, withdrawn island girls. But he smiled back—he liked her honesty.

"I'm Jason . . . how do you do? Your father forgot this suitcase at the dock and I brought it over."

Petros appeared from the doorway of the house and Joanna made the introductions.

"So you're Jason," he said after thanking him for the suitcase, "I've heard a great deal about you son. I'm happy to meet you."

His friendliness touched Jason. He was going to like this family.

"Come visit us soon. Your mother will be coming here often now . . . she's going to instruct Joanna in needlework." Petros put his arm around Jason's shoulder. "Whenever you can, son, you're always welcome."

Jason liked the way Petros said "son." He smiled to himself. They're not familiar with our ways, he thought. Chiotes didn't often invite boys into their homes when they had pretty daughters. Not unless they had marriage in mind. But he would like to come. Perhaps he could get Joanna to work in the movement. Every pair of hands counted. What about the Captain, Jason wondered, what were his feelings? He must find out. Yes, he would be back soon.

As he walked to the carriage, he turned and waved goodbye to the two standing in the courtyard. They looked so much alike. A stab of pain went through Jason as he thought of his father. I wonder what it's like, he thought, to stand beside your father with his arm on your shoulder? Sadness swept over him . . . he suddenly wanted to cry. Ashamed of his feeling, he reprimanded himself.

"Only children cry, you fool," he muttered through his teeth.

The man-child leaped angrily onto his carriage and hurried back to town, fighting back the tears.

* * *

Karanikolas' coffeehouse was filled by early evening. Several of the tables concentrated on *tavli* (backgammon) while discussions on the crops and the weather dominated the others. The owner hurried the orders of Turkish coffee, retsina and *mezedakia*, the hors d'ouevres the villagers preferred this time of day. His wife placed more *souvlakia* on the coals—tender pieces of pork and lamb on skewers. Business was good, as usual, but tonight was a special night.

"The rifles arrived this morning," a boy whispered to the others at his table.

"I know . . . they're at the schoolhouse. What did Fatouros say?"

"He's coming by tonight."

At that moment, as though in response, the tall villager appeared in the doorway. He was fair, big-boned, with a chiseled face. A simple man with little formal education, Fatouros was wise in the ways of life, clever in the scheme for freedom, and impatient to see his island free. His large frame enclosed an innocent heart and a stubborn nature. He felt it his duty to convince every villager that revolution was the only answer to the Turks. And since he was a night watchman at the farms, he was skilled with the rifle, an expert in hunting and tracking. For years now, he had been organizing . . . first the youth, then the adults, so they would be ready when the time came. All these months he had been in touch with the Greeks of the mainland who were planning the Spring revolt. The time was nearing and he could not wait . . . his hand itched to grab the rifle against the barbarians.

Jason left his table and walked over to Fatouros.

"The crates are unloaded in the cellar," he said in a low tone, "nine of them sir . . . two hundred sixteen rifles and all the ammunition."

"Good. Fatouros looked around at the men who watched him thoughtfully, anxiously.

"We'll start training tonight. Come to the hill at the farm . . . around nine . . . bring two rifles with you and five boys from your group. I'll have a fire going in one of the caves."

"We'll be there."

The boys in Jason's group ranged in age from sixteen to twenty. There were over a hundred of them. And each one would eventually be trained to use the rifle, to aim, to scout, to protect himself. Fatouros knew that when the signal came, every able body must take his stand. The Chiotes must join the battlecry . . . they would show the other Greeks that they could not be bought with comfortable lives and Turkish bribes . . . that they wanted independence as much as the others.

Fatouros looked at Jason for a long moment. He has potential, he thought, remembering the shy, withdrawn boy that came to him five years ago. Jason would not even hunt then, lest he take an innocent life. And now he had become the best marksman of them all. He had spirit and love of country. This is our future, thought Fatouros in his wise, peasant way . . . with boys like Jason we *must* win freedom.

* * *

It was nearly midnight when the boys returned from the hill. They were tired but excited from their first exercise. Every night they would rotate, five at a time. In a month they would all be proficient.

Helena was embroidering beside the oil lamp when Jason walked in the door.

"You're tired, son," she kissed him as he bent towards her, "how was it?"

"It's going well . . . I met Captain Petros and his daughter this morning."

"Oh?" She tried to sound casual.

"Very nice people. Mother, how does the Captain feel about the Turks . . . and about the Revolution?"

"I don't know, Jason. I haven't known him long enough."

"He says you'll be going to his home often."

"Yes . . . Joanna is beginning embroidery lessons in about a week."

"He could be a great help to us. His daughter, too . . . she has nerve."

Helena smiled. "Well, don't tell me you've finally noticed a pretty girl!"

Jason was annoyed. "You know me better than that. I'm thinking about the work ahead of us."

The vein in his neck throbbed.

"We've got to be ready for Spring . . . to join the others when they give the sign. And you talk about pretty girls . . . "

"Jason, son, there's nothing wrong in noticing a

pretty girl. Some day you're going to fall in love, get married . . . have children."

"I'm not!" His tone startled her. "That's not for me . . . what really matters is the Revolution . . . and finding Joseph." He shook his head. "Mother, you just don't understand!"

The color left his face . . . he seemed to be trembling.

Jason's attitude had always disturbed Helena, but now she was beginning to feel alarm. The other boys were in this struggle too, but it did not stop them from reacting to life as boys should. But then, how could Jason remain unaffected by all the tragedy in their lives? He was sensitive . . . dangerously so. Perhaps his zealousness with the Revolution was a blessing in disguise . . . an emotional outlet. She must talk to her uncle Xenophon—he understood Jason. He always seemed able to reach him.

Xenophon Andreadis, the merchant of Thymiana, was the guiding force of the village. A tall, stout, wise man of fifty, it was to him the villagers came with their problems and plans. He was their link to the Elders in the capital city. He loved Jason like his own son, and since he had no children, became Jason's unofficial guardian from the moment they arrived in Chios. His wife Maria loved the boy, too, and opened her home and her heart to him. Helena was grateful that Jason had a man to turn to, someone to share his problems and thoughts. And yet through the years, Jason remained closed within himself. He rarely went to Xenophon for advice or comfort. But when he did, he always found understanding and compassion. Xenophon knew that Jason longed for his father, for the man who should rightfully be with him.

* * *

"Well, and how's the rebel today?"

Xenophon smiled at the glum Jason who stood before him. He closed his ledger and rose from his desk, looking questioningly at the boy's face. Something's disturbing him, Xenophon thought, he doesn't come to me so easily. He slapped Jason on the shoulder.

"Let's have lunch together. I'm not going upstairs because I have to work on these books. We can eat and talk."

He laid out the fresh bread and olives, stuffed grape-leaves and scallions his wife had brought earlier. He handed Jason some hard-boiled eggs to peel while he took out a bottle of his better wine.

"We have a feast here . . . join in."

Xenophon ate with gusto as he always did. He loved good food and enjoyed the produce of his village, especially the brown olives. As he ate he watched Jason who was pre-occupied. He waited for the boy to speak.

Jason remained silent. He sipped a little wine but ate nothing.

"What's the matter, Jason? Do you want to tell me?"

Still nothing. Jason bit his lip and looked the other way.

"Did you have a falling out with your mother?"

Jason related his conversation with Helena, her references to Joanna, his annoyance at his mother's attitude, his own passion for the Revolution. Xenophon listened with interest. Like Helena, he too, was worried about Jason's intensities, but he said nothing. He's a good human being, he thought, wise and serious beyond his years. But something's wrong . . . and I pray it soon passes. Xenophon felt there would be little joy in Jason's life.

"Uncle Xenophon, is it so wrong to have more important things on my mind than girls? I certainly can't think of romance when the whole world is blowing up. Can't my mother see that? You tell me."

It hurt Xenophon to see the tormented look on the child he had helped raise to manhood.

"Jason, listen son . . . it's hard for your mother to understand. You must not condemn her. One who doesn't follow the pattern is always considered strange." He paused a moment, searching for words.

"This isn't the first time, you know. She's always questioning . . . making me feel self-conscious."

"I know how important the Revolution is to you," Xenophon continued. "And I can see that you have your priorities. But youth is only a short while, Jason, and it demands some pleasures. Enjoy it son . . . your work will not suffer. Remember," he smiled, seeing that he was reaching Jason, "all things in moderation."

"Except the Revolution," Jason smiled back and the somberness was broken. They both laughed.

He'll find himself one of these days, Xenophon thought. And yet, he wondered, would he? He patted Jason on the back.

"The time will come, I'm sure, when you'll be anxious to run after someone like Joanna."

Jason's smile faded and Xenophon thought he saw fear in his eyes. The boy lowered his gaze.

"But if the time doesn't come, Jason," Xenophon added gently, "you'll still be the young man we all love and admire."

Jason felt a lump in his throat. The pain had returned, but he felt this man reach out to him . . . and it was comforting.

Embarrassed, he mumbled an abrupt "thank-you" and hurriedly walked away.

V

Christmas and New Year's came, the island teemed with activity. Everyone was in a festive mood. People rushed about in their holiday preparations. Church bells rang. And the winds blew more fiercely than ever. The wealthy matrons of Kambos planned their holiday socials with a flutter of excitement. They ordered their silk gowns and made ready to welcome friends from the neighboring estates and villages. Turkish overlords, anxious to honor their Christian friends, arrived with lavish gifts for the season. Wine, *raki* and barbecued lamb scented the air. Tables spread with white embroidered cloths offered pastries and various delicacies. Music overflowed from the terraces, and white kerchiefs fluttered in the air, as the men danced to the sounds of the oud, the fife, and the drums. It was a time of joy and brotherly love in Chios.

On the Greek mainland, a different mood prevailed. An undercurrent flowed beneath the holiday preparations, a wave of hurried anxiety, solemn hope. The people here were busy with other things—guns and powder, meetings and decisions. The time had finally been set. The Revolution would burst on the twenty-fifth of March. It would be an historic date for the Greeks. 1821—a date to be carved with swords and polished with blood. A dual holiday their descendants would celebrate in years to come. March 25th, the day of the Virgin Mary's Annunciation.. March 25th, the day of Greek Independence. Quietly, hopefully, the Greeks of the mainland drank their toasts: "Happy Birthday Christ Child, lead us to our liberation!"

This would be their last Christmas under the Turkish yoke.

Maria spent weeks preparing for her first social in Chios. She and Joanna had ordered their gowns a month ago; Helena was just finishing the embroidery on the sleeves. The house, also dressed in its fineries, was spotless. Servants hurried about while the two cooks were buried among their kitchen-ware preparing varied delicacies and pastries for the guests. Maria looked over all this with growing enthusiasm. For the first time since her arrival she was beginning to feel her old self. She thought of their holidays in Constantinople with nostalgia. How upset she had been to leave the life and the people she loved. She thought she would die here in Chios, but it was not so bad now. Their old friend, Ali Bey, had closed his home in the Turkish capital and set up residence in the neighboring estate. It was good to have an old neighbor close by again. Perhaps things would work out after all. She felt a tinge of conscience. Was it shame? But she had done nothing wrong—she often wished she had. All his life her husband had enjoyed his own love—the sea. It had meant more to him than any woman or any home. Why should she not have filled her own needs? But her strict upbringing forbade it. She tried to fight it but she could never quite build up the courage. So she had endured a sexless life by filling her time with parties and charitable work. It had helped drive away the loneliness. She wondered why Petros had bothered to pick up their lives at this late stage. For a moment she felt sorry for him. He must be a very lonely man, she thought.

The outside gate slammed shut. It was Helena with the gowns. Maria sighed contentedly. I'm so glad we have her, she thought. She's not only a gem in her work but a true friend. I really should confide in her—there is so much I want to tell her. But would she understand Maria's thoughts, her dreams? Would she sympathize or simply think of her as frivolous? She is a strange woman, so sedate and proper, Maria thought. She wondered about Helena's loveless life. How had she managed it? How did she fill the void? Had she suffered as much as Maria? At least Maria had drowned her frustrations in luxurious living. She could not have endured, otherwise. And now Petros was back. Now, when Maria did not care anymore. When the feeling they once shared had been left to die. How dared he be so inconsiderate as to expect her to fall at his feet. Her thoughts turned elsewhere and she felt a new blood coursing through her veins. One day she would tell Helena her secret—but not now, she was afraid.

Helena fitted the dress on Maria and smoothed out the folds of the delicate silk. It was soft, gentle to the touch, the most expensive fabric available. Maria was pleased with Helena's work. The fine satin stitches on the sleeves, interwoven with beads, had been applied with great care and love—so typical of Helena's handcraft.

Captain Petros stood in the doorway and watched the two women. Helena's back was to him; she did not turn when Maria greeted him. Her voice was cold, emotionless. Helena was disturbed that Maria could not be more affectionate towards her husband. He needed love—she could see that his whole being cried out for it. One day she would talk to Maria about this, when the right moment came. She felt it would be soon. Helena sensed that Maria needed to talk to her. Something was troubling her. She hoped it was not what Helena suspected.

"Do you like it? Isn't Helena wonderful? We're so lucky to have her near."

Yes we are, Petros thought to himself, yes we are. He smiled and approached the women. Helena turned and bowed her head in greeting. It infuriated him that she was still so distant. She had been in and out of his home for three months now, sharing Maria's life and his, adding her touch to everything around him. Yet she constantly avoided him, always careful to stay out of his way. He was jealous of the time she spent with Maria, of the time she spent in her own home. Still, he knew she was doing what she felt was right, and he respected her for it. Perhaps it is better this way, he thought. No, it's not, he quickly contradicted himself, she's a fool, arrogant. He knew she was neither of these. She was wise, well-bred, intuitive. The turmoil inside him increased. He must talk to her.

* * *

Jason arrived early to find the Sofronis home filled with guests. He felt uncomfortable and wished he had not come. But Helena had coerced him by cleverly suggesting it would be wise to meet the overlords and prominent Chiotes of Kambos. Who knows when they might prove helpful to the cause? Jason looked about, at the grandeur and aura of the surroundings. A hum rose—the chatter of busy voices, the rustling of women's gowns. The wealthy men of Kambos with their black, frocked suits, their thick moustaches and deep voices, greeted their hosts with well-wishes and gifts. For a moment Jason was caught up in the excitement of the evening. It was the most festive New Year's Eve he had ever experienced.

Remembering the main reason he came, Jason situated himself at a place where he could view everyone. This is not so bad after all, he thought, as he watched the guests intently. He shook hands with many wealthy landowners, taking mental notes for the future. As the crowd drifted through the two large rooms devoted to the festivities, he caught sight of one of his young friends from the movement and tried to get his attention. A smile lit the other's face when he recognized Jason.

"Come over," Vangeli motioned him and turned to his parents as Jason wove his way through the crowd.

"Mother, father, this is Jason Delipetros, a friend of mine who works at the library."

Jason was delighted to run into his friend, and

further, to meet the parents.

Mrs. Xydas eyed him carefully.

"Delipetros? That's not a Chian name. Are you from the mainland?"

"No, I'm from Thymiana. But my father was from Zagora."

"Oh?"

Vangeli sensed the further questions in the air and took Jason's arm. Excusing themselves, they left to find other young people who wandered about.

The Xydases nodded.

"What a nice young man. So dignified. I wonder why he never comes to the house." She frowned, remembering the many hours her son was away from home. She was concerned about his friendships and recent mysterious activities away from home.

The boys were lost in the crowd as the musicians began tuning up for the dancing.

"That was close. My mother would have cross-examined you the rest of the evening."

"They seem nice. Are you sure they don't know about your involvement with us?"

"I don't think so. I certainly cover my tracks well. But sometimes, the way my father looks at me, I just wonder . . . " Vangeli had a pleading look in his eyes as he added, "You know, Jason, all wealthy people aren't that bad. They just try to protect their interests."

"That's not bad?"

"I mean . . . well," Vangeli was at a loss.

"Oh, don't worry about it . . . you're making up for them." Jason playfully punched Vangeli's arm.

The music of a *tsamiko* rang in the air and Captain Petros waved a handkerchief to one of his guests.

Captain Tsangaris rose and stretched out his arms, clicking his fingers as the two began twirling and leaping in the air. The guests watched approvingly and drank to the dancers' health, eating the hot tidbits the servants passed around the room.

"He's from Kardamylla," Vangeli said to Jason, nodding towards Captain Tsangaris, "owns three ships and I hear he's using one of them to bring in guns for the village."

"Kardamylla is doing pretty well, they tell us. It's one of the towns that are already prepared for the big day."

"Well," Vangeli smiled, "the Kardamylliotes are wealthy, I notice you don't resent *them.*"

"All right, you win." Jason turned to a newcomer that was drawing some attention.

"It's Dr. Glarakis," Vangeli said, "he returned from Europe last year. Used to teach mathematics here, remember? They sent him to Paris on some island matters and he stayed and got his doctor's degree."

Dr. George Glarakis had done more than receive his medical degree. At the hospitals he served in Vienna, Holland, Italy and Paris, he won over many friends for the Greek cause. A staunch patriot and lover of freedom, he returned to his island home in 1820.

"He must know something's coming to a point," Jason said. "I'll bet that's why he came home."

It was proving to be a rewarding evening. Jason was glad he came.

Joanna and several other young ladies sat across the room eyeing Jason and Vangeli who had been joined by a group of other youths. She was sullen, trying to think up some reason to be near Jason. These islanders were so proper—the girls and boys never mingled. Her annoyance grew until she suddenly jumped up and ran over to the musicians. She whispered something to the oud player and the group broke into the music of a Chian *syrto.* Joanna gathered the girls and they formed a semi-circle in the room. Jason watched them dance, holding their kerchiefs between them. It was a simple dance, but a spritely one. The parents stood on the sidelines admiring their children, and many mothers calculated marriages in their minds. When it was over, the girls hesitantly followed Joanna to join Jason and his group, chatting amiably, though a bit self-consciously. Joanna looked up at Jason with sparkling eyes and he smiled as he thought how different she was from the girls of Chios. Helena eyed them lovingly from across the room. They looked so handsome together, so well-matched. She sent up a secret prayer. If only she would live to see Jason married and happy.

The heavy scent of perfume and *raki* filled the room. Jason turned at the sound of rustling silk. The young people around him followed his gaze, resting on the imposing figure that stood in the doorway. Flanked on each side by a servant carrying a tinsel-covered box, was their old friend, Ali Bey. His haughty air masked the desire that appeared on his face when he saw Maria across the room. She quickly excused herself from her guests and came to greet him.

Bey's eyes, deep and fiery, penetrated Maria's. She laughed to mask her nervousness and bowed her head to hide the look of pleasure there.

Helena saw them from the adjoining room. She would not go near Bey, near any Turk. She despised them. And if Maria persisted in trying to introduce her, she would keep busy in another room.

Jason watched them silently, morosely. The thought of sharing an evening with Turks infuriated him. He could never accept the fact that the Sofronises and their friends in Kambos socialized with the conqueror. When two other Moslem neighbors arrived, Jason was certain he had had enough for the evening. Sometimes he thought he hated these Chiotes for what he considered their treasonous behaviour. He looked around for his mother but she was nowhere in sight. On second thought he decided to stay.

* * *

The festivities ended and the island settled back to its daily routine. Thymiana bustled with building and quarrying. Kambos' orchards thrived in the winter sun. The famous Chian tangerines became ripe for picking, and hands sped to pack the fruit for export to Europe and Russia.

It was past noon when Helena and Joanna finished their embroidery lesson. The girl was doing exceptionally well. She was a gifted, lovely child and Helena was delighted with her. She would make Jason a loving, devoted wife. It was obvious that Joanna was experiencing her first love, painful and unrequited. Helena felt sorry for her. If only Jason would take the time to look at Joanna with different eyes. Still, friendship is a good beginning, Helena consoled herself, a strong foundation. Helena's thoughts were interrupted as Petros appeared from the terrace steps. He walked to her side, a grim look on his face.

"Please, I want to talk to you." He saw her hesitate. "It's important," he insisted, "please. Meet me at the end of the olive grove."

He hurried down the steps and past the orchard. Helena looked around, worried. No one was in sight. She did not want to go. She would not. How dared he? A moment passed. She picked up her skirts and hurried down.

When she reached Petros he was leaning against the olive tree near the wall, at the end of the estate. He was pale, his lips chalk white, a look of misery on his face. Her heart went out to him but she stood there waiting, not speaking. What could she say?

It came light lightning.

"Helena, I'm in love with you."

Helena said nothing. Though she had sensed it for a long time, it came as a shock.

"It's killing me to be near you like this . . . " His voice had an urgency that frightened her.

"Sometimes I can't stand it . . . and yet, I was nothing before . . . " He shook his head. "I can't believe this has happened to me."

How dare he, she thought, trying to be angry with him and not succeeding.

"You have no right to say that."

Her voice was cold, stern. Yet her heart was warm. She knew he was not toying with her feelings, for she felt the same about him. But he must never know.

Petros waited a long while, biting his lip as though he were trying to reach a decision. He went to touch her. She quickly drew back.

"Don't be frightened, I won't hurt you." His voice was gentle. "It's hard loving someone without touching them, Helena. And it's painful . . . but it's possible."

He felt silly, like a lovesick schoolboy making a

confession. Yet he knew she would not laugh at him. She was not the kind.

"Just the thought of you makes me glad I'm alive." He paused and looked at her intently. "I know it sounds ridiculous." He turned away, embarrassed.

She could not answer. The words stuck in her throat.

"Is it so wrong?" His eyes pleaded for understanding.

She wanted to say, yes, it's wrong. We're both married . . . but she could not utter a sound.

He went on. He wanted to get it all out now that he'd begun.

"Don't say it's absurd for me to love you . . . Helena, I think I loved you always. I really believe that now."

He told her of the times he'd seen her in the harbor and at the festival.

"Those scenes stayed with me all these years . . . doesn't that mean something?"

She stood there not knowing what to say or what to believe. Her heart pounded as she fought to keep her composure. She turned the other way so he would not see her turmoil.

"Doesn't it prove I love you?" he grasped her shoulders and made her face him.

She was silent. Then, realizing how painful it must be for him to say all this, with no response from her, she answered softly . . . "I'm sorry . . . "

She wanted to say, I don't love you, forget this, but it was the first time she had lost control of her senses—they refused to obey.

He looked at her and all his love and agony showed in his eyes. Her heart twisted. Oh God, why do you let things happen this way? You are so great, but You plan things so impractically. She was frightened by the feeling that stirred within her. A part of her tried to fight it but another revelled in the joy. If they were both free . . . if she had met Petros first . . . now it was hopeless . . . Maria, Stratis, Jason, the Revolution . . . suddenly she wanted to tell Petros she loved him too. She ached to say it, but she knew she must not. He knew it too, but it only strengthened his love.

Finally she spoke, a faint whisper.

"It's difficult for me, too, Petros . . . "

Oh God, I can't bear it, she thought, to feel alive after all these years, and to be so helpless. She wondered where all this would lead.

Helena smiled to herself as she thought of God again. Her mother used to tease her about her conversations with the Almighty. "What is it child," she would say smiling, when she caught Helena talking to the icons in the vestibule. "What is with you that you talk with God? Who do you think God is, your playmate?"

"Never mind," Helena would reply, "God understands . . . we have our own secrets."

And she would run to Him with her little girl's problems. Please God, don't rain tomorrow, we're going on a picnic . . . please God, don't let the kittens die . . . please God, let me have a new dress. Until she grew up and realized God had more important things to do, that she had no right to ask for trifles when the world was in chaos. And when real troubles came . . . her parents' death, the nightmare of Stratis, she merely asked God to help her face them and endure them. Even when they took Joseph away, she knew it was foolish to ask God to stop it. She merely asked for strength. And now that Petros had entered her life, she would need more strength. Thank God, this, at least, was a prayer that was always answered.

But whatever happened now, Helena could not deny that the whole world had taken on a new light . . . a new meaning. It was bittersweet. Beauty and despair again, she thought, that strange coupling will haunt me all my life.

Petros interrupted her thoughts.

"I didn't mean to upset you . . . forgive me . . . it's the last thing I want to do."

He drew her to him. The sun glistened through the branches of the olive tree as they leaned against it. He bent and kissed her gently on the mouth. It felt cool and sweet, like water to a thirsty man. It was tender, like first love. Helena stood there for a moment motionless, unresponding. Then his longing engulfed her and she returned his kiss with a passion that surprised them both.

Just this once, she told herself, just this once. She clung to him as though she would never let go.

Then she pulled abruptly away and hurried towards the house, promising herself they would not be alone again. The promise died on its way from her brain to her heart.

Maria was standing on the side terrace watching Helena as she came into view. Helena's breath caught . . . could she have seen them? No, the trees were thick, the orchard deep. Yet the terrace was high . . . it looked down into the estate.

"I've been looking for you, Helena," Maria called out. "Come here my dear, I want to talk to you."

No, she had not seen them. Or could she have, and

not cared? It worried Helena.

Maria smiled and turned to someone standing in the doorway. Silken clothes glistened in the sun. It was Ali Bey. He'd made a practice of dropping by more often these days.

She could not bear the sight of him, or the gleam in his eye when he looked at Maria. Helena always managed to keep out of his sight or to leave by the back way when he arrived. Now she walked cautiously up the stone steps to the terrace. How can Maria stand him, she thought, seeing how her eyes lit up whenever the Turk appeared. It disturbed Helena, for she believed Maria had depth and character underneath that facade of the frivolous, social matron. She knew it was only a substitute for the attention Petros had denied Maria all these years.

"Ali Bey stopped for coffee . . . this time you won't get away, Helena."

Maria was determined to get them together. Helena's attitude toward Ali Bey had not escaped her.

"I understand you are a very talented lady," he smiled and bowed his head. "You must visit my home one day. Perhaps you would consent to teach my wives your craft."

Indeed, Helena thought, your wives sit on silken pillows chewing mastic all day. I'll teach them a thing or two. She was amused at her picture of Bey's wives sitting propped up on their luxurious pillows chewing away like goats. Helena smiled at Bey unknowingly as a thought suddenly crossed her mind. How convenient to have access to a Turkish nobleman's home. Perhaps it could help Jason's plans. There must be something she could do from within the Turkish mansion.

"I would be most pleased to accept your invitation, *effendi,*" Helena lowered her eyes, trying to hide the sly pleasure that flickered on her face.

Maria watched, pleased that the two were finally getting on friendlier terms.

Something's going on between them, Helena thought. She hoped she was wrong. Her mind turned to the lessons Bey suggested and to the possibilities they offered.

She could not wait to tell Jason.

Her son was gone when Helena arrived home. She remembered that he would be with Fatouros again tonight, helping train the younger boys. They would be late. She pictured Jason's exuberance, his excitement, and she was glad. All this was good for him . . . it sustained him, gave his life a new direction. He had been such a sad child, growing into a withdrawn, melancholy youth. Books and studies took up all his time, until talk of the Revolution reached his ears and pushed his personal frustrations aside. Now, even with the added agony of Joseph, she knew her boy would survive. He had the spirit of his Greek heritage . . . and he was strong-willed, determined, like his mother.

Helena thought about Petros. Jason should approach him about joining the movement. If necessary, she would help persuade him. There was a great deal he could do. She wanted Petros to be a part of all this, perhaps because she realized the Revolution would be their only bond, their only communion, from now on.

The scene in the orchard flashed before her eyes as she put chamomile tea on to boil. The warm liquid would sooth her, help her sleep. Her nerves were shaken from Petros' confession . . . from their kiss. She sighed and chastised herself.

"Oh God," she whispered aloud as she so often did, "what am I going to do?"

All her sternness and dignity melted at times like these, and she became a lost, frightened little girl. Fortunately no one had ever seen her this way, for she was careful, and she could rally quickly. But she knew this new problem would not be an easy one to solve.

Helena undressed and stood before the large mirror, looking broodingly at her reflection. The old saying came to her mind . . . "women without love are like flowers without the sun, they wither and die." Helena had lived a manless life for twenty years. Yet she had blossomed in this darkness. She smiled sadly as she pondered her image in the mirror. Perhaps this was God's way of making things up to her, a small compensation for all the tragedies. Her tall body was slender, inviting, and her olive skin was smooth, without a wrinkle. The many tears and sleepless nights had graciously left no traces behind . . . her eyes were clear and bright, without a single line to mar the edges.

She wondered what it would be like if she were married to Petros now. He would walk in and put his arms around her. He would hold her. She could almost feel his touch, see the love in his eyes. They would like side by side on their bed and he would caress her face, her breasts. Chills went through her at the thought and she closed her eyes, as if to savor the sweetness of her fantasy. She was astonished that such feelings could stir within her. So she was not dead after all . . . her emotions had merely lain dormant all these years, waiting for Petros to come and waken them.

Exhausted, she sat down, still staring at the mirror across from her . . . still feeling Petros' fingers up and down her body. She remembered his kiss . . . and she was on fire.

"No!" she cried aloud, covering her face with her hands, "please God, no!"

She felt tainted, ashamed, as she sat there sobbing. When she finally opened her eyes she was trembling. She looked at her reflection again, and saw that her face was white, drained. Embarrassed at her emotions, she shook her head angrily to erase the memory of this scene. It was painful . . . bittersweet . . . but it reminded her that she was a woman, with all the fire and passion of her maturity.

The sound of boiling water made her jump. She ran to the stove . . . the tea had spilled over. She left it and went to bed.

The hours went slowly Helena could not sleep. Her heart ached and with it her body. Just once, she had said to herself when Petros kissed her. But she was afraid it was only the beginning of a feeling she would not be able to overcome. She had fought so many battles in her life and survived . . . yet this new experience, this new emotion was one she did not know if she could fight . . . or if she wanted to. No man had stirred her since her tragic marriage. When she first looked at Petros she saw someone who could be a friend, perhaps like Costas. But this was more, and it surfaced more each day. She had refused to admit it, but the feeling stirred each time she saw him. It was growing unknowingly, innocently, and now, three months later, their kiss made her realize it would never stop. She wanted Petros, she wanted to belong to him . . . and she was ashamed. She would die before bringing dishonor upon them. He had a wife and daughter . . . and she was bound to the ghost of Stratis, to a marriage that was a sham.

"God," she whispered as she lay there, "God, I always believed you were testing me . . . that you allowed all those tragedies so that in the end I would be rewarded. The end honors the beginning . . . isn't that what they say? Petros should be the end to my story, the happy end to my life, yet You sent him to me only to torment me."

The first rooster crowed as Helena fell asleep. She woke an hour later when the door opened and Jason rushed in. He ran to her bed, elated.

"Fatouros just told us. It's definite, he got the word from Uncle Xenophon. The Revolution is set for March 25th. At last the Greek mainland rises! That means Chios will soon be following."

He got up and paced the floor nervously, swinging his arms, clenching his fists.

"March 25th, the day of the Annunciation . . . oh God, the glorious day the Greek banner rises, and the world knows at last we'll be free . . . after four hundred years, mother, think of it . . . free!"

He sat on the edge of her bed and put his arms around her.

"You don't know, you can't imagine what I feel inside at this moment."

His face shone . . . he was ecstatic.

"And then to find Joseph . . . to find him and bring him back. Please God, help me do it, help me!"

They clung together and his enthusiasm surged through her, giving her new life and hope. Oh my

Jason, my flesh and blood, she whispered to herself. She prayed, how she prayed his dream would be realized. Could it be possible, that one day Joseph would be back with them? She was so afraid . . . their destiny was strange, ill-starred. Somehow she felt neither she nor her son were meant to find happiness . . . or peace. She brushed these thoughts aside to rejoice with him now. Jason at twenty-one, she thought, is twice the man his father ever was.

"Wait til you hear what I have," Helena teased Jason, "you think you're going to be the only hero in this Revolution?"

She told him about her meeting with Ali Bey and his invitation to teach his wives. Jason was delighted at the new prospect.

"You've got to start the lessons as soon as possible. Meanwhile, we can study the possibilities of this new development." Jason beamed. "What a Godsend! Do you realize what this could mean? I've got to find Fatouros and tell him about this."

They spoke of Captain Petros. It was time to approach him about joining the movement. A Greek from Constantinople would be a great asset to them. They would speak to him as soon as possible.

"Why don't you lie down a few hours, son?"

"I can't now . . . later." Jason rose. "I want to tell Fatouros about this. And from there I'm going straight to work. I'll see you tonight."

He kissed his mother on the forehead.

Helena watched her son leave. Spring, she thought, in Spring he would have been returning from Paris with his teaching degree. She decided Jason's wisdom was no less for lack of it. She was not sorry she had encouraged him to follow his conscience.

I wonder where we'll all be by Spring, she mused. What will happen to us?

A sense of fear gripped her, a dread that she tried to dispel. She listened quietly to Jason's footsteps crossing the courtyard.

VI

It was March 25th, 1821. Kambos lay peacefully shaded in its greenery. Chora bustled with shipping activities. Thymiana quarried its famous stone. And the Greek mainland exploded with Revolution. Bishop Germanos raised the banner in southern Greece and led the freedom fighters against the Turks at *Agia Laura.* The Greek spirit would no longer be squelched. Those four centuries of slavery, of shame and torture, had burst forth in a rocket of anguish and disgust. The Greeks were determined—Freedom or Death was the cry that rang out in the hills and valleys of Hellas. Freedom or Death! They would take no more humiliation. They would be proud, free men or die. The determination of these suppressed people was so great that it multiplied their strength. And the Turks, in all their numbers, were no match for them. The Greeks rushed into the villages and towns with swinging sabres plunging into the bellies of their conquerors. Blood for blood! At last they would avenge their raped women and pillaged homes.

The news reached Chios a week later. Jason watched the ship approaching at the harbor, the sailors waving frantically from the bow, and he knew it was a signal of joy. This was what he had been waiting for—the moment that seemed forever in coming. The ship docked, the details were breathlessly relayed, and Jason's jubilance knew no bounds. His heart beat wildly. He felt his blood surging, his excitement rising. Soon Chios, too, would rise!

Within a month the Greeks took the Peloponnese and set out for Thessaly and Epirus. Eager to take up the fight, the islands of Hydra, Spetsai and Psara rose and declared their independence before the Turks could retaliate. The Turkish navy scattered in chaos and terror at this sudden strength of the *giaours.* When did the faithless ones prepare, they wondered, where did they get this power, this support? And the reprisals began. Christians in Constantinople were rounded up and slaughtered. The clergy, too, were not excepted, they were the first to be hanged. Among them was the Holy Patriarch Gregorios, spiritual leader of the Orthodox faithful. The christian world was stunned to learn of the holy man's demise. But the Turks cared little for rank or position . . . they must stop the rebels at all costs. But this did not stop the Greeks. The cruel reprisals only strengthened their purpose, their will. Ten will die that thousands will live, they shouted. Reprisals meant nothing when a nation was at stake. They were determined it would be a fight to the end. Nothing would hold them back. And nothing did.

Bent on stopping the Greek rebels, and believing the Chiotes were impervious to all that went on around them, the Turks were at ease with matters on the island. After all, they had the best of two worlds . . . they were content. What other Greeks shared the favors of the Sultan? What conquered peoples enjoyed the wealth and prosperity of Chios?

It was a surprise to both sides when, on April 27th, twenty-five Greek ships appeared in the horizon. They sailed from the islands of Hydra and Psara with orders to initiate the rebellion in Chios. Anchor was dropped at Pasha's Fountain in Vrondados, to the north of the island, and immediately word was sent to the chief Elders to meet with Commander Tombazis. The Elders came, but against their better judgment. Disturbed by this sudden development and fearing the consequences from the Turks, they gathered hesitantly to greet their fellow Greeks.

Commander Tombazis stared at their grim faces, sensing their reluctance to welcome him. The rotten bastards, he thought as he handed them the proclamation, they couldn't care less about freedom. One hundred twenty thousand Chiotes dangling on strings, mere puppets in the hands of these aristocrats. Curse them, he felt an urge to push them aside and rush into the villages himself, waving the proclamation he had brought from the mainland. It was a statement of urgency, direct orders from Ypsilantis himself. Knowing full well the spirit of Chios and her desire for freedom, the newly formed Greek government was calling them to arms. Brothers, rise and fight! Rise and declare your independence!

Jason and Fatouros stood at the side, not allowed to join the discussion, clenching their fists and trying to catch wisps of the conversation. They saw the nature of the scene, the grimness, the cool attitude of the Elders, and longed to be able to speak, to shout their objections. But according to law they had no right. Only the Elders handled these matters. Jason was aware of their political views and he knew there was only one reason this fleet had arrived. So he hurried down with Fatouros the moment he heard, telling no one, hoping . . . hoping what? He did not know. All he could do was pray the Elders might be shamed into joining Tombazis. Jason and Fatouros watched the scene anxiously. They must remember all the details to report back to Thymiana.

The group talked quietly and the Elders listened to Tombazis' plan, wishing there were some way they could be rid of him without embarrassment. They shook their heads patiently. Yes, they would consider the proclamation. No, they could give him no immediate answer. They must return to Chora and consult the other Elders. Then they must consider the opinions and wishes of the general populace before reaching a final decision. Tombazis was not sure the Elders would give much attention to what the common people wanted. He knew what their answer would be. But there was nothing he could do.

"Give us a few days and we will bring you our answer. Please know that we want to do what is best for Greece and for Chios. But bear with us for we are a trading island. We have few fighters here and even they are unprepared."

Diomataris was being patient with Tombazis, hoping he did not sound condescending. But Tombazis was fuming.

"What have you been doing all these years,

Diomataris, while the rest of us were preparing?" He could not help spit out the words. Did they think Tombazis was a fool, that he would believe an island as rich and powerful as Chios was unable to prepare for a Revolution?

There was no reply. Nothing the Elders could say would justify them, for they controlled the wealth and the movements of the island.

"We are traders and educators," Diomataris finally replied, "we told you this before, Commander. Chios can help you with money if you like." He paused a moment. "At any rate," he spoke slowly, emphasizing the words, "we will bring you our decision in four days."

Jason itched to have his say, but Fatouros held him back. They stood there together, angry and defeated, watching the aristocrats of Chios sell their countrymen to the foe.

Tombazis watched the group walk away . . . he turned to his second-in-command.

"I think it's hopeless, but we'll wait and see."

"It's a pity," the other man shook his head, "but it's their loss."

Tombazis felt it was also his.

Jason and Fatouros waited until the Elders were out of sight, and walked up to the rejected men. They wanted Tombazis to know the truth, that thousands of Chiotes, the villagers of the island, were with them. And that their hands were tied because of the wealthy landowners and traders of Chora, Kambos and the mastic region.

Tombazis shook his head sadly. It did not matter now. They had wasted their time coming here.

"I'm sorry for you lad," he spoke kindly to Jason,

admiring his fighting spirit. He turned to Fatouros and offered his hand.

"I know there are others like you. And I wish there was something more we could do." It was hard for him to believe his mission to Chios had failed. "But you heard . . . nevertheless, we will wait for their reply. And then we'll sail for other Greek shores that will welcome us."

The two Chiotes were ashamed. They could say nothing. Tombazis noticed the defeated look on their faces and smiled sadly.

"Come aboard a while," he slapped their shoulders. "Come let us drink a cup to Chios, and to the freedom that will come some day."

And noting the defeat on Jason's face, he added, "Don't worry, fellow Greek, the day will come for you too. As long as there are Chiotes like you two, it cannot fail to arrive."

With bowed heads Jason and Fatouros followed Tombazis to the ship.

* * *

Big Ears lifted the last of the flour sacks and piled it on top of the others. He brushed the white powder from his hair and his patched shirt, wiped his brow and turned to see Helena through the doorway, walking up the narrow street. He watched as she stopped to adjust the bundles that were slipping from her grasp and rushed to help her, his words tumbling over themselves in his anxiety.

"Here *Kyra* Helena, I'll . . . I'll . . . here, give them to me."

"Thank you Yorgo," Helena never called him Big

Ears like everyone else.

She smiled gratefully as she gave him some of the packages she had brought from Chora—skeins of yarn, knitting wool, threads and canvas for her handcrafts.

"Big Ears" adored Helena. She was the only one in Thymiana, besides Jason, who did not laugh and make fun of his big ears and stumbling walk. He did not mind the nickname they gave him in childhood, for he knew his ears were at least three times their natural size. He had even become used to the taunts and good-humored jokes of the villagers. For in their crude and often tormenting ways, they accepted him as a part of their village and their lives. Helena and Jason accepted Big Ears as a human being who had a heart and feelings like everyone else. And he would do anything for them. Often at dawn he would steal quietly into Helena's courtyard, before she awoke, and water her plants, her small garden, pull the weeds, clean out the magazine where the goat and a few chickens roamed. When Helena smiled at Big Ears his heart overflowed with a feeling he could not understand—a feeling of warmth and happiness. The sun seemed to shine brighter and the burden of his ugly ears protruding for the world to see was not quite so unbearable. Once Helena had even touched them, smiling sadly. At that moment he was ecstatic. For the first time in his life he was glad he had big ears. Otherwise would Helena have touched them with such tenderness?

He walked behind her now, holding the packages lovingly, and she turned to him, slowing her pace. He was ashamed to walk beside her but she did not mind. He wanted to laugh and cry. He giggled nervously, a squealing sound he wished he could control. Why was he so different from the others? Now, at the age of forty, he still found it difficult to understand his mother's explanation that God creates man as He chooses. What had Big Ears done to God that He should punish him that way? He never hurt anyone and he always obeyed orders. He washed his face every morning like his mother told him, and his feet every night so they would not smell. He hated to wash and often tried to get under the bedcovers with his dirty feet, only to have his mother shake her finger at him and scold gently.

"Come on now Yorgo, I saved some nice, warm water for your feet."

He would make a face and, seeing his mother's persistence and growing impatience, hurry to do her bidding.

They reached her house and Helena invited him in. They put the packages down and she brought out the jar of fig preserve she kept for company. Big Ears watched her spoon some into a tiny dish. She poured fresh water from the jug and he noticed the copper cup was one of those she used herself. It puzzled him that his ugliness and stupidity did not offend her. At that moment he would gladly have given his life for Helena.

"Big Ears, eh Big Ears, where the devil are you?"

The voice of Xenophon the merchant rang through the narrow street and reverberated through the stone archway leading to Helena's house.

Big Ears thanked Helena quickly as he gulped his water down and ran to answer his employer's call. He shuffled down the street yelling in reply, his hoarse voice stuttering.

Xenophon scolded Big Ears for wandering away again, but his tone was good-natured. He tried to be stern with the man who needed to be disciplined and guided like a child.

Xenophon Andreadis was a brilliant man, well-read, self-educated. But he was also practical, a man of logic who was seldom swayed by emotion and false idealism. Today he was greatly disturbed to learn about the Greek ships at Pasha's Fountain, and the proclamation Tombazis had brought. One of his men set out to gauge the pulse of the islanders and was now riding from town to village to talk with them. Andreadis' keen instinct and knowledge of conditions told him that grave consequences lay ahead if the island agreed to revolt. It would be suicide at this stage. Yet he knew the villagers were headstrong, they wanted to fight. He must find a way to stop them or, at least, to stall for time. He was never more wrong in his life and the months ahead would prove it.

"Big Ears, I want you to find Fatouros and tell him we have a meeting tonight. Evening vespers. You got that? Tonight, evening vespers. Tell him to be at St. Efstratios at five and to tell the others."

Big Ears could not understand all this confusion about meetings and churches and vespers. He always thought church was for praying and for lighting candles. But while the priest chanted and sprinkled holy water, the men gathered in a group and spoke in low tones of guns and ships and Ypsilantis. It was all a confusing jumble to Big Ears. The only thing he knew and understood was that he was never to repeat what he saw or heard. Especially to anyone from Kambos or Chora, and particularly to Turks or servants. Once Jason had tried to explain all this to Big

Ears—something about being free. Big Ears understood a little, but he was not quite sure if he wanted to be free. True, it was a nuisance to have his mother stand over him scolding and shaking her finger every so often, but then who would fix his supper and wash his clothes? And who would pour water over his dirty feet and hand him a clean towel to wipe them? He thought about this often. No, he really did not care to be free. But he would never do anything to stop the others who seemed to want this freedom so badly. Perhaps there was more to it than he understood. Jason said he would explain it more clearly some day. But Jason was always in a hurry. It bothered Big Ears that his friend always looked so sad, so preoccupied with deep thoughts. Maybe his mother shook her finger at him too. Maybe Jason didn't like to wash his feet either. Big Ears giggled at the thought. But no, Jason was a fine gentleman, not like Big Ears. And Helena would never shake her finger at her son, or at any human being. Big Ears sighed. He felt so fortunate, so rich to have Jason and Helena as his friends. He hurried off to find Fatouros.

* * *

"Kyrie Eleison, Kyrie Eleison." Father Stelios' chant rose in the air and mingled with the incense. Saint Efstratios looked down from his position on the iconostas, his elongated countenance a grim sight. Beside him was the Virgin; further to the left the other saints, their Byzantine forms lending a somber mysterious air. They faced the few old women and widows that came to pray every evening, measuring them silently, judging, convicting.

Kyra Perdika with her fresh mourning clothes stared at the saints stubbornly as though daring them to judge her. Let them! Last month she had buried her daughter. The town was shocked, jolted by the sudden loss of the young wife who was barely twenty and carrying her first child. No one could understand the tragedy. Only her husband and her mother knew the truth . . . and the saints staring down at Perdika.

Olga had arrived home from the fields earlier than usual that day. Finding the kitchen deserted, she walked into the bedroom to discover her husband under the sheets with her mother. The girl stood frozen in her tracks, staring at the two panting figures on the bed, their startled expressions making them look almost comical. Olga could not believe her eyes. She thought she might be dreaming, but at that moment the child inside her kicked spiritedly and she realized she was awake. She let out a terrifying scream and ran out into the street, up the hill and down to Megas Limionas, the Great Harbor. The next morning her body floated ashore.

Perdika was annoyed. She should have been more careful. That foolish child of hers, running off and drowning like that. Fortunately no one suspected, or even mentioned the scream that pierced the air that fateful afternoon. Was it possible such a sound went unheard in all that stillness? Dimitris had wanted to run after Olga, but Perdika held him back. There was no point in creating a scene, she insisted, the girl would return and they would work something out.

Perdika and Dimitris had been sharing stolen moments for nearly two years now, since her daughter's betrothal when he had moved into the house. The innocent Olga had been none the wiser. Perdika needed love. Her strong body ached those long evenings her seaman husband sailed the seas. It was his fault, she kept telling herself, for leaving a sensuous woman alone at the prime of her womanhood. And so Perdika had carved her own course. The villagers, who had savored juicy gossip about her daring escapades in the past, had little food for it now. With her daughter's marriage, Perdika appeared to have settled down. She was pleased; it was safe with Dimitris inside her own house. All was well with her world.

Now Olga was dead. She stared up at the saints tight-lipped. Yes, they knew. Her look seemed to taunt them. The thought of having Dimitris to herself sent chills up her spine. She could not wait to have him touch her again. But he was cold, withdrawn, since the funeral. Guilt tortured him and he lay in bed night after night, sleepless, cursing himself and his sensuous mother-in-law. He wished he could leave the house immediately but he did not want to make it obvious. The first period of mourning must pass. After the forty-day memorial service he would take his clothes, spit in Perdika's face—hadn't she made the first move?—and walk out. Yet he felt excitement at the thought of her, remembering her naked body, their stolen moments together. She had been almost maniacal in her desires, sharing with him an ecstasy he never knew with young Olga, whose purity only he had known.

Father Stelios stood before the small congregation swinging his censer while the incense permeated the air, its smoke drifting among the women and up to the dome. He looked at Perdika who had bowed her head piously. The poor woman, he thought, what greater pain than to bury one's own child. I must stop at her home one evening . . . and comfort her.

The priest looked towards the church entrance and watched the men of Thymiana gathering. They had come to discuss the proclamation. Father Stelios' face showed deep concern. Chios was not an island of fighters. What would happen to them all? It was only the second month of the Revolution on the mainland. He hoped their decision would be a wise one.

"You've heard about the ships at Vrondados, men." Xenophon spoke quietly, somberly as he looked the men, one by one, in the eye.

"This is the moment we've been waiting for." Fatouros spoke up. Hadn't he been training the men, planning each one's role in the struggle? His hand itched for the rifle.

Christos the butcher spoke his mind. "I've been waiting for this moment too, friend, but don't you think we should be more practical? Are we really ready to fight?"

"We're as ready as we'll ever be." Fatouros was adamant.

Michalis the stonecutter was annoyed. "What about the other villages? Most of them haven't a weapon to their names."

"That's right," another offered. "We're one of the few villages with guns and ammunition."

"I say we can all use a rifle," Monogios interrupted, "and those without rifles can use pitchforks and sticks. We've got to join the other Greeks in this fight."

Xenophon watched them silently. Let them all have their say. He wanted to know what his people thought. He would speak last.

"You don't stand up against Turkish swords with pitchforks and sticks, compatriot," the solemn Karanikolas spoke. "I say we must weigh this carefully."

It was a moment of indecision. The villagers knew the Elders were against the Revolution. "They're looking out for their own welfare. They've got the best of two worlds now."

Indeed, the Elders enjoyed wealth and power in government. They shared the friendship of the Turks while they filled their own coffers. Revolution would only demote them to common people, not the statesmen of the island. Their only decision would be refusal to fight.

"Forget the Elders and let's be practical for our own sakes."

All eyes turned to Xenophon who could remain silent no longer. He was the wise one, the ultimate decision-maker; they trusted him. Xenophon Andreadis seldom steered them wrong. They must hear him now.

"Now listen men and listen carefully. The Elders have their reasons but we have ours. We all know that Chios is unprepared to fight."

"What about all the guns and powder we've been storing in the caches?" Until now Jason had remained silent out of respect for his uncle. But Xenophon's rationale made no sense.

"Why have we been training and preparing all these years, uncle? I don't know about the rest of Chios, but here in Thymiana we're ready to fight, now. My God, then the whole thing was pointless." He looked his uncle in the eye. "Forgive me sir, but I say we can fight and we must."

"Sorry Mr. Xenophon, but I tend to agree with the lad." It was Fatouros again. "I've been training riflemen for a long time now."

"You call that adequate training for war? A few nights of target practice in a cave?" Xenophon could hold his patience no longer. "Do you really think you can stand up to all those Turks? A handful of farmers and stonecutters? What do we know about fighting?"

Silence fell over the men. Xenophon continued, "And what about the other villages? What happens to them?"

"Let them speak for themselves. We're deciding for Thymiana now." Jason would not be crushed.

Xenophon's tone softened. He knew these men were determined. He knew the obsession that spurred them on.

"I understand how you feel, believe me. There's nothing I want more than to see us free, to see us our own men. But we've got to face facts. Listen to me, men. The Greeks of the mainland have been training and planning Revolution for hundreds of years. But here in Chios you know the situation. We're a great trading power. We've got the greatest scholars and library renowned throughout the world. But where does that place us in the Revolution? Our knowledge of fighting is insufficient. I say let's help the struggle some other way—with money, ships, transport."

"Who said we can't fight?" Tsimbinos would not hear of it. He was furious with Andreadis. "The Chiotes are as good as any Greeks."

"I didn't say they're not."

"Who said we can't fight?" Another voice repeated the enfuriating phrase. "We're the best hunters in the Aegean. Give us a chance at the Turks, you'll see."

The one thing Xenophon could see was that the men would not be swayed. He tried again.

"Hunting is one thing and fighting is another. Look here a moment. Do you realize that Turkey is only an hour's sail from here? If we rise now, help from the mainland could never reach us in time. We'd be ashes before you could say the word 'freedom.' I say refuse Tombazis' offer."

The group buzzed. Doubt crept in the men's minds. Andreadis had a point. And he was usually right. Perhaps they should wait. The priest chanted louder to drown out the noise.

"No! I say *now*, I say we accept the proclamation." Jason spoke with passion. "Otherwise we'll never live it down. Do you want them to say we were afraid?" He was pleading desperately now. "How ready do we have to be? There are twenty-five ships out there in Vrondados. And only a handful of Turks on the whole island. If we join Tombazis now, we can finish them off. I know we can."

The men were weakening. They respected Jason for his maturity and his patriotism. A boy was showing them the way and they could not refuse. One of the men put his arm around Jason's shoulders.

"Chios needs more than spirit to win a Revolution." He hesitated, reluctant to disagree with Jason. "I'm afraid I must side with Mr. Andreadis. And it's because I love this island too, Jason. I love it and want to see it free. But the risk is too great."

"You too, Christos?" Jason's face was red, the blood ramming against his temples. Were they fools? "Are you asking me to believe the Chiotes are a bunch of cowards? I'm ashamed to think that. I won't!"

A firm voice came from behind. It was not one of

them.

"Chios will not shirk her duty, Jason, you can be sure of that."

Everyone turned to see Captain Petros.

What's a man from Kambos doing here, wondered Andreadis anxiously. Sofronis no less, a man from Constantinople! This will never do. Who the devil let him through? Andreadis turned to the watch at the door who gave him a positive sign. Nonetheless Xenophon was puzzled. Up to now Sofronis had given no indication of his political allegiance.

Petros continued, ignoring the merchant's scrutinizing stare.

"We owe it to ourselves and to Greece. Perhaps to the world. We *must* take up arms—we will! History must show that the Chiotes are as valiant as any other Greek. We're not swayed by wealth and luxury. We want to be free, too . . . and we *will* be free!"

There were tears in his eyes, and in the others'. No one remained unmoved. But slowly suspicion clouded their vision. Was Sofronis to be trusted? After all, wasn't he a close personal friend of Ali Bey the Turk? Didn't their families socialize for years?

"Those are noble words, indeed, your captaincy, but your friendship with Ali Bey is no secret here. How do we know this is not a Turkish trick?" Karanikolas eyed him carefully.

Angry voices rose up from the anxious men, bounced against the dome where the Pancreator stared down, and drowned out the *kyrie eleisons* of Father Stelios. As the turmoil increased, Fatouros signaled them to stop.

"Wait—I believe there is something you should know." He turned to Karanikolas. "My friend, as well as the rest of you." He looked at the others. "Do not look upon Captain Petros Sofronis as an enemy. He is one of us, and he has been risking his life helping prepare for the Revolution."

A murmur rose. Fatouros continued in a bold voice.

"I had been sworn to secrecy, but now Captain Sofronis has come forth and I am free to tell you . . . that the rifles we received last October were arranged and paid for by the good captain . . .

The men were stunned. Joyful shouts filled the church. Jason gave Petros his hand, exuberant at the news. The priest signaled from the portico while the sexton gestured frantically for quiet. Ah, these Thymianousi were incorrigible. They would be the death of him. He wished he were back in his old parish in the capital city where no one spoke of Revolution. Or in the village of *Tholo Potami* high on the mountain. The most beautiful women on the island lived in *Tholo Potami.* They said it was the drinking water, or perhaps the altitude. The sexton smiled, carried away by his fantasy.

Father Stelios noticed Perdika wiping her eyes. The poor thing, he would go to her tonight. He made the sign of the cross as he spoke his last *Kyrie eleison.* Then, with a hurried "Amen," he ended the vespers and the meeting.

The men walked out, satisfied that they had arrived at the only decision possible—they would fight. If Captain Sofronis, gone from his home for twenty years, could do this much for them and for his island, they would be with him and with the cause, one hundred per cent.

Xenophon was defeated. For the first time he could remember, his advice was rejected. He shrugged his shoulders.

"I'll leave for Chora now," he said, "to tell the Elders of Thymiana's decision." His heart was heavy with foreboding. He hoped he would be proven wrong in his judgment.

Xenophon had no idea that only an hour earlier forty of the leading Chiotes had been taken hostages by the Turks, to ensure against such decisions as the one Thymiana had just made.

* * *

The sun cast its warm rays over Vrondados. It was a beautiful April morning, a day of God's joy, marred only by the sight of the warships anchored in the placid waters of Pasha's Fountain. The wind blew softly, as though it, too, were afraid of disturbing the stillness. Only the faces of the group that stood near the shore speaking in low, angry tones betrayed Nature's tranquility.

Diomataris, Patrikousis and Vlastos stood together facing Commander Tombazis once again. The council had taken all things into consideration, they said, and at the will of the people had voted against joining the revolt. Vlastos explained the reasons a successful uprising was impossible at this time. What he did not tell Tombazis was that the Elders had taken it upon themselves to make the final decision, ignoring the consensus of the towns and villages who had voted to fight. After all, the council reiterated, what do villagers know about military strategy? As leaders of the Chiote government, the Elders believed it their sacred duty to take every precaution to save the island from disaster.

Tombazis saw through them. He listened patiently, saying nothing, but in his heart he refused to accept their feeble excuses. His two men watched their superior anxiously. They knew their commander was fighting a battle within. He did not want to say anything he would later regret. These Chiotes are indeed a strange people, they thought.

Vlastos tried to hide the annoyance that grew with Tombazis' accusing silence. He wanted him to leave now, with those ships of his and the men that came to stir up trouble.

"The presence of your ships has infuriated the Turks. They've already taken hostages. Go before we have more serious consequences."

Patrikousis was calmer. He did not want to antagonize Tombazis.

"Don't be annoyed with us, Commander Tombazis," he said. "You came here to liberate us, yes, we understand that. But how? Where are your reserves?"

The man is mad, thought Tombazis.

"You have one hundred twenty thousand Chiotes on this island and you want reserves, compatriot?" I'm wasting my time, he thought, but I won't give up so easily. His tone softened.

"We brought you shiploads of rifles and ammunition. And there's only a handful of Turks on the island. Surely we can beat them on numbers alone. Others have done it with much less. Come now, friends, these are Greeks we're dealing with."

"These are Chiotes we're dealing with, commander," Vlastos corrected, "Chiotes—traders, seamen, educators, not fighters!"

"What makes you think Chiotes can't fight?" An

angry voice interrupted the conversation. Captain Hadjinikolas Kyladitis, the Elder from Vrondados stepped from behind the other three. He had been silent long enough. He knew he was outnumbered, that the majority of the Elders were with the three men here, but he would have his say regardless. History would not say that this man of Vrondados shirked his duty.

Diomataris and Patrikousis frowned at Vlastos. The three turned an angry glare upon Kyladitis. They should not have allowed him to come. He was always a rebel in their midst. But he was a rich man, a powerful one and they must not offend him.

"Hadjinikolas, you insisted on coming with us. We hope you will respect your position as well as ours. We reached our decision at the assembly in Chora by lawful means. There is no room now for changes or reconsiderations. Your opinion was heard, but it was voted down. Please remember that."

For months now Kyladitis' ships were carrying arms and supplies to the revolutionaries on the mainland. The captain-shipowner had given up his own trading routes to help the cause in the one way he could—by transporting what the Greeks needed in their struggle. Now he wanted to aid his own island. But he was helpless. He turned to Tombazis.

"Commander Tombazis," he stated solemnly, as though he were in a courtroom, "let it be noted on this 31st Day of April, 1821, that Hadjinikolas Kyladitis of Vrondados, Chios, dedicates his ships and his life to the liberation of this island. And let it be further noted that the Elders of Chora have taken it upon themselves to vote against Chios' declaration of independence."

Vlastos was embarrassed. He did not want

Tombazis to think they were cowards . . . they were only trying to do what was best for the general welfare of the island.

"You know very well, Captain Kyladitis, that they are holding forty hostages in the fortress." Vlastos would make them see. "Forty of the greatest minds of Chios. Our leading citizens, and many of our Elders . . . those who led our people and must lead us again until the day of freedom comes. If we make one move they are all dead. Will you take their blood on your hands?"

"Will you take the blood of the whole island on *your* hands, friend Vlastos!" Kyladitis would not be swayed.

"Don't be a fool, Kyladitis," Diomataris' anger rose. "All the Chiotes on this island combined aren't worth those forty minds in that fortress prison. Think about it man, think who's locked up in those dungeons. The Bishop Metropolitan, Skilitsis, Rodokanakis, our leading educators, our clergy, our traders and sea captains. Forty who will soon become one-hundred-twenty. One-hundred-twenty heads that hold Chios together! If we lose them we lose the island!"

Kyladitis retaliated quickly. "And who offered the Turks these hostages?" Nothing escaped him. "Who went to the Turks and assured them Tombazis would leave? And, who guaranteed his departure? You, my friend! If you recall, Diomataris, the Turks asked for ten hostages, yes ten! But you made a more generous offer, you wanted to show your good faith and gave him forty instead."

The Elders were outraged. Kyladitis was exposing facts that embarrassed them. How could they explain that these actions were made in good faith, in complete trust of the Turks, who had never misled or mistreated the Chiotes?

Diomataris had no ready excuse. He spoke with resignation but there was sadness in his voice.

"Some day history will understand our decision. Some day it will explain our stand."

"Some day history will call us cowards. Men will make jokes about the Chiotes and their mastic, and their friendship with the Turks."

Kyladitis stormed off, unable to continue. He would leave the island, go with his ships to ports that needed him. He would not taint his name by being a part of a group who valued their comforts above ideals.

Tombazis gave up. Even the Elders of the island could not agree amongst themselves.

"I believe we are wasting each other's time." Tombazis shook his head in defeat. "Our work does not end with Chios. There are other places waiting for us, others who need us."

There was silence. It was over. Vlastos offered his hand to the commander.

"God be with you Commander Tombazis. Do not think badly of us. Remember that we love our country as much as any Greek. We are merely fighting in our own way."

"Before we leave, let us give you the weapons we brought." At least Tombazis could help arm the Chiotes. "One thousand rifles and ammunition. Give them to the villagers. I am certain the time will come when they will be put to good use."

He knew, his scout had reported to him, that the villagers had also hidden fifteen thousand rifles these past years, and they were waiting for the signal to use them. But it was no use arguing with these Elders.

Their minds were closed.

The men shook hands and thanked Tombazis. They would distribute the rifles immediately. It would not be long, however, before they would convince the Chiotes to surrender them up to the Turks, as another sign of good faith, and as guarantee against future revolts.

Tombazis watched the Elders leave, biting his lip, cursing inside him. He was a respected man who had been appointed National Committeeman of Hydra in 1818 by Prince Alexander Ypsilantis himself. He could not understand this attitude, this flagrant disregard for honor at such a crucial moment. No one could imagine, then, what confusing chapters would be written in future annals. One side blaming the Chiotes for selfishness and cowardice in their refusal to fight, and the other blaming Tombazis for igniting the spark that was to bring bloodshed and annihilation to an innocent, unprepared people. No one would ever know which side to blame. Perhaps they were both right and both at fault.

In October of that year, the three Elders—Diomataris, Patrikousis and Vlastos—were added to the list of hostages by orders of the new Governor. They were herded into the prison inside the fortress to begin a year's discomfort and humiliation. The very people who had won the respect and admiration of the Sultan were now treated like animals, locked in caged dungeons to wait their doom. The newly appointed Governor Bechit Pasha, followed by Elezoglou and one thousand Turkish soldiers had arrived from Constantinople to take over the reins of government once held by the Chiote Elders. The Pasha would now rule the island—the friendly, fatherly hand of the

Sultan was removed. The carefree lives the Chiotes once enjoyed was coming to an end. Bechit Pasha made certain of this. To begin, he ordered the Chiotes to assume full expenses for maintaining the Turkish forces on the island. He then ordered one hundred fifty people, men from the villages, to start the back-breaking task of digging and enlarging the moat around the fortress. The workers were driven for long hours, with little food and constant abuse. The hostage list was lengthened and the Turks decided to rotate the leading citizens—Elders and clergy, traders and sea captains. Soon the exempted workers from the precious mastic fields were brought in. A rumble of fear spread over the island. This was not what the Chiotes expected. Who had issued these orders? No one could understand this complete reversal of policy. The Elders had said the Sultan would be pleased at Chios' refusal to rise and fight against him, that he would show his gratitude for their loyalty. Was this their reward? The Elders' decision had boomeranged, then, in spite of their wisdom and diplomacy. It had worked against them, against all the Chiotes. The peace and prosperity of the island, the cooperation between Greek and Turk were soon a thing of the past.

As time went by Bechit Pasha increased his demands. He borrowed thousands of *grossia* from the Elders, money he never returned. He forced them to turn over sacks of wheat and barley without payment, contrary to Turkish agreement. News of Bechit Pasha's cruelty spread throughout the island, and the Chiotes felt the yoke tighten around their necks.

In a few months the Chiotes were leaderless. All the Elders had been taken hostages. The Turks wanted no

Chiote to lift his head again. They confiscated every weapon on the island, including those left behind by Tombazis. And now the Chiotes were completely powerless. Pasha was pleased. There was no danger of Chios rising, of asserting herself in any way. The security and power the island once knew no longer existed.

As time passed, Turkish soldiers became bolder. They roamed the villages at will, raping and pillaging, supposedly without the Sultan's knowledge. Every day the yoke was pulled tighter. And every day Chios realized, more and more, the need to revolt. Now at last the Chiotes saw signs of what the other Greeks had endured for four centuries. There was no alternative now. The Chiotes must rise to save themselves.

Jason was heartsick at this turn of events. He could not help blaming the Elders, although they were now paying dearly for their errors. But his despair only spurred him on in his determination to help bring about the day of Revolution.

This time Chios must be ready. Yet how? Without weapons, without freedom to circulate as before? When the Turks on the island had turned from friends into tyrants? When the coast of Turkey, only an hour away, was constantly on guard, watching the island's every move?

Jason cursed silently. Why did they let this happen? Chios had had all the opportunities, all the wealth to feed armies and man ships. They could have done this while they were still in the Sultan's favor. It seemed hopeless now. More and more Chiotes felt the same as Jason, but it was too late. They didn't stand a chance unless they could rally full support from the Greeks on the mainland. They needed ships and ammunition to back them. But the Greeks there had their hands full. Their struggle was still in its first year, there was a great deal of ground to cover on the mainland and little funding to support the huge costs. A second expedition to Chios was impossible. The Friendly Societies abroad had done what they could. The organization's phil-Hellene members raised funds throughout Europe and the Americas, but even this was not enough. The European nations looked with disfavor upon the Revolution, upon any revolution. It did not suit the Great Powers to encourage revolt, for they had their own interests, their own possessions to guard. The United States Congress debated over whether to grant support to the Greeks, and their proposed bill for aid was defeated because of public opinion. The world's advice to Greece in 1821 was "wait until a future date." But the Greeks would not wait. And the world left Greece to her fate. The powder keg was filled, the wick was lit, the dynamite exploded. And Chios, by her own leaders' hesitance, was now caught in the crossfire.

VII

Christmas came again and there was joy and renewed hope on the Greek mainland. The new year found them closer to their goal, to complete liberation. And as large areas overthrew the conquerors, many of the Greek islands followed suit and raised the Greek banner. The Cyclades, Hydra, Psara, Spetsai; Samos, Sifnos. One by one they became free, these small, determined islands. One by one inexorably, for they had prepared years for this moment. They had built ships, hoarded arms, planned their strategies, while biding their time. Those islands who had no fighters hired mercenaries to do the work. There were no excuses, no doubts, no hesitations. When the time came they stood up like their ancient forefathers.

But Chios remained static. Chios, the wealthiest island in the Mediterranean was unprepared, confused, hesitant. The island whose men held high offices in foreign governments and trade—men of great influence. Chios, with her wealth, position, and power. Chios did not rise.

Jason thought constantly about this, turning the facts over and over in his mind. He could find no adequate explanation, and in his desire to excuse the Chiotes, often rationalized. Did history not prove that the great liberators were not statesmen but common people, men of the hills, men who worked with their hands, not their minds? On the other hand was Ypsilantis not a statesman in Russia? Did he not plan and was now running the whole Greek Revolution? Jason tormented himself in his search for the answer. During his slower hours at the library he pored over books on Chios, learning about the island, its history, its people. The conclusion was that the Chiote villagers wanted their freedom, wanted to rise, while the wealthy noblemen of Kambos and Chora were holding them back. How unfair that a few should trample the bodies of many.

Jason admired the Chiotes and hated them. They had many virtues but many faults. At times Jason wished his mother had kept him on the mainland where he could live to see the day of liberation. His native Zagora was free now. He longed to see it again. He wondered how it would be now. But he longed to see Chios free, too, with all his heart. Would he live to see it? It was an ache inside him.

* * *

The shores of Chios were dim this Christmas of 1821. There were no festivities in the villages, no socials in Kambos. The people stayed close within their homes, behind the walls that offered temporary protection. These were somber holy days for Chios, and the islanders prayed before their icons, huddling their children close to them. And when the new year came, there was no gaiety, no singing, no tables spread with delicacies and pastries, no dancing with white kerchiefs fluttering in the air. Somehow the Chiotes feared the coming of 1822. They felt a strange premonition of disaster. They gathered their families together and went to church. They lit their candles, received communion, the old women fell prostrate on the floor and made the sign of the cross over and over again.

"Holy Virgin Mother," they murmured with fear, "help us, protect us and our children, and their children."

"Oh heavenly Father, in the name of Your only begotten Son, keep us safe from the terror that stalks us."

Within their churches they were under the benevolent eye of the saints. But outside these walls the eye of the conqueror, their former protector, glared with hatred and suspicion.

Silver coins tinkled in the offering boxes and filled them to overflowing, while gold-encrusted designs on the walls and rubies on the icons sparkled in the candlelight. Gold and rubies that could have bought arms and manned ships to free Chios. The saints, in their luxurious surroundings, looked down upon their huddled believers, looked upon them wistfully, sadly, and waited for what was to come. And if among these saints there was a rebel, he may have whispered, "Prayer is good, but move your hands a bit, too."

Yes, there was much gloom in Chios this holiday season, but no one was as pained as Ali Bey, who looked upon the turn of events with sorrow and embarrassment. He had lived well among the Greeks both here and in Constantinople, and he felt a strong kinship to them. Particularly with the Sofronis family who looked upon him as a dear friend. Ali Bey knew the worst was yet to come and he was frustrated with his position. What would he do when the island rose against the Sultan as it was bound to do? The Chiotes could not go on like this much longer. He dreaded the moment when his own world would collapse. Could it be, he wondered, that Allah was preparing to show his wrath because Bey had come to violate the code of friendship? But his god was generous, practical, luxurious beyond belief. It was the other God, the God of the Greeks that frowned upon forbidden joys and pleasures. Somehow this God of the *giaours* frightened him. Bey wondered if he had incurred His wrath. But the Greeks' God had no power over Bey, let Him deal with Allah!

Ali Bey sat on his silken pillows this night, the week of New Year's, smoking his *nargyle,* watching the bubbles of water, following the smoke rings he blew in the air. He remembered other holiday seasons he had shared with the Sofronis', the food and drink, the gaiety and friendship. It was a pity all this had stopped. But tonight he would forget the past and whatever curse awaited him in the future. He would not think of the moment when a part of him would be torn out, leaving him empty, without purpose in life. Tonight he would revel in the ecstasies Allah blessed. The beauty of a woman's body, the softness of her touch, the warmth of her love.

Mehmet the Eunuch appeared before his master. The women were settled for the night in the *haremliki*, the women's quarters on the other side of the house. He came to report all was well there, and to see which wife his master preferred for the night. It was Mehmet's task, each evening, to fetch the female of Bey's choice. Ali had not brought all his harem from Constantinople. He had tired of them. So he had sold the concubines and kept only his legal wives—two Turkish girls, an Armenian and a Lebanese. Bey was not a greedy man. Here in Chios, even his interest in his four wives was diminishing. His passion and desires were as strong as ever, for Bey was a rested man still in his prime. But he knew the reason his pleasures were meaningless. That other feeling, surpassing all things physical, had rooted itself inside the Turk and would not let go.

Ah, sighed Bey when Mehmet left to carry out his orders, poor Mehmet, he will never know the thrills of his sex. But then he will also never know the pain.

Bey felt sorry for this tall, soft-fleshed Spartan who had come to him many years ago. Mehmet had been abducted as a child from Greece, brought to Turkey and designated to be trained for the Janissaries. What better qualifications for a member of the crack Turkish regiment than a stalwart, healthy Spartan boy of heroic ancestry to serve the Sultan? But an error had occurred and the boy's name was placed on the eunuch's list instead. He was castrated before the error was discovered. The Turk who made it never lived to make another.

Ali Bey's thoughts were interrupted when his personal servant came in to make him comfortable for the night. It was time to retire. Ali was breathless—he must hurry. She would be here soon.

* * *

Maria put down her canvas and turned to Helena.

"I'm tired . . . and I'm bored!" Her exasperated tone startled Helena.

She turned from her knitting and looked at Maria. Something was bothering Petros' wife tonight. She was restless, moody. Everything irritated her. And several times Helena had caught her looking out the window furtively, as though she were expecting someone.

The two women had been close friends for over a year now. Helena had been what Maria needed in this strange land of walled-in estates and secluded living. Maria loved Helena and trusted her. She had tried for months now to confide in her, to tell her what was innermost in her thoughts and in her heart. She wanted to pour out the pain to this woman who had lived in pain herself. But she merely skirted the edges of her despair. Helena was so stern, so proper, that Maria was ashamed to confess her thoughts.

Poor Helena, Maria often thought, she is so much worse off than I am. I have been alone too, but I have known luxury and comfort. Yes, and even love, from afar. How can she bear her life? I would die! Maria was not as strong or courageous as Helena. Tonight, she did not want to be. Life is to live, she often told herself. She had smothered her sexual drive with charitable work and social affairs. But now, even that had proved meaningless. She could not live an empty life any longer. She had decided she would not.

Maria looked at Helena, wondering if her friend, in her uncanny perception, were reading her mind. But the look on Helena's face was one of concern. Was there a touch of sadness, a glint of understanding? Can she know, Maria wondered, can she sense what I am feeling tonight? What I have been feeling this past year? But no, she thought, only a woman in love can understand another.

She is suffering, thought Helena as she watched Maria now. Poor Maria, you want to tell me something to unburden your heart, to share what bitter joy you have, and you are afraid. Oh God, what is this strange game You play with us? Like the chessmen on the table inside, you place us—a king here, a queen there. You push us forward, backward, kill us off, at your will. And we are powerless to react.

"You're upset, Maria, aren't you?" Helena's voice was gentle, compassionate. "Why don't you tell me what's bothering you? I've watched you this past year. Whatever it is, trust me."

"How can you understand, dear Helena?" Maria was suddenly impatient with her friend, "How can you understand, when your own life is so empty and loveless?"

Maria saw a glint of tears in Helena's eyes and was sorry for having spoken. But Helena had conquered tears long ago and they rushed back obediently.

"Forgive me, Helena, oh my dear, forgive me for being so cruel. I didn't mean it the way it sounded."

Maria put her arms around Helena and began to cry softly. Helena held her for a moment, then took out a handkerchief and wiped Maria's eyes. She looked anxiously toward the adjoining room.

"Maria, hush or they'll hear you."

Jason and Captain Petros were playing chess in the library. Their voices, interrupted occasionally by Joanna's chatter, drifted into the salon where the two women sat. Joanna was delighted that Jason came to their home so frequently these days. He spent hours in deep conversation with her father. They seemed to have so much in common. But it annoyed her terribly when they sent her away during those mysterious, secret talks of theirs.

Joanna was certain Jason liked her. Yet he had a strange way of showing his affection. He would smile at her absent-mindedly, as one does to a child. When she tried to talk with him, his thoughts were far away. She had to scold him to get his attention. Why couldn't he see that she was not a little girl? The other young men did. But when she looked at them she saw Jason, only Jason. Why is first love so painful, she wondered. Why doesn't Jason see me, truly see me? She refused to understand that his every thought and concern was with the approaching Revolution, the passion of the uprising, and the fierce, secret hope that he would find his brother. He had never mentioned Joseph to her. The Sofronis' had no knowledge of that part of Jason and Helena's lives.

Jason could not explain this new feeling that was constantly with him. It was a premonition that grew with the passing weeks, the premonition of a meeting. Could it be with Joseph? He knew that they would come together soon, he felt it. How could he think of pretty girls and romance? He wished Joanna would leave him alone.

Petros' daughter brought a tray of pastries and set it down before the two men. Petros looked at her and smiled. My child, my own daughter, he thought, what joy and contentment it is to be with you again. He tried so hard to make up for the years he was away, leaving her to grow up fatherless. But are years ever made up? He did everything in his power to make her happy now, to make the most of their time together. He would never leave his daughter again, or his home. He did not realize that Joanna did not need him any longer—those years were gone—now she needed someone else.

Petros' thoughts were endless. And what of Helena? Would he go to her if she wanted him? He thought of his daughter, and felt torn inside, unable to answer this question. The time will come, he comforted himself, when Joanna will not need me. Then I will think of myself. Perhaps some day there will be time for me . . . and Helena. But what of Maria? Could anything be salvaged with her? Their life together was strange. He had tried, even while his heart was with Helena, to bring Maria close, to pick up their relationship. But she was cold, unresponsive. She complained of headaches, of being a light sleeper. So he left her alone. Before long they occupied separate bedrooms.

Petros looked at his daughter. She did not hold anything against him. She was a loving daughter, a fine, sensible girl. He watched her as she offered Jason the pastry. Jason took it and thanked her, smiling absently.

If I had a son, Petros thought for the hundredth time, I would want him to be like Jason. And seeing the two young people before him now, he added, perhaps if we are fortunate, I might have him as a son after all.

Jason and his mother had come to the Sofronis

home early this evening. They all had supper together and the men withdrew into the library to talk and play chess until the hour came for them to leave for Thymiana. There would be an assembly of all the neighboring villages, including a few renegades from Kambos and Chora, to announce the latest communique. Doctor Logothetis, the Naval Commander of the forces at Hydra, was discussing a Spring expedition to Chios with Bournias. It would probably take all night.

Helena worried when Jason was out late. Every hill had a Turkish watch and she feared the consequences of his discovery. But Petros assured her it was safer than the daytime when Turks took to wandering about everywhere. And their secret meeting place, the *koufes,* was impossible to locate. The Turks would never suspect they were gathering in the deep caves of the stone quarries, Petros promised Helena he would not let Jason out of his sight, that he would protect him as though he were his own. And her fears were quieted. She trusted Petros and felt relieved knowing he was with her son. After all, Jason was still a boy, regardless of the maturity of his twenty-one years. I have a lot to be grateful for, she told herself. Jason and I are loved and protected. The scales, once again, were balanced.

It was getting late now. Within the half hour the men must leave. The carriage would take them as far as Helena's house. They would leave her there and go the rest of the way on foot.

Maria had stopped crying and now stood at the window looking down over the orchard, watching the branches bending in the wind. She did not speak for a long while. It was cold outside and the winds blew across the island with fury. Maria hated the winds. It was always calm in Constantinople.

"Do you want me to stay with you tonight?"

Maria seemed not to hear.

That's strange, Helena thought, she doesn't want me to stay. Maria usually pleaded with Helena to remain with her.

"It's no bother, I have nothing to do." Helena tried again. "And we can talk."

She watched Maria carefully with suspicion.

"Maria, you shouldn't be by yourself tonight. You don't look well. Why don't I stay over?"

Maria turned suddenly and Helena noticed her nervousness.

"No, really, Helena, I'd rather be alone tonight. Truly I would."

She avoided Helena's eyes, looked at the floor, the ceiling, then turned back to the window.

She's in love, thought Helena with resignation. Of course, I saw it on her face. It's Ali Bey. And she's doing something she's going to regret. Helena thought of Joanna, of Petros, of Kambos and the taut Greek honor. It allowed no explanations, had no room for emotions. She shuddered. But there was nothing she could do. She would go to her home, with her own thoughts and her own problems. Yet were they her own any longer? Her life had become interwoven with the Sofronis family in so many ways. Her friendship with Maria, her feeling for Petros, her devotion to Joanna. Want it or not, Helena was a part of the Sofronis family and they a part of her.

She rose and gathered her knitting.

"Whenever you need me, Maria, I am here. I will

always be here." She wanted Maria to know this, to believe her. "Remember I am your friend."

"Thank you Helena." Maria smiled sadly.

Suddenly she wished she were like Helena, strong and able to cope with life. She knew Helena was fighting her own battles, some which Maria did not know, and she admired her friend's stand. Yet at times Maria felt sorry for her. Helena would never know the full joys of life.

Helena's own feeling for Petros—she was afraid to admit the word "love"—suddenly overwhelmed her. She wished she could dismiss it as quickly as she dismissed her thoughts. But it had the fervor of a mature woman, a flower thirsting for sun and water. This would be the other cross she must bear. She accepted it.

Maria smiled at Helena. Poor thing, she thought, poor Helena, life has cheated you. But I won't let it cheat me. Tonight Maria had made her decision. Her gaze followed Helena who went into the library to rouse the men.

* * *

Mehmet helped Maria through the steel door in the wall that separated Sofronis' estate from Ali Bey's. It was dark, there was no moon, but the eunuch knew the way. Maria held his arm and stumbled beside him. How tall he is, and flabby, she thought, and loyal. It was well-known that eunuchs repaid their masters' confidence with unswerving loyalty, to the point of death. Maria felt safe, there was nothing to fear with Mehmet close by. Her heart beat wildly, as though it would burst. She placed her hand over it, afraid he would hear the pounding.

What am I doing here, she thought, am I mad? Why, after all these years, now, at this crucial moment in everyone's life, have I decided to break the rules? She shook the thought away, not wanting to think of the consequences.

They hurried up the stairs to the main house. Mehmet opened the terrace doors and they stepped inside. The doors closed behind her and she stood facing Ali Bey. His huge form filled the room. The smell of incense and *raki* permeated the air. He was tall and stately, resplendent in his silks, a heavy man with handsome, kindly features. There was warmth and longing in his eyes. Not a sign of the animal passion that lay hidden. Bey was a gentleman, a man of culture and manners. All those years in Constantinople he had loved Maria and said nothing. He had respected her home and his friendship with the Sofronis family. Maria never suspected. Only once she thought she noticed something, but she quickly dismissed it as her imagination. Or was it a feeling? She was not sure. In the past she had been attracted to Bey. Strange warning signals went off inside her when he appeared in her home. But Maria never allowed herself to think of Ali Bey as anything more than a friend. Bey never gave the slightest indication of expecting anything more. He was a man of principle, and she respected him for this. Had he not always kept his place? Only when Maria was preparing to leave Constantinople did Bey reveal the secret he had kept so long.

It was Joanna's name day and Ali Bey had arrived with gifts for the young girl. They had coffee, in the presence of her servants and his two attendants. When the time came for him to leave, Ali Bey took her aside in the vestibule.

"I honor your household, Kyra *Sofronis," he said, in a formal tone, but his eyes shone tenderly. "I respect your husband and our friendship. But I must speak to you now. Before you leave, I want you to know that you have always been in my heart, that I have yearned for you many years."*

He ignored the stunned look on her face.

"Your leaving will create a great emptiness in my life. I wished to speak to you before, but as a man of honor I could not."

In spite of her surprise, Maria could not help feeling flattered at his confession. It must be difficult for a man of Bey's position to humble himself this way. Yet he spoke with dignity. He was controlled, calm. Only his eyes betrayed his turmoil.

"May Allah go with you, Kyra *Sofronis, I wish you every happiness."*

His voice faltered. "Perhaps I should not have been so honorable. My god teaches no restraint in the luxuries of life. But I respected your *god,* Kyra *Sofronis, out of my feelings for you. And your god says no one shall take that which belongs to his neighbor."*

Maria was deeply moved by his words. How sad, she thought. To think he never said anything all these years. How wise he is. And how honorable. Yet there are times when the heart tramples honor in its anxiety to fulfill itself. It takes a great deal of courage, she thought, and for a moment she wanted to put her arms around him. But she was silent, unable to move.

"All these years I was content to be near you, watching you from a distance." He paused,

embarrassed, then went on. "The holidays at your home were cherished moments for me. I would leave your house and go to my hanoums, *trying to forget, but I could not. Only at night, in my dreams, did I possess you."*

Maria thought she saw a tear in his eye. But Ali turned away for a moment and when he looked at her again it was gone.

"Take this," he handed her a small package, "take it and remember me. I will never forget you."

He turned quickly and left her standing there, speechless. She wanted to cry but waited for the privacy of her own room where she unwrapped the package. It was a lovely gold box encrusted with rubies and sapphires. When she opened it she gasped. On the red velvet lining was a teardrop diamond. She held the box against her and wept. Nothing like this had ever happened to her before. Nothing like this tenderness, this generosity. The years of loneliness, of lovelessness, of abstinence now came rushing forward in an interminable flow of tears. Finally spent, she fell asleep over the covers, the box in her hand.

A few months later when the Sofronises had settled in Chios, they received word from their new neighbor. One of his servants arrived with greetings and tokens of friendship—a bottle of raki *and a container of incense. Captain Petros was overjoyed to learn their new neighbor was Ali Bey. Maria was shaken. He* did *love her. He had uprooted himself to come to Chios.*

When Petros returned the greetings with an invitation to take coffee and pastry with them, Bey wasted no time. He arrived within the hour and they sat on the veranda sipping the thick Turkish brew and eating loukoumades, *the famous cruller of the*

Turko-Greek cuisine. Maria fought to hide her excitement. She was amazed at Bey's composure. Did that afternoon in Constantinople really happen? But she had the gold box and the diamond to prove it. Could Ali Bey have been joking, toying with her affections? But Bey was not a man who played games. And then Maria handed him a napkin and saw a look in his eye. It was only a soft light but it was her answer. His feelings had not changed. She wondered what would happen now. Surely he knew it was impossible for any relationship to develop between them. And yet he came all this distance just to be near her. Maria could not believe men were capable of such deep feelings. She thought love to them was only a matter of sexual fulfillment. Yet here was a man, a barbarian by all traditions, who loved a woman from afar and was content to be merely within sight of her. Was it possible? Bey had remained silent throughout their friendship in Constantinople. Ten years! She did not know that her own husband was fighting a similar battle.

Since then, only once had Bey spoken to Maria of his love. It was the night of their first New Year's social in Kambos. The guests mingled in the salon and, in the heated excitement of the festivities, Maria had stepped out on the terrace for a breath of air. In a few moments Bey stood behind her. She turned when she heard his servant close the terrace doors from inside. Bey was very handsome in his silken finery, and very serious. Maria's heart missed a beat, but she maintained her composure.

"Kyra Sofronis, I have few opportunities to speak alone with you. I hope you will permit me."

She smiled faintly and he went on.

"I wanted you to know why I came to Chios."

As though she could not guess.

"I tried very hard, but I found life unbearable without you." His voice was calm and dignified. "If your god wishes me to suffer, I will accept it, but at least I will suffer near you."

How strange that Ali Bey, who had all the women he wanted, would stoop to opening his heart to a Christian woman in this manner. How strange that he should care about her god. Maria found this incredible.

"I am a man of great wealth and great means, Kyra *Sofronis." He could not resist trying to win her. For a moment he forgot honor and spoke quickly, before his conscience could stop him. "I can offer you anything in the world, whatever you wish. But I will never force you to come to me. I believe you will come one day. For my love is so strong it will draw you to me even against your will."*

He could not help himself. He would not be human, or a man, if he made no effort to possess her.

"I will be waiting," he hesitated, . . . "to take you . . . when you are ready . . . to make you mine."

Maria gasped at his candor. He ignored her reaction.

"I think of nothing else but you, Kyra *Sofronis. And by Allah, neither friendship, nor your god's laws can stop my love and my longing for you."*

He had finished, and he sighed in relief. But he wanted to say more . . . just one last word.

"You will come to me one day, that is inevitable . . . it is Kismet. But do not wait too long. Life is short and the future is uncertain. Who knows how long we will be on this earth?"

His words left Maria weak. She held her composure but was too embarrassed to speak. She wanted to reprimand him, to tell him he was insane to even consider such a possibility. A Turk and a Christian woman? And each married? Surely he was mad. But when she opened her mouth to tell him so, she saw the love in his eyes. His dignity and aloofness had melted. How strange that such tenderness could lie within this bulk of a man, she thought. She looked at him startled. My God, he means it, he really means it! What on earth will I do?

The terrace doors suddenly opened and Helena stepped outside carrying a small tray of liqueurs. She looked at the two figures standing there and, seeing their embarrassment, glanced quickly away. What could they have been discussing? Did they know she had come out purposely? That she had seen them go out to the terrace, and was worried about what people would say? Fortunately the crowd was so caught up in the gaiety that it paid little attention. And Petros was unaware that his wife had left the room. His main concern was Helena, always Helena. His eyes followed her everywhere. When he lost her, he went in to the kitchen where she had gone earlier to instruct the servants.

"It's . . . it's a beautiful night . . " Maria stammered.

"We were speaking of other New Years in Constantinople," Bey said, looking at Helena in his usual aloof manner. "I have shared many holidays with the Sofronises. I was telling Kyra Maria of my deep respect for her husband and her household."

He took the liqueur Helena offered and handed another to Maria.

"I think Captain Petros is looking for you Maria," Helena told the lie well.

I must watch Maria, she thought, she is becoming careless. She needs guidance, like a naughty child.

Maria sensed Helena's thoughts. She turned and went quickly into the salon.

Helena looked at Ali Bey who was silent.

"Captain Sofronis is a fine man . . . an honorable man. He respects you, Ali Bey, he is proud of your friendship."

"And I have the deepest respect for him too, Kyra Helena," Bey bowed to her. He looked her straight in the eye and added in a tone that puzzled Helena. "Yes, Captain Sofronis is indeed an honorable man, like your humble servant, Ali Bey. We have much in common, it seems."

What did he mean by those last words? Before she could answer he turned and walked inside.

Those were the only moments Maria had been alone with Bey. Only twice. But these were strange times, fascinating times. The world turned, and love stirred, shackled and restrained as it was, shouting to be let free. These were days of history and romance, of adventure and passions. Greece was fighting for her life. But the heart continued to beat, to feel, to nurture love. For one thing that never stops living, in all ages and all times, through revolutions and evolutions, is love. Love unfulfilled, undaunted, fought the greatest battles.

Now they stood alone together, once again, in the shelter of Ali Bey's home in Chios. Maria was a little frightened, a little ashamed. But she knew this was where she had to be and her shame slowly left her.

Her inner instincts followed their course. Ali Bey's heart cried out to her and she had answered.

Ali Bey moved toward Maria.

"Welcome," he said, looking into her eyes. His face looked tired, as though he had been fighting a battle too. And his eyes, whose light Maria could not escape, held pain mixed with tenderness. He was calm. Maria had expected him to be excited. What a strange man, she thought again. He offered her a pillow, clapped for Mehmet—he trusted no other servant tonight—to come and make her comfortable. Then he handed her a sweet liqueur and sat back watching her solemnly as she sipped it.

When Mehmet disappeared, Bey turned to Maria.

"I do not wish to offend you. But I have waited many years for this moment. Allah be praised."

He saw the look of fear that crossed her face.

"Do not be afraid. I will not hurt you. I have four wives. I am not sexually deprived. If you like, we will only talk. Perhaps you will allow me to kiss you. And you will go."

He did not want this to happen. He said it only to calm her fears. Yet he knew that if she did not want to give herself to him, he would not force her. Curse the Greeks, he thought, they have ways of making us Turks jump through hoops without moving a muscle.

The liqueur went to her head and Maria began to feel a warmth inside her. Her face became flushed. Ali watched her intently. He bent and kissed her hand. She touched him, felt the silk of his turban, the roughness of his face, his beard. He pulled her to him and kissed her on the lips. Maria went limp. It was never like this with Petros, not even in their early days of marriage when they were young and passionate.

Bey was pleased at Maria's response. She lay back on the pillows and closed her eyes. Once the thought of all this would have stunned her. Now she did not care—she was proud to be here with this man. He was strong, generous, dashing . . . and he loved her, wanted her as Petros never had. Her rigid upbringing, her years of being without her husband, her strong will-power were now tossed aside in this room. She would find herself with Ali Bey, give herself to him gladly, willingly. She felt a tremor go through her, as though lightning from his body had pierced hers. She went to him and her eyes told him he had not waited ten years in vain.

He picked her up and laid her on the silk cushions of his bed. He pulled the thin curtains around them and laid down beside her. Then he kissed her, gently at first, not to frighten her. She was not a *hanoum*, a slave, he reminded himself. He had not bought her. He must be careful . . . she needed tenderness to submit. Maria responded far beyond his hopes. He had never cared about a woman's response before. But this christian female had changed him. His heart beat wildly. Gently, carefully, he undressed her. Her blond hair fell over her firm rounded breasts, and her face was flushed. She was all warmth and softness. He kissed her mouth, her neck, the spot between her breasts. She moaned at his touch, twisting her body in a way that drove him wild. His lips moved over the soft white skin of her belly. He was no longer Ali Bey, the Pasha, but Maria's slave. She sighed and muffled a scream. She had never known such ecstasy. And it was not degrading, for it came naturally, with tenderness and love. He would not spend his mania on her and toss her aside, she knew that. She also knew, at that moment, that she would never leave him. They twisted with passion, the gentleness forgotten now. It lasted a long time . . . they were both unwilling to let the moment end. When it was over and they lay back exhausted, smiling, in each other's arms, they were silent, each content in his own thoughts. Ali Bey had never felt this way before. Once in every man's life, he mused as he looked at Maria lying beside him with her eyes closed, once in every man's life there is one woman, only one, who brings him complete fulfillment, who feeds both his body and his soul. And joy to the man who finds her. Ali Bey knew Allah was pleased, but he wondered about her God. Why should He hand down such rigid laws? What could be more beautiful, more sacred than love so fulfilled?

The hours passed and the two were oblivious to time. They shared this incredulous joy, kissing, caressing, making love as the night crept away. And yet they could not speak, afraid of saying something that might mar these moments. Maria was not sure this was happening to her. Bey could not believe she was here. Finally they stopped. A look passed between them and they smiled, embarrassed.

I am not ashamed, Maria thought, this was not degrading. It was the most beautiful thing that had happened to them. And then Maria had a frightening thought. What would happen now? How could she live without Ali Bey?

He saw the look on her face, sensed her doubts and kissed her gently.

"Do not worry, my flower, I will take care of everything." He did not want her to worry, for fear played over his own heart. "We will see about the future. Some day we will be together, Praise

Allah, for always."

It sounded difficult, even to him. For there was no immediate answer to their dilemna.

A rooster crowed and Maria leaped from the bed. Realizing her nakedness, she grabbed the silk cover to hide her body. Bey looked at her and desire leaped into his eyes again. He did not have to speak, she understood. Without a word, she let the silk cover fall and went to him. She did not care about the rooster's crow. Petros would not be home until late that morning. Bey knew this too, as he knew everything that went on in the Sofronis home. He pulled her to him and held her as though he would never let go.

They were dressed and standing in the center of the room when they heard the sudden confusion in the outer quarters. Maria turned a frightened look at Bey. There was a sound of shuffling footsteps and then Helena's voice.

"I want to see your master. I must see Ali Bey."

They composed themselves and Bey went to the door.

"Mehmet, let the lady in."

Helena was flushed, angry, as she walked into the room. She stopped, looked at the two figures, the disheveled bed, and sighed deeply. She had expected this.

"Come Maria," she spoke sternly, like a mother to a child who had misbehaved, "hurry, Captain Petros will be back soon."

She turned a scornful look at Ali Bey. Her voice was calm, spiteful.

"You are a barbarian, like all the rest of your countrymen!" Her eyes shot daggers. "If I were a man . . ." She could not finish the sentence.

Bey did not lose his composure.

"Do not be so condemning, *Kyra* Helena. We are not all as you picture us."

Helena laughed scornfully. She waved her arm indicating the sunken pillows, the scattered silks, the liquor cups.

"And what of your honor now, Ali Bey?"

"Love is not hateful or barbaric, *Kyra* Helena. I am sorry you have not been fortunate enough to learn this in your time."

He looked at her with pity, and she wanted to spit in his face. She had never been so quick to reveal her anger before, but she was frightened for Maria . . . and for Petros. She could not stand to have him learn of this betrayal. Greek honor was above love . . . whatever Petros' feelings were for Maria, his family name must not be disgraced. It would destroy him. He had struggled so, to keep his own loyalty intact. Why should not Maria? She was frivolous and childlike, as Helena suspected. She turned to her now and saw the crushed, embarrassed look on Maria's face.

"Come, let's go. I came through the orchards. No one saw me."

Bey looked at Maria with such love that she wondered how Helena could doubt him. Helena saw it too, and was surprised. Could it be that he really loved Maria? Was any Turk capable of loving a woman? They were beasts. Had she not seen them raping and killing her neighbors in Zagora? They thought nothing of holding a woman in their arms, making love to her, then plunging a dagger into her heart. She suddenly remembered the day a Turk had passed her home with a sackful of loot. He stopped along the way and opened it, gloating. When she saw what he held up, she shuddered and held onto the door to keep from falling. "Greek breasts," the animal shouted, "see my war loot. A sackful of Greek breasts."

She had hated the Turks passionately since that day, and would have welcomed the opportunity to kill any one of them. She thought of Yusbasi Hassan and shivered. She had not wanted to kill him, in spite of her hatred. But it was his life against theirs. She had no choice. She realized that she was not as cold-blooded and hateful as she appeared.

The two women hurried through Bey's orchards and reached the dividing wall. Mehmet stood there holding the steel door open. Maria turned and smiled wanely at him. Helena stopped.

"He's a Greek, Helena," Maria whispered, anxious to draw the subject away from herself. "He was abducted when he was a child, for the Janissaries. But he was castrated by mistake. A terrible tragedy."

Helena's heart leaped. She looked at him carefully. He was at least twenty-eight years old. No, he could not be Joseph. She wondered about this boy's mother and felt her pain. How many lives these cursed Turks had destroyed. How many mothers had wept. Surely there is a god of justice somewhere, she thought, why doesn't he act? Why does he allow these things to happen? It was the eternal, unanswerable question.

They were in Maria's bedroom when Helena finally released her exasperation.

"Maria, how could you? Is this what you wanted to tell me? Is this what I wouldn't understand?"

She found it disgusting that Maria would let a Turk make love to her. That she could so callously betray and dishonor her husband. On my darling Petros, she thought, this whole vicious circle is hopeless.

"Helena, please don't judge me. Don't judge any of us. I swear to you this was the first time. All these years he never touched me, never said a word. I swear it!"

Maria began to cry. And then she told Helena the whole story, pouring out her shame and her passion, her past loneliness and her new joy.

They sat on the bed together, and when Maria finished, the tears stopped too. She watched Helena's face for what was to come, her reprimands, her disgust. But Helena was not angry any longer. There was a softness there, the fury was gone. For a moment Maria thought she saw envy. But Helena was not an envious woman.

"You are wrong in what you did, Maria." Helena said. "But surprising as it is, I understand. Perhaps the heart must leap over honor in its desire to find its other self. I would die before I allowed that to happen to me. But we are not the same. You are foolish, Maria, but I am still your friend. . ."

She wiped Maria's eyes, suddenly feeling old enough to be her mother. A part of her cried for the lost, strayed child; a part of her rejoiced that Maria had found fulfillment. How many are born, go through life and die without having achieved that goal, she thought. Helena would not be one of the lucky ones. Honor forbade it.

"How did you know?" Maria's voice was hesitant.

"I couldn't sleep . . . I was worried. You seemed so upset, so preoccupied when I left . . . so I came back. When I found your room empty, I told the servants not to disturb you, that I would sleep in the next room. Something told me you would be at Bey's . . . so I came."

"You walked all the way from Thymiana, alone?" Maria was amazed at Helena's strong will and constitution. She was indefatigable.

It was late morning when Maria fell asleep. Helena sat in the chair near the bed watching her breathe. She finally decided to go down to the kitchen and brew some chamomile tea.

VIII

Helena answered the knock on her door and looked at the tall stranger standing there. His chestnut hair was gray at the temples, gray streaks ran through his tapered beard and thick mustache. He smiled wryly and she froze. The hazel eyes, cold beads, pierced hers. She recognized the look.

"Good morning, Helena." He said it with audacity, as though daring her to recognize him. "Don't you remember me?"

She could not believe he had the nerve to appear before her like this.

"Stratis," she said tonelessly. Her face was blank. As always, she masked the turmoil within her. She had been afraid of this moment. Thank God Jason was not here.

"Aren't you going to ask me in?"

When she did not answer he pushed her gently

aside and entered.

"Is this the way to greet your long-lost husband?"

He watched her for a long moment. Then, embarrassed at her silence, he turned to the three-legged pot in the fireplace. He picked up the wooden spoon beside it and casually stirred the contents. He turned to her, smiling.

"Smells good." He tasted the food. "Mmmm, you always were a good cook, Helena. I was right when I said Chiote women are the best cooks in the world."

How like Stratis, she thought, to walk in after twenty years and taste her food, as though he had just arrived home from work. For a moment her heart began to melt. He was like a little boy, a lost child, not knowing how to say he was sorry for being bad. But she remembered the years of misery with him, his unfeeling, uncaring attitude towards her and the twins, towards his home and responsibilities. She thought of his mother and the way she had manipulated him. Stratis was not a man, he never would be. Now, after his youth had gone, spent on women and drink, he had come back, a tired man of fifty to rest at her hearth. But he would not. She bit her lip in determination, staring stonily at him. He looked at her and smiled bravely to hide his fear of the rejection he was almost certain would come.

"What do you want, Stratis?" Helena was calm, bitter.

"What do I want? What kind of a question is that to ask your husband?"

He moved toward her and pressed her against the wall, blocking her with his outstretched arms. She could not believe his lack of feelings went this far. What could she say to this man? There was no substance to him.

He tried to kiss her and she turned her head, a look of disgust on her face. Infuriated he turned her to him and kissed her roughly on the mouth. He softened and took her in his arms. His touch repulsed her. She stood there unmoving, unfeeling, wishing God would strike them both dead. She could not bear the thought of picking up life with Stratis again. Why does God keep torturing me this way, continuously, she wondered in crushed defeat. What have I done to bring this curse upon me?

Stratis could not believe that Helena would not melt in his arms. He remembered the other times he had hurt her, humiliated her, and how easily she forgave him. He would embrace her, kiss her, tell her he loved her over and over again, and she would give in. She was a girl then. And she had loved him with all her heart, all her innocence.

Love is forgiving, she realized, but love can be killed, as Stratis had killed hers. And what he had professed to be love for her was merely a shallow, selfish means to his own end. She could not live with it again. But it was hopeless to explain all this to him. He could not, would not understand.

He pushed her away, his ego hurt.

"What the devil is the matter with you?" He could not believe that any woman was strong enough to resist his advances. None ever had.

Helena did not reply, unable to believe the impudence of his question. What was wrong with her? A cold, hateful look was her only answer.

He was about to ask if she had found someone else but he thought better of antagonizing her. He wondered if she had. A part of him knew she would not, but he remembered his mother and his philosophy that all women are whores. They were all alike to Stratis. He fought the instinct in him that defended Helena, that said she was good. He knew he did not deserve her but he would never admit it to himself. Now he was uncertain about what to do. Should he move into the house? She could not stop him. What about his sons? The thought jolted him. He had forgotten them in his anxiety over Helena.

"Where are the boys? I want to see them."

Helena was silent. The words she wanted to hurl at him lay crushed inside her, knowing it was hopeless for them to come out. They would only fall on deaf ears, wasted, rejected. She went to the cupboard and took out a jar of quince preserve. She brought the jug of water from the corner. Stratis watched her curiously. Why didn't she answer? Were his sons dead? He smothered the fear inside him, afraid to reveal it lest she know he had some feelings somewhere. Then he smiled, relieved. She was only playing with him, taunting him awhile as he had so often done to her. He would show her it did not matter.

"Have you got any *raki* in the house?" He watched her grim face and wondered what she was thinking.

Helena did not dare offer him a drink, remembering how the fiery liquid set him off in drunken rages. She wondered if he were still like that. Why not? Do leopards change their spots?

"You're not going to be stingy about a little liquor now, are you?" Damn this woman, she irritated him.

Helena finally spoke. "I think first you should learn about your sons. Sit down."

Another flash of fear passed over him. So they were

dead. He was surprised that he cared. All these years of wandering had brought nothing more than passing thoughts of the children, where they were, what they might look like. And of Helena, and the strange, annoying feeling of her absence. He would then shrug those thoughts aside and wait for the next port, to spew out his frustrations on the local whores. Stratis loved women, but only for one reason. He had no use for them outside his bed. And he hated Helena for making him feel differently. It annoyed him and disturbed his life. He was not meant for that.

Stratis sat down and took the small saucer with the quince preserve. He watched her pour water into the cup. It was a good-looking cup, copper, probably part of her dowry. He looked around the room, noticing the beams, the high ceiling, the embroidered doilies, the crocheted pieces on the shelves, the small table. The room was spotless. It was a good house, well furnished, well-kept. He raised his cup.

"To your health . . . to ours," he grinned ironically and winked his eye.

His attitude infuriated her. To your demise, she said silently to herself. Then, as though in remorse, she added, to what you could have been. Sadness flushed over her like water, drenching her, leaving her weak. She knew Stratis was what he was, and nothing would ever change him. She must remember this and not weaken. She could not turn this man out of her house. Legally he was her husband, but nothing could make him welcome in her bed. She thought of Petros and her heart sank. Then she composed herself and told Stratis about their sons, and the years between.

He said nothing. He was dumb-struck. Never in his wildest dreams did he imagine that his son could have been snatched by Turks, taken away and raised to hate his people. For that was surely what had happened. Something inside told him that. He thought of the years that had gone by, the short time he had known the children. He struggled with his confused feelings and felt a nausea in his stomach, a pain in his chest. He did not want Helena to know this. He was, as always, ashamed to show emotion.

What's the matter with him, she thought, why is he so afraid to appear human? Does he think I'll laugh at him? What did that evil mother of his do to him? She had destroyed her son—made him useless to the world and to himself. But in her hatred for Stratis Helena pitied him. She felt a sudden urge to put her arms around him and cradle his head the way she used to do when he knelt down and begged forgiveness after his drunken rages. But she held herself back, knowing it was hopeless. Any regret on Stratis' part was temporary. He would go on ruining himself and everyone around him. She suddenly wanted to be cruel. Let Jason see his father as he really is, she thought as she brought out a bottle of wine and placed it before him. Was it cruelty or perhaps the hope that Stratis might prove he could fight temptation? Only then would he be entitled to his son. Without another word she walked out of the house.

Helena set out to find Xenophon. Only he could speak to Jason at this difficult moment. He would tell him about his father in his own way, man to man. She wondered how Jason would take it. My poor Jason, she thought, my lonely, sensitive boy . . . life has been so cruel to you.

Xenophon was not in Thymiana. Her uncle Mihalis told her he had gone to Kambos, to Captain Petros'.

He offered to take her there. So Petros was meeting with Xenophon now. That meant plans for the Revolution were still on. Petros had become a hero since knowledge of his secret support. She was proud of him. He had gone against the opinions of the people of Kambos, caring little about his position or wealth. She loved him for this—a different, mature feeling from the foolishness of her youth. It's so easy to mistake love when one is young, she thought. Can it be that there are different forms of love, various levels one must pass before arriving to the lasting one? She rejected the unladylike thought. Women do not fall in love at various levels, she scolded herself. It was unheard of in her time.

Petros and Xenophon were waiting outside the Koraes Library when Jason appeared from the great stone entrance. The boy was surprised to see Petros' carriage and the two men watching him somberly. Had something happened to his mother? His heart almost stopped.

"Your mother's alright son," Petros assured him, and Jason breathed again.

The ride back to Thymiana was slow and painful. Jason could not believe what he heard. His father was back. He did not know whether to laugh or cry, to be happy or sad . . . or angry. Angry, yes, the thought burst inside him and his face twisted.

"I don't want to see him."

How dare this man drop out of nowhere after twenty years, without a word or a sign. Who did he think he was? But the anger began to melt. What was he like? What would he say to him? Again the anger took force. What could he say to a son he'd deserted without a qualm? No, Jason would not see him. Yet he knew that in the end, he would, if only for curiosity's sake.

Xenophon and Petros looked at each other anxiously. If only I had a son like that, Petros thought, he doesn't deserve all this.

He is my son, too, thought Xenophon, the son I never had. I helped raise him and I love him. Who is this man? But he knew the time had come for his real father to claim him. Would he? His sharp instinct told him he could not.

Helena was waiting in the courtyard. She would remain here while the two men faced each other. Jason must be alone with Stratis. He must not be embarrassed by his mother's presence.

Xenophon and Petros patted Jason on the shoulders.

"We'll be down the street at Karanikolas' when you're finished. Come down." Petros looked Jason deeply in the eyes, a look that told him he was loved and wanted.

"Good luck son." Xenophon felt the anguish in Jason's heart. "I'm taking your mother to the house with me. Your aunt Maria's baking pastries—stop over later."

Jason smiled weakly. He was grateful and felt fortunate to have their love and concern.

Helena could say nothing. She kissed her son on the cheek.

The three figures watched the boy they loved walk up the steps into the house where twenty years of his past lay waiting . . . three figures whose love intertwined, whose agony was interwoven. In her pain Helena was thankful that God had given her these pillars of strength, these men she loved, to stand beside her in her time of need.

Stratis hid the empty wine bottle behind the water jug. He had regreted drinking it now, and in sudden panic made himself a double brew of thick Turkish coffee to clear his head. It helped. No one would suspect he had drunk so much. I always could hold my liquor, he murmured.

He turned at the sound of the door.

The two stared at each other.

"Jason, I'm your father."

Jason's voice was faint, almost choked. "My father is dead."

"I'm alive Jason, and I'll make it up to you son." Stratis took care not to slur his words. Jason must not know he had been drinking.

"I'm sorry." The boy's words were cold as steel, "my father is dead." He fought to keep his composure. I must not cry, he thought, I won't.

Stratis did not know what else to say. Fear gripped his heart, the fear that his son would send him away.

"I . . . I promise I'll make it up to you."

"I don't think you can, sir . . . no one can make up twenty years . . . not even God."

Stratis tried to get through to his son. Everything depended on Jason's accepting him—there was nothing else in his life now.

"People make mistakes, Jason. I came back, didn't I?'

The blood rose to Jason's head . . . the veins in his neck throbbed. He could not speak. He was torn between hugging his father, sobbing on his shoulder, and spitting in his face.

"Your mother did a fine job," Stratis continued, "you're a good boy . . . a man now."

He looked at his son anxiously, waiting for recognition . . . longing to hear it. Jason could not remain quiet any longer. The fire inside him leaped out with the pain.

"You destroyed her . . . and me too." He paused and looked in his father's eyes. "All the time I was growing up I kept wondering where you were, why you didn't come to see me. Did you ever ask about me?" Jason's voice softened, "Whether I ever needed anything . . . If I was lonely . . . or hungry?"

His voice was barely audible, as though he were talking to himself. "Do you know what it's like to wonder why your father doesn't come home? Why your father doesn't want you?"

"But I do want you . . . I always did . . . I just . . . I just didn't know how to show it." His words were feeble, meaningless, and he knew it.

Fury rose in Jason and he fought to control it. His words came out calm, distinct.

"I used to wonder if I was a bastard . . ." his voice trailed off.

"You know damn well you're not!" Stratis shouted. He was getting impatient with this son of his. "You're crazy, boy. What's wrong with you? How can you say such a thing?"

Jason smiled and shook his head at the stupidity of his father's questions.

"What's *wrong* with me?" He laughed bitterly. "You don't understand what I'm trying to say . . . how can you possibly know what I feel?"

He shrugged his shoulders as he looked at the older man, at this stranger who came to claim him now that he had the notion.

"Don't keep saying you're going to make it up to

me. Why, you don't even know what there *is* to make up."

Stratis was going to keep trying. He would not give up.

"Look son, I'm sorry . . . I really am," his voice was that of one reasoning with a naughty child. "Let me try . . . please."

Then, in desperation he tried to grab at anything . . . at the one thing he knew.

"Look, you're a man now . . . you need fatherly advice . . . I'll teach you . . ." he laughed nervously, embarrassed. "I'll take you along . . . you know . . ." he hesitated and he was almost comical, "sort of show you the ropes. We'll pick up some pretty *hanoums* . . . I'll wager you've never had a Turkish girl, have you? You don't know what you're missing!"

Hope sprang in Stratis. Maybe now he would reach his son. They would be friends, they would share the best things in life together.

Jason could not believe what he heard. He stared at his father with disgust.

"I think I'm going to throw up," he said, and turned to leave.

Stratis realized he had said the wrong thing. He was furious with himself . . . and with Jason. He was desperate now.

"What's the matter son, you don't like girls?" he raged, "maybe you'd like a nice, fat Turkish boy." He wanted to hit out at his son. "I thought you were a man, like your father!"

Jason stopped. He turned, looked at Stratis and walked back to him. His voice was calm, but it cut like steel.

"If you're an example of a man, sir, then I'll gladly

reject manhood." His voice was low but the words fell like a thunderbolt.

Stratis struck Jason across the mouth. The boy reeled. He touched his lips, looked at the blood on his hand, then at his father. There was deep pain in his young eyes.

"Thank you," he said slowly, "now I can't say you never gave me anything."

He turned and walked away.

Jason might as well have put a knife in him. Stratis stood there, dumb, watching his son walk out the door.

It was one of the few times in his life that Stratis showed any feeling, any sensitivity. He could not cope with it. He ran outside.

* * *

The Harbor was bustling with activity when Stratis stepped down from the carriage in front of the Cafe *Aman*. This was what he needed . . . music and women. He was glad to be out of that wretched village, Thymiana. This would help him get over his anger, his disappointment at Jason. This always helped. The boy could go to hell . . . Helena too, for that matter. He thought of Helena again. Her propriety makes me sick, he muttered to himself. She had looked at him as though he were nothing . . . as though he were dirt. He felt a tinge of sadness, remembering that once she had looked at him differently. But he pushed the thought aside. His mother was right . . . Helena was not for him. He eyed two girls who approached him, smiling seductively . . . Armenian beauties with tantalizing bodies. This was his type of woman. He chose Ismini, the tall one, and they sat down to drink. It was warm and the music was loud. A girl with long hair danced the dance of the veils. Armenian women always excited him . . . he would show Helena. He felt exuberant. This was his idea of an evening . . . he never tired of it. This was a man's life . . . the sea, wine, beautiful women . . . not wives, babies, responsibilities.

When they had finished the bottle of *raki* he asked Ismini to take him to her room.

"House, room, whatever you have, girl . . . anyplace where there's a bed."

His tall good looks aroused Ismini . . . she was overly eager to please. Work had been monotonous lately.

Stratis could drink many times a normal man's capacity and still stand on his feet. Yet tonight he was reeling. When they entered Ismini's room he walked to the window, opened it and breathed deeply. He remained standing there, staring out past the harbor. The girl undressed and lay on the bed, not speaking. He's a strange one, she thought, watching him curiously. Stratis turned and looked at her a moment, then stared out the window again. He thought of Helena and wished she were here instead, but quickly erased the idea from his mind.

"They're all alike, aren't they?" he suddenly muttered, as though to himself. "This whore, my mother, Helena . . . they're all alike."

He shook his head, trying to clear it, and went to Ismini.

"Let's see what you can do," he looked hungrily at the voluptuous girl. He laughed, and it was a choked cry. "I've made love in every part of the world and with every kind of woman . . . I know what's good."

The *raki* had gone to his head. He stumbled and fell on the bed. Ismini caressed him and began to remove his clothes. Her heart beat wildly . . . it had been a long time since a man had affected her like this.

Stratis felt the room spin. He felt Ismini's lips on his body. He closed his eyes and smiled . . . his hand touched her head, pressed it against him. He was fifty years old and his greatest pleasure was, as always, making love to a woman and having her make love to him. It was always a personal conquest. But for the first time he could not lose himself in his game. His mind wandered . . . he cursed softly, and Ismini stopped, looking up at him questioningly. He pushed her head down again.

"Go on," he said between gritted teeth, "go on . . . you're doing fine."

He lay back again, furious at himself, at the emptiness that suddenly seared him. Perhaps he was getting old . . . the thought terrified him. What else was there? When this was over, what would he fall back on? There was nothing, no one. He sat up abruptly, hurting Ismini as he did. With a moan he grabbed her.

"This is what women are for," he whispered, "the only thing they're good for."

He threw her back on the bed.

"Let's go woman," he hissed, and looked down at her, a twisted grin on his face, ready to move in for the conquest.

Suddenly the figure before him became a blur . . . and Helena was lying there waiting to receive him. He went to her, anxiously, gently, not wanting to hurt her. In all his moments of passion, even when he was drunk, he had been gentle with Helena. She was special, not like the others. Stratis had never been with women who were not whores. And those moments with Helena were revelations, precious ones for him. He had never admitted it to himself or to her, erasing it from his mind once he left their bed.

Now he moved into Ismini and sweet passion surged through him. Ismini swayed her body with his, bewildered at his sudden change, wondering what had caused it. She wished he were more rough with her, that he would hurt her, push into her until she screamed. Yet she enjoyed this. He was a well-built man . . . his body still firm and strong. And he kissed her mouth, her face, her eyes. No one had done this before. Men did not kiss whores on the lips, she recalled wryly as she felt Stratis' moist mouth on hers. She was thrilled. Later . . . later she would awake the animal in him too.

He finished, but Ismini held him tightly, not letting his body move from atop hers.

"Oh no," she whispered, careful not to anger him, "not yet . . . so soon?"

He did not reply and she tightened her arms around his back.

He looked bewildered for a moment as he realized where he was, with whom he lay. He smiled ironically.

"That was just a starter," he tried to excuse himself, "Now I'll show you what I can really do." And he began again, anxious to show his prowess.

They lay back on the bed exhausted. The minutes passed as Stratis stared up at the ceiling, silent, his mind far away. Ismini watched him, knowing he was troubled, feeling sorry for him. She wanted to speak but was afraid. He looked so somber, so morose. Yet he had had such pleasure tonight. Slowly, with hesitation, she touched his chest and stroked it. He took her hand away without turning. Then he spoke in a whisper, still staring ahead.

"You know something Ismini? You're pretty good in bed . . . but then, that's what you're all meant for . . . to get . . ." His voice trailed off. He bit his lips. He wanted to talk, to get it all out.

"My mother was a whore too, you know that? Not a prostitute like you . . . at least you're honest about it . . . she was a whore! And she made sure my father wasn't around to see it. Her lovers, the Turks, saw to that. So I left because I couldn't stand the sight of her."

His voice trailed off again . . . she could barely hear him.

"I don't know why I went back, or why I took my wife there. What was I trying to prove?" Anguish rose in him. "God, I don't know what the hell I was trying to prove . . . Helena was good . . . I wanted to show her to my mother . . . to prove I could get a decent woman . . ."

His voice rose and there was anger in it. "But Helena was a woman . . . a whore too . . . like all women . . ."

Ismini watched him wide-eyed as his voice grew angrier.

"All women are whores, Ismini, aren't they?"

He grabbed her by the shoulders and shook her. "Aren't they?" He threw her back on the bed, as the sobs came out, uncontrolled, pitiful, like a child's . . .

Stratis was five years old and he was back in Zagora, that mountain village above the sea. He remembered his father sitting him on his knee, singing to him songs of the mountains . . . and his mother, Christina, joining in with her sweet, melodic voice. He remembered how she held his hand as they stole quickly through the village streets. Women seldom appeared outdoors alone in Zagora. But his mother was not afraid. Soon she was going out alone. Often times she was gone a long while, returning late at night. Stratis remembered the shouts and the fury of his father, and his mother's sometimes taunting, sometimes soothing laughter. Then he would watch the door close—he slept in the kitchen near the hearth—and he would see the lamp go out, from the crack under their door. The fighting would stop and Stratis would hear moans and curses, soft purring sounds, giggles, and finally his father's snores. Sometimes his mother came back out and leaned over Stratis, kissed him or stroked his head.

"Don't worry dear," she would whisper, "it's all right. Your father isn't angry any more. Sleep now."

She would smile and the look on her face puzzled Stratis. He was too young to recognize it as the look of evil, or of shrewd cunning. To him it was joy, relief, that another storm had passed.

By the time Stratis was eight years old he noticed his father was not the same. The life seemed to have gone out of him. He hardly ever smiled, and he never sang his happy mountain songs. Stratis watched him sit at the table or near the fireside, drinking more wine each day, as though something tortured him, something he wanted to drown in drink. Stratis knew something was wrong in their home but he could not understand what it was. His father did not fight much anymore, or curse his wife. He seemed to have given up. Christina, in turn, seemed to blossom. She sang as she went about her work. She primped and strolled out into the village more frequently and was gone longer periods of time, always past the evening hours. On those nights, she would come up to her husband who sat with his bottle near the fire, caress his head, kiss his thinning hair and go into the bedroom.

It was a cool Fall evening, that last night Stratis remembered his parents together. His mother had left at noon and returned after sunset. Her husband called her into the bedroom. He closed the door solemnly. Stratis was worried, sensing that his father was at the breaking point. The boy crept up to the closed door and listened. He knew it was wrong but he could not help himself.

"How can you do this to us?" His father's voice was a whisper, pleading. "How long is this going to go on? Aren't you ashamed? Think of the boy!"

It was the cry of a defeated man pleading for the last time.

She laughed tauntingly. "I'm not doing anything wrong. I can't stay cooped up like a prisoner in this dungeon."

"Nothing wrong? They saw you sneaking out of the Turks' post again last night. Have you no shame, woman, no dignity? Don't you care what people say?"

"That much for what people say."

Stratis heard the snap of fingers.

"I hate this place. You took me from my lovely

Smyrna and brought me to this God-forsaken mountain. And you expect me to shut myself up like a nun."

Her voice suddenly lost its sting. It was soft again.

"You should be glad we're on good terms with the Turks. Do you realize our house hasn't been touched, that nothing's been taken since we got to know them better?"

He was enraged.

"Nothing's been touched?" he shouted, and struck her across the face. She reeled.

Stratis heard a crash. He beat on the door, pleading to be let in. There was silence from within, then his father answered, in a tired, old voice.

"Go to bed son, it's alright. I just dropped something."

He was sick at what he had done. He had never laid a hand on his wife before.

"Stratis, go to bed." His mother's voice was calm, sweet.

That night Stratis did not hear the familiar sounds that followed their quarrels. There were no whispers or sighs, no moans and giggles. And his father was not snoring. The lamp burned all night. No one slept. Stratis could not understand his mother. She seemed to enjoy making her husband miserable. She was always sweet to Stratis, but more often than not, she was a devil to his father. The boy felt pain in his heart, a deep sorrow for the disillusioned man. Perhaps now his father would stand up to her . . . perhaps this was what Christina needed.

The next morning his father did not go to the fields. Christina would not let him. They had all had a sleepless night and he looked pale, tired. She hovered over him with concern and remorse, wanting to make amends. Stratis was happy seeing his father smile—he felt a ray of hope. The older man, too, was touched by his wife's sudden transformation. She is not a bad woman, he thought. Perhaps I wronged her. She was such a spirited girl when we ran off and came to Zagora. He never forgot his shock on the first night of their marriage when he discovered that his sixteen-year old bride was not a virgin. But she unleashed such animal passion, that his joy knew no bounds. She satisfied and fulfilled his strongest sexual needs as no other woman could. For this passion he forgave her many things.

It was noon and Stratis watched his mother warming the milk for his father. She was so devoted that morning, going back and forth to him, tucking in his covers, feeling his forehead.

Christina thought Stratis was in the next room when she spooned the white powder into the milk and stirred it briskly. She turned suddenly and saw her son standing in the doorway. The blood drained from her face.

"How long have you been standing there?" she hissed between her teeth.

Stratis was frightened. He could not understand the reason for her anger.

"I . . . I . . . just came in this minute."

Why should she be so upset because he was watching her?

"Did I do something wrong?"

Her voice softened immediately, the way it always did.

"No, dear, don't mind me. I'm just nervous lately. Here, take this milk in to your father. And see that he

drinks it all. I'm going out to feed the chickens."

How sweet she could be to his father when she wanted to. Perhaps she had changed. Happiness would reign in their home again. Stratis was glad for the chance to wait on his father, to show him he cared. He handed him the cup of milk and watched him drink it slowly down. The older man grimaced. Then he smiled at his son.

"Thank you," he said and tousled the boy's hair. "You're a good boy, Stratis."

He paused a moment, licking his lips. He wondered if the milk was sour. No, Christina would never have sent it in if it were.

They buried him the next morning. Under Turkish rule no death certificate and no coroner were necessary.

Stratis never drank milk in his mother's house again.

Ismini put her arms around Stratis, cradled his head on her breast, muffling his choked sobs. He cried like the child still in him, like the man he could have been. Then he stopped and looked strangely at her. It had all come out at last. He was ashamed and humiliated to admit what had been hidden there all those years. His vision slowly focused and he saw Ismini clearly in her nakedness, her serious pitying face. He did not want pity, not from a woman, not from a whore. Fury and lust returned to his eyes. This was all he knew—the only way of asserting his manhood. He grabbed her and they wrestled on the bed, squirming like two animals, toppling onto the floor. She shrieked with delight and pain at his coarseness. His body closed over hers, pushing, heaving, all passion and hatred. She loved it.

"Take me with you, take me with you," she whispered hoarsely, breathlessly as the room spun around them. She would go anywhere with this Greek.

He finished, but it was not enough . . . the pain was still there. He took several breaths and began again, like a maniac. Ismini felt deep pain and ecstasy as she sank into unconsciousness.

They sailed at dawn. Once again Stratis was running away . . . this time it was with Ismini . . . tomorrow it would be someone else. It was the curse of his mother's sins, and he did not care. There would always be ships to sail and wine to drink and whores to bed with. It was enough for him.

IX

January, 1822 on the neighboring island of Samos . . .

Lycourgos Logothetis stared with knitted brows at Rallis. Anger and frustration throbbed inside him and he clenched his fists to control himself.

The other man was calm. He met Logothetis' gaze.

"You proved yourself when you freed Samos, Logothetis. But in all common sense we cannot go forward with the rebellion in Chios . . . you know that."

The Samiote did not know that, but he said nothing. What he knew was that he wanted to free Chios now . . . at this moment. Common sense or not, he must continue the struggle they had begun. Once before the Chiotes had refused to fight and it had sealed their doom. Now they had no choice. He would make them rise. Words like "logical" and "sensible" were for weaklings.

"I've written Ypsilantis and explained the circumstances. I expect you to abide by my decision."

"But Ypsilantis sent you to plan the onset in Chios. And Ypsilantis himself appointed me to lead the revolt."

"He didn't know the conditions I found here. Chios is not prepared for a revolt. For God's sake man, don't you see they have no arms, no manned ships, no trained men for such a move? How can you think of risking so much, with Turkey only an hour away? You can wait. You *will* wait."

If only they had joined Tombazis last year, when there was ammunition and only a handful of Turks on the island. But the Chiotes were hesitant then. It was unthinkable now. He noted the sparks in Logothetis' eyes and added with understanding.

"Be patient compatriot. I well understand your desire to finish the task. Every Greek here and abroad dreams of the day of complete liberation. But we are not children playing games. We can't afford to start something in Chios we can't finish. The time will come when we will go forward together to free the island, as we freed the others. But we will do it like adults, with strategy and preparation. And we will not fail. Do you understand?"

His tone was that of a father to his stubborn child. The child relented . . . at least for the moment. Logothetis was anxious to be left alone. He wanted to think. Bournias, the man from Chios who helped plan the island's uprising, would be arriving soon. Logothetis would decide what to do then.

The two men shook hands and Rallis left, pleased

that he had proven his point. It was a wise decision. The risk was too great in Chios. For the time being they must concentrate on the mainland. The Revolution was going well there. God was with the Greeks. Their banner had begun to appear in many areas along the coast. The glory that had been dimmed these many centuries was appearing again. He hurried to board the ship that would take him from Samos.

It was February when Bournias arrived in Samos. 1822 and Samos breathed free at last. He smelled the air, clean and fresh, liberated air, victorious. Soon it would be like this in Chios. Bournias could not wait. But he was surprised to find Logothetis despondent, confused. The Samiote had promised Rallis he would wait, but his heart spoke otherwise. Bournias understood; he was not confused, he was determined. Chios was his home and he wanted it freed. He would convince his partner they must act on their own, and soon.

Don't listen to anyone, Lycourgos. Do what you feel is right, do what your heart tells you. Come with me, help me free my home like you freed Samos. You are the leader here, you have been appointed to guide us. Forget Rallis."

If the Elders had followed Tombazis last year, Chios would be free now. Bournias would not make the same mistake. Yet the two men did not consider that this time the odds were indeed impossible. All the weapons and ammunition had been rounded up by the Turks . . . the Chiotes were now completely powerless.

* * *

Jason watched the ball of fire move slowly behind the hill. He sat quietly on the slope below the chapel of the Prophet Elias and stared at the glow in wonder. For a moment the storm in his heart subsided and his pain and disillusionment were forgotten. The sudden arrival and departure of his father was like a morning dream, a fleeting moment, a passing scene, then awakening. He could not believe it came and went so fast, that it would leave him so crushed and disappointed. He had not expected it to be like this. So this was his father . . . this was the man he had been waiting for all these years. Jason felt a deep void inside him, as though he were alone on this hillside, alone in the world. There seemed to be no one and nothing to look forward to. The plans for the Revolution had disintegrated. The years he had worked and dreamed and sacrificed were meaningless now. A handful of men had killed his dreams and the lifeline of Chios. His father had come to write the epitaph.

"You never get tired of watching sunsets, do you Jason?" It sounded foolish but Joanna could think of nothing else to say. He had completely forgotten her presence.

She looked at him with desperation, feeling helpless, unable to offer a comforting word. Her father had told her to go to him, knowing that only the young can understand the young. But Joanna felt like a stranger. Jason had never allowed her to enter the inner circle of his life.

She looked at him now, thinking how much she loved him, wondering why this feeling was not contagious, this beautiful feeling that overwhelmed her. How could he be so uncaring when she felt such fire, such longing, all the passion of first love? And yet she felt some comfort at being able to share even this moment.

She was thankful for that. True, she had practically forced herself on him, trailing after him as he climbed the hill, until he finally relented and accepted her presence.

She wanted desperately to comfort him now, to console him with her words, but her tongue was tied.

Jason looked at Joanna as though reading her thoughts. He smiled sadly. She's sweet, he thought, a beautiful child. He suddenly felt very old. If ever there was to be a girl in my life, he thought, I would want Joanna. He saw the love radiating from her face and hated himself for not being able to return it. Yet there was something inside him, even in this moment of confusion, something undefinable that he felt for her. He pushed the feeling away. There was no room in his heart for such trifles. He had too many problems now. He was dedicated to important tasks—the liberation of Chios and the search for his brother. And his father? He would forget the man ever existed. The ache inside him swelled each time he thought of him . . . and of Joseph. He must think only of Joseph now. He knew the time was near . . . that his brother was near, too. Word had come that Logothetis and Bournias were ready to sail for Chios. Jason's heart pounded as he envisioned their arrival . . . he would be waiting at the harbor. Perhaps there was hope after all. Joseph, Joseph, he whispered to himself, we're going to meet soon. We've got to meet!

"What are you thinking about, Jason?" Joanna persisted. It frightened her.

The look on his face dissolved. He was teasing now.

"I'm thinking that you're terrible, always following me around like this. You're going to get a bad name, my girl, and no one will want to marry you. Proper young ladies don't trail after men over hills and valleys."

"I don't care about being a proper young lady, she pouted stubbornly, hope rising inside her. She looked like a kitten wanting to be petted. "I don't care if no one marries me."

Then she added on impulse, quickly, before she could stop, "Except you, Jason, only you."

He turned to her startled. Why am I surprised, he wondered, I knew it all the time. His manly pride soared in spite of himself. But he felt sorry for her. Was it only sorrow? He refused to ponder it. A stern, reproaching look came over his face.

"Jason, please." She placed her hand on his lips shyly, before he could speak. "Don't say anything. Don't send me away . . . I love you, Jason."

She was ashamed of her boldness but glad that the words had finally come out.

A strange feeling spilled over in Jason's insides—warmth, joy, sadness. He was confused, ashamed to feel emotion. His obsession must not be blocked by anyone or anything. But he could not help it now and he smiled sadly. He looked at Joanna and her heart skipped. She had never seen that look on him before. Shyly, tenderly, he felt her hair, stroked it. He touched her cheek and his fingers lingered there a moment. There was gentleness in them. But his face changed, and she was puzzled. Did she see compassion? There was no desire, no longing there. She did not care. This was more than she had hoped for. She did not know he was fighting these emotions within, holding them back, as though it were a crime to reveal them.

"I love you, Jason." She said it again. She could

say nothing else.

Jason wanted to turn and run. But Joanna looked up at him and he could not move. He leaned over, brushed his lips against hers; she wrapped her arms around his neck. He felt her body pressed against his and was panic-stricken. Why am I so frightened, he wondered. Suddenly his father's words rang in his ears. "What's the matter son, don't you like girls? Maybe you want me to find you some nice, fat, Turkish boy."

Repulsion swept over him. He hated Stratis more that moment than ever before. Torn with these mixed feelings, he wished he could show his father that he was a man. Joanna's sigh brought him to reality. She was his for the asking, but he was afraid. And he could not hurt her, not to prove something, or to avenge himself against an irresponsible, heartless father. He felt ashamed again. Joanna deserved a ring and marriage vows for her purity. He wished he could give them to her.

Joanna was startled to see Jason turn away. He helped her up, avoiding her eyes. Then he smiled and kissed her on the forehead.

"Let's go, it's getting late."

The ball of fire disappeared behind the hill. They stood there holding hands, watching the red glow in the horizon. He saw the tears fill up in her eyes.

"Some day I'll explain everything to you, Joanna. You are very special, and I don't want to hurt you."

"But you *are* hurting me," she answered, "you hurt me every time you treat me like a sister."

He was embarrassed, at a loss for words.

"Jason, why don't you try . . . you could love me if you wanted to."

He could not stand to see the pain in her eyes, to be the cause of someone's unhappiness. His fingers touched her lips and remained there.

"Joanna, you're sweet," he said softly, patiently, "but you want to play games when the world is falling apart."

His words infuriated her.

"What's the matter with you, Jason? Don't you know that life has to go on? Worlds have always been falling apart . . . but people don't stop living! They build new ones. They live and love and have babies and grow old."

She paused at his startled expression.

"And if they don't grow old, Jason," her voice softened, was gentle now. "If they don't grow old, they thank God they lived while they did. *Lived* Jason, not existed."

The profoundness of her words surprised him. He could not believe the wisdom of this eighteen-year-old, a wisdom which came with her first love. Love, the great teacher, a wise, able instructor. He could not help being moved.

He tried to speak, to answer her, but could not. For he suddenly felt small, very small beside her. Look at this girl, something inside him said, look at her Jason, she's not a child, she's a woman. And you are no longer a boy, you're a man. Find your answer here.

He drew her to him, suddenly discovering why she was here, what he meant to her. He kissed her gently, once, twice, surprised at the feeling that surged through him. She was startled and delighted that she had finally reached him. This was what she had wanted from Jason.

"Jason, Jason," she whispered breathlessly, "I love

you Jason. Whatever happens to us or to Chios or to the world, it can't change that."

He looked at her again, the startled expression still on his face.

A great weight was suddenly lifted from his shoulders. Jason felt lightheaded, able to soar with newfound wings.

He laid Joanna gently on the ground and fell down beside her. She smiled and stroked his hair, looking deeply into his eyes, seeing the world there.

Jason could not believe this feeling . . . it was so new to him. Was this what his mother had meant? Had she felt this way about his father? The thought of his father jolted him. Joanna saw the sudden look of fear on his face.

"No! Don't let something come between us now, Jason, please. This is the real you . . . here now, with me. Please Jason . . ."

She would not allow anything to enter and spoil their hallowed moment.

"Look at me," she took his head in her hands, the tears flowing down her cheeks. "Jason, don't torture yourself. I love you and you love me. Why won't you accept that?"

He could not stand to see her cry. He was afraid he would cry with her. I'm not going to let these shadows haunt me, he thought, I won't let them. Not my father or Joseph or the Turks. Only Joanna counts at this moment . . . this one special moment.

For the first time, Jason saw Joanna as a woman, a woman who loved him. He accepted it, believed it. He knew she was offering her self without question or conditions, knowing no other man would marry her without her purity. It was a revelation to him. Joy swept over him as he took her in his arms.

They were shy and daring, gentle and passionate. It was the most beautiful moment of their lives. Joanna felt the pain of her womanhood mixed with unbearable ecstasy. She would gladly endure much more pain for Jason.

When it was over they lay silently against the grass, Joanna's head nestled in Jason's arm. She could not believe her happiness. And Jason, the boy turned suddenly man, sighed as he looked up at the first star that appeared in the sky. He had never felt such contentment and peace. All the agony and loneliness, the longing and anxiety of his life dissolved into this warm feeling that spread over him, soothing his body, warming his veins. This was a part of life he had never planned, never expected.

"Someday, Joanna," Jason's trembling voice cut into the stillness of early evening, "someday, when this is all over, if we're alive . . ."

She winced at the words and placed her hand over his lips.

"Don't say it, don't be so pessimistic." She would pour new life into Jason, make him see the world as he had never seen it. "We'll be alive Jason, and we'll be together, and we'll have children . . ."

She watched his expression as she said the words. It softened. He turned to her with a look in his eyes that left her limp.

"I hope so, Joanna. I want to be able to marry you . . . when this is over. I won't leave you." It did not occur to him to marry her now. The Revolution and his brother still were paramount in his thoughts.

Fear clutched Joanna. She felt a shadow suddenly fall over them. Shuddering, she snuggled closer to

Jason. He hugged her to him, kissed her forehead, her lips. She did not care anymore. Jason loved her. No matter what happened, she belonged to Jason . . . nothing could change this.

* * *

Bishop Kyrillos of Samos stood at the Holy Gate of Saint Spyridon's church, dipped the cluster of green basil into the holy water and sprinkled it over the bowed heads of the two men standing before him. He turned to the large congregation gathered from all parts of Samos to witness the blessing of the leaders who would soon set out to liberate Chios.

"In the name of the Father and the Son and the Holy Ghost, Amen."

The doxology ended. Archimandrite Makavrios gave the blessing. Logothetis and Bournias were ready. Fifty ships and twenty-five hundred men waited to set sail for the island of the mastic.

Logothetis had hesitated in his final decision, and he was uneasy now. It also disturbed him that they had sent no formal notification to Chios of their planned arrival. He wondered if he were right to listen to Bournias again. Yet, recalling Tombazis' welcome, he agreed with Bournias that it seemed pointless to notify the Elders of Chios. They would act quickly, giving no one a chance to turn them away. Let Kambos and Chora sleep in their false contentment. The other Chiotes would rise and fight, and these two would lead them.

Yet Logothetis could not erase the doubts that persisted. He had promised Rallis to wait. He had also written Ypsilantis that he would abide by the new government's wishes to postpone the Chios mission until a future, more appropriate date. Why did he allow Bournias to sway him? And yet he did not believe that the Chiotes were completely powerless, without arms and ammunition.

Bournias had not let Logothetis rest. He arrived in Samos swearing not to leave there until the Samiote accepted the co-leadership of his mission. Bournias, a drunken peasant, coarse and insolent but brave in battle, as he proved in the service of Napoleon, hid a twisted ego behind the face of patriotism. Yet he had succeeded in convincing Logothetis where others, more educated and able, had failed. Bournias smiled now, gloating in the idolatry and praise of the crowd in the church. His dark eyes gleamed under his thick brows, and he stroked his bushy moustache as he watched the crowd lining up near the door to shake his hand. He grinned, remembering his own visit to Ypsilantis. He had gone personally, all the way to the mainland at the Peloponesse, to present his plan for the liberation of Chios. But Ypsilantis had been unimpressed by both the plan and its architect. Not wanting to offend the Chiotes, he referred Bournias to a fellow revolutionary, the phil-Hellene Maxim Raybud, who also hesitated. Again Bournias was referred elsewhere, this time to the Chiote educator Neophytos Vambas. Vambas, most anxious to free his homeland, but also mistrusting Bournias, sailed to Samos and begged Logothetis to take over joint leadership of the Bournias expedition. Bournias was satisfied. Even Ypsilantis' arrival in Samos and his conference with Logothetis could not change their minds. Bournias' clever manipulating convinced Logothetis to go ahead. And now they were about to begin. They were setting sail for Chios today. Unprepared or not, the Chiotes would be liberated, and Bournias' name would go down in history. How was he to know it would go down anathematized, as a bungler, a fool and a thief? And that Logothetis, who had proved himself a true hero elsewhere, would lose face, control, the battle and his good name. How strange the Fate that writes the chapters of history!

* * *

It was an hour before midnight. Jason and his mother looked at each other silently. The time had come . . . they rose. Jason went to get his rifle and jacket. He gathered up his bullets as Helena stuffed her embroidery into her satchel and picked up a white shawl. The carriage would be here soon to take her to Kambos where she would spend the night. There she would be safe. In the morning, if the attack was successful and all went well, she would return home.

The ships would soon be here. Word had reached Father Stelios that morning—thank God for the wisdom and foresight of Bishop Kyrillos. Without the clergy the Revolution would not have had its foothold.

The Turks were asleep in the fortress while the villagers quietly gathered together. Jason's heart leaped in anticipation, in renewed hope. Once the liberators arrived, the two-thousand Turks on the island would be crushed. He could not believe that after all these years the time had actually arrived.

"Son," Helena looked into Jason's dark eyes with anxiety. The thought of something happening to Jason terrified her.

"Oh my son," she pressed him to her. "Remember I love you. We all love you. Be careful!"

"Don't worry mother, I can't afford to get myself killed. There's too much ahead of me . . . Joseph . . ." He paused a moment and smiled . . . "and Joanna."

A glow came over Helena's face. So he did care for the girl. Her eyes asked him a hundred questions, questions he had no time to answer now.

"Yes, mother . . . Joanna." He said no more, but his mother read his heart.

He loves her, she sighed deeply, thank God . . . thank God.

"But I must find Joseph first."

Sadness covered her face again.

"I *will* find him, you'll see." He tried to calm her fears. "And it won't be half as bad as you think. I've heard of Janissaries finding their Greek families and returning to them . . . it *does* happen you know."

He tried to sound convincing, knowing full well that such cases were rare.

From your lips to God's ears, Helena prayed. Would they be so fortunate?

A whistle pierced the air. It was Captain Petros with the carriage. His driver would take Helena to Kambos while he and Jason headed for the shore of Megas Limionas on foot.

The door opened and Petros entered. Jason sensed something in his look and offered to wait outside. Petros' face was clouded. Helena's heart ached for him.

"Helena, there isn't much time. I wanted so much to talk to you. About us . . . about Maria. But it will have to wait. We'll talk tomorrow . . . or later . . ."

"What about Maria?" Helena had noticed another change in her lately. The newfound joy she had gloried in a few weeks ago had turned into deep gloom, a sadness that seemed to be eating her, like a disease. Was it guilt? Had Bey tired of her? She would find out tonight . . . she would make Maria tell her.

"Maria's not well. I'm worried about her." Petros was genuinely concerned. "But that doesn't mean I've stopped loving you Helena, not for a moment."

He doesn't have to reassure me, she thought, but she drank in his words nonetheless. She seemed to sense that their days together were limited and wanted to savor every word, every gesture.

She smiled sadly.

"You won't say it, will you?" Petros grinned ironically. "My darling, beloved Helena, so proper and so refined. You think it will lower your dignity to admit you love a man."

He saw her eyes cloud, her lips tighten.

"I didn't mean to hurt you, my dear. Don't you know that even my criticism comes with love? I love you Helena, no matter what you do or say."

He drew her to him and kissed her passionately. She could not move, afraid it was the last time she would see him. He held her away from him and stared at her, wanting to remember her face. He stroked her hair, caressed her cheek, and she stood there, embarrassed, letting him.

"I'll be back as soon as I can. Take care of yourselves."

He turned to go but she stopped him.

"Wait."

She put something in his hand. He looked at it and

smiled, deeply touched by her gesture. It was a small gold cross on a chain. She was telling him she loved him in the only way she could. He stood there flustered, unable to speak.

"Here, let me put it on you."

She took the cross from his hand and fastened it around his neck.

"To guide you and keep you safe."

He watched her eyes wanting desperately to cry but not daring. He had rarely seen such discipline in a woman. She has the spirit of a Spartan, he thought.

The door burst open.

"What's the matter? It's late and the men are waiting for us." Jason looked curiously at the startled pair.

"Captain Petros was telling me about his wife," Helena explained to her son, afraid he might suspect. "She seems worse."

"She'll be alright, mother. It's just battle nerves." He laughed nervously, still watching his mother and captain Petros.

"I'm ready son," Petros took Helena's arm and helped her to the door.

"By the way," Jason stopped his mother, forgetting his curiosity at the scene. "I didn't get a chance to see Joanna. She was expecting me. Tell her that I'll be back and not to worry. And please tell her . . ."

Helena watched him carefully. He was like his mother, afraid, so afraid of his emotions.

"Tell her what, son?" She smiled to encourage him.

Jason paused, embarrassed. Then he changed the words that came to his lips.

"Tell her I'll see her the moment I can get away."

He waved and ran ahead. Petros helped Helena onto the carriage. Once more his eyes told her he loved her. He turned and walked away, pausing once to wave. In the darkness Helena made out muted figures. It was the villagers, carrying pitchforks, scythes, knives, sticks, whatever they could find to use as weapons. They were on their way to greet the ships from Samos and to help launch the attack on shore. Father Stelios led the way, with Fatouros at his side.

X

The sentry blinked in the darkness. He looked again past the black mist into the sea. A light . . . two lights . . . three. There were ships in the horizon. The Greeks were coming!

Quickly he gave the signal to the watch below. Call out the soldiers, man the rifles, the *giaours* are coming. Within the half hour, Turkish soldiers had gathered along the shores of Megas Limionas and Kontari ready to meet the Samiotes.

Jason and the villagers crawled slowly up the hill to the rear of the Turks who were preoccupied with the oncoming ships. Silently, there in the darkness, the first pitchfork found its mark and the Chiotes rushed headlong into the surprised Turks. The Moslems had little time to aim their rifles or draw their swords. Knives and scythes, shovels and sticks struck the flesh of the conquerors, pierced it with a furious mania. The villagers had no guns, but this did not stop them. The Turks may have taken their weapons but they could not touch their determination. Thymiana and Vrondados, Kalimasia and Neohori, all the surrounding villages were represented tonight. Several of the Greek ships landed and the men disembarked and joined the hand-to-hand fighting. The other vessels remained at sea to shell the fortress in Chora. It was swift and victorious, this first skirmish, for the people of Chios. One hundred fifty Turks lay dead along the shore, while the others scattered, running in all directions to save themselves. Only a handful of Chiotes were lost. God grant that the rest of the battle would be so easy.

The boom of the cannon jolted the night, rousing the surprised citizens. Inside his tower in Chora, Bechit Pasha frothed at the mouth, cursing and screaming at the "bastards" who dared cross the Sultan, who dared break their promise. Quickly he ordered the rounding up of the hostages for execution.

It was dawn when the drawbridge was raised and the last of the Turks was safe within the fortress walls. Captain Petros threw himself on the ground, exhausted and out of breath, his clothing torn, his face and hands scratched. But his spirits were high. Thank God, he prayed silently, we have survived the first ordeal. Thank God for sparing us so far. Yet he was leery, victory had come too quickly. Was freedom, after all, so easy to achieve? He lay there, resting, pondering the situation. The sun had begun its climb. Where would they be by sunset, he wondered. The crucial moment of their lives was here. Petros felt a shudder as he realized they had only just begun . . . there was so much that could happen to them. He thought of Helena and sighed. Then he remembered where he was and quickly looked around. The others were crawling from everywhere, behind the mounds, the hills, from behind the bodies that lay scattered about. He saw Jason wandering about, bending over the Turkish corpses, turning them over to look into their faces. There was a frantic look about him.

"Did you see them run?" Petros said as Jason fell down beside him, sighing dejectedly, exhausted from the ordeal. Petros noticed the hopeless look on Jason's face. What was bothering the boy? They had had their first triumph. They had both looked forward to this day for so long.

"Well son, it's a happy day in our lives. Although I must say you don't look too happy about our victory." Petros watched Jason intently. "This is what we've been waiting for, isn't it?"

Helena's son was not one to thirst for blood. But he had wanted battle, had looked forward to the fight for freedom. What was wrong with him now? Was he sorry? Was he afraid? Petros looked at Jason with these questions in his eyes.

I suppose, thought Petros, offering his own answers, I suppose this was a shock to Jason. Poor lad, it's not his nature to be a killer. He's a sensitive one . . . and this has affected him. But he'll survive. It's only the beginning. He'll learn, as we have.

Jason's thoughts wandered too, as he sat there, feeling frustration at this turn of events. He had wanted to fight, yearned to free Chios, but now he found it painful, disillusioning. The sight of the Turks' bodies strewn on the shore brought a sense of degradation. Somewhere, past those white hills in the east, wives and mothers and children would mourn. He pictured them weeping, and he felt a chill run through him. But death is life, another part of him said. The Turks' deaths would mean life for the Greeks, freedom for the Chiotes. And we have had enough of slavery, Jason said to himself. He thought of the thousands of mainland Greeks who suffered these long centuries of subjugation. Death to the conqueror, was the cry. Why then, when the day of liberation had arrived, should Jason feel this way? He could not help himself. It was an empty triumph. This was not at all the way he imagined it would be.

"Why were you looking through those bodies, Jason?" Petros' voice broke into Jason's thoughts.

There were tears in his eyes when he turned to Petros. The older man looked away to save Jason embarrassment. And the boy, wanting at last to pour out what was hidden in his heart all this time, found the opportunity now, on this hillside near Megas Limionas. He looked at the water sparkling in the morning sun. He had played here as a child, and now as a man, he was playing games of war and searching for his lost treasure.

"I'm a pretty good listener, why don't you try me?"

From the day Jason learned about Joseph, he had spoken to no one about it. Now he turned to Petros. The thought suddenly came to him that he loved this man. He wished his father were like him. He looked at Petros, shook his head as though trying to push away his thoughts, and began to talk.

The story came out in spurts. He talked about Joseph during their childhood days, of the abduction, the final question of his whereabouts. At the end,

Jason was grateful he had poured out his pain to another soul, to someone who would understand, who loved him and sympathized with his obsessive desire to find his brother.

Petros listened grimly, then smiled with understanding.

"We'll find him Jason. I know God will help us there, too. Have faith."

A man appeared in the distance, then another. One by one the villagers gathered around Petros and Jason. Some had just returned from Chora, bringing the latest news. The Turks were closed within the fortress, afraid to come out, helpless to do anything. They had been told by the foreign consulars friendly to the Greeks that Logothetis' men numbered many thousands. You don't have a chance against such odds, they exaggerated, surrender and save yourselves. The Turks were sweating it out. But their one weapon was the hostages locked within their walls. Petros' men had more details. The fortress at Chora was being attacked on all sides. Logothetis' ships bombed it from the sea and Fatouros on shore led the rear attack. Those villagers who were able to obtain rifles gathered on the hilltop behind the fortress, at Trouloti, while the men from Vrondados and Thymiana set up cannon and prepared for the large-scale attack. It appeared that luck was still with the Chiotes.

* * *

Logothetis and Bournias strolled through the streets of the empty capital. Chora was deserted. The local citizens had locked themselves in their homes, afraid to appear. Who were these men, this Logothetis and Bournias who dared bring this new terror upon them? Who asked them to come? The Sultan would surely be infuriated. The Turks would be roused to violence . . . they would hang the eighty hostages. God help us all, they moaned inside the comfort of their lavish homes. Damn these uninvited adventurers who came and stirred up this holocaust. Yet the holocaust had not really begun.

"What a welcome for the freedom-fighters!" Bournias grunted sarcastically as the two men walked towards Aplotaria. He tried to laugh it off but the laughter stuck in his throat.

"Your fellow Chiotes don't seem too happy about our arrival, friend Bournias." Logothetis smiled wryly.

Then, in serious afterthought, he added. "You came to Samos and begged me to join you. You said the Chiotes were waiting for us, that they had pleaded for someone to lead them."

Logothetis wondered if his partner were a liar. "Except for those few villagers on the shore, where are your Chiote freedom-lovers now?"

Bournias was embarrassed, but only for a moment. He had no answer to Logothetis' questions, no explanation for the disorganization. But, he decided, he would not let that bother him now, he would think of a way to waken the Chiotes.

"They've run to hide like squirrels. Don't mind them. It's not that they have anything against us. I guess it was the shock." Bournias rattled on, saying whatever came to mind to cover his confusion.

"Remember these people don't know much about fighting. But we'll teach them. They'll come out soon." He watched for Logothetis' reaction.

"Well, what do we do now, *Signore* General?" Logothetis addressed Bournias by the title he had requested. The vain Bournias did not notice the irony in Logothetis' voice. "How do we get them to come out?"

The Samiote could not hide his disappointment. This Bournias was nothing after all, his words and schemes were merely hot air. The people of Chora were obviously not in sympathy with the villagers. They resented this intrusion.

"We'll set fire to the *dzami** and the Turkish coffee-houses. Then you'll see how quickly the Chiotes will come rushing out to watch the show."

The fighters had disembarked and scattered throughout the town. They gathered in groups, some in the square, passing on Bournias' suggestion. The idea of setting fire to the buildings appealed to them. They hurried towards Aplotaria, looking at the shops and the merchants' stands with greedy eyes . . . there was much wealth here in Chios. As the flames went up, the Chiote townspeople ran to watch the Turkish buildings burn, and Bournias' men found their chance to help themselves. They streamed through the shopping area, grabbing armfuls of expensive silks and cotton fabrics, copperware and silver which they carted to the harbor. Linens and delicate laces, hand-woven rugs—they could not believe their luck. They heaped their loot aboard the fastest ship in the fleet, and prepared to set sail for Samos, unload their spoils and return for more. As the Moslem buildings went up in flames, the startled

**dzami - Turkish mosque*

Chiotes watched their carefully gathered wealth being snatched by their liberators. Expensive, indeed, was the price of freedom.

Logothetis chose to see nothing. He was too busy with his own problems—how to rid himself of this madman whose illusions of grandeur were ruining the mission. And Bournias watched the chaos with unconcern. Let the men take what they wanted. Freedom at all costs. Later, as the acclaimed liberator of Chios, he would rule the island and bring order.

"Where are the Elders?" he cried. "Bring them to the cathedral at once. We must speak with them."

"Our leaders are held hostage inside the fortress, master Bournias."

Bournias stared blankly at the man. He and Logothetis had neglected to inquire about the hostages.

"*Signore* General, if you please," Bournias corrected, demanding the respect due him. When would these fools realize he was not a mere soldier?

"Forgive me, *Signore* General, our Elders are prisoners inside the fortress."

"Then bring those who are in their place. You must have *some* representatives here."

Frangias, Tziropanias and Manousos stood before Logothetis and Bournias in the silence of the great cathedral. In their first official appearance since their predecessors were imprisoned, the new Chiote leaders lacked the calm, self-assurance of the other three. There was no arrogance on their faces, no attempts to send these fighters away. They did not know where to turn, who was the foe and who the friend. They remembered that Diomatris, Patrikousis and Vlastos had sent Tombazis away last Spring. And this was the result . . . a worse fate that came to them unexpectedly, suddenly. They wondered now if conditions would have been different if Tombazis' offer of liberation were accepted last Spring. At least then, the Chiotes were armed. Now it was hopeless.

The three stood before these so-called liberators, shocked by their pomposity, curious to hear what they had to say. The two leaders had ascended the bishop's throne and looked down at the Chiotes with hands extended for the spiritual kiss customarily bestowed upon the archbishop. What manner of fools are these, the Elders thought as they bent hesitantly to kiss the hands that were offered. Bournias and Logothetis did not notice or would not notice the look of astonishment on their "believers'" faces.

In a matter of minutes—during the shuffling of the audience, the rendering of the spiritual kiss—Logothetis had surveyed the interior of the huge cathedral. With hidden amazement he noted the gold and jewels abounding, the priceless candelabra and chandeliers, the marble floors and mosaics, the tall windows, the offering boxes bulging with coins. So much wealth segregated in one building. The Chiotes are prosperous beyond all heresay, Logothetis mused while the egotistical Bournias gloried in the luxury of their new, self-appointed posts.

The door burst open and Jason and Captain Petros entered. Behind them were a handful of angry men, all stunned at the chaos they had witnessed outside. God, what was this devastation? What had gone wrong? The new arrivals stopped and stared with open mouths at the sight of Frangias kissing Bournias' hand. They pushed forward, angry questions on their faces, holding their tempers to see what answers they would receive. Surely there was an explanation to all this. As they walked down the aïsle Petros turned to see Fatouros entering the church, panting, in a fury. He, too, had seen the turmoil in the streets and set out to find Petros.

Bournias motioned to them.

"Come forward men." His tone was a welcoming one. "I want you to hear this too. This is for all Chiotes."

"I would like to identify myself," Petros addressed Bournias from the center of the church as his men formed a semi-circle around him. "Captain Petros Sofronis of Kambos."

He explained his position in the Revolution, the work he had done and the details of last night's skirmish at Megas Limionas and Kontari.

"It was to me the first news of your arrival came."

"And who sent you the word?" Bournias had made no such arrangement.

"Bishop Kyrillos of Samos . . . to the priest, Father Stelios of Thymiana."

The men of the cloth were the true fighters. They left nothing to chance. Was it not a Bishop who had raised the banner that first day on the Greek mainland? In every part of Greece the clergy led the way to freedom. And now the clergy had corrected the errors of Chios' liberators.

The two leaders looked at each other. This Sofronis was an intelligent man but a critical one. They hoped they would not have trouble with him. He bore watching.

"We're pleased to have you with us, Captain Sofronis," Bournias smiled in welcome, "and to have you lead your men through the difficult days ahead. We're counting on you. Please come forward."

The villagers followed Petros to the front of the cathedral. Bournias motioned Petros to sit on the benches against the wall. Then he braced himself, in comic dignity, to begin the speech he had rehearsed.

"Be advised that upon orders from the revolutionary leader Dimitrios Ypsilantis himself, we are herewith dissolving the present system of the Elders as a governing body in Chios. They will be replaced by a six-man committee which General Logothetis and I will appoint."

The Elders were stunned. The villagers were pleased. They had had enough of the wealthy landowners and the government that benefited mainly the Elders. Perhaps these two men were not so bad after all, in spite of this ridiculous beginning . . . and yet, the villagers were hesitant, worried.

Bournias continued.

"My friends, as you can see we came to liberate Chios. Things may seem strange to you now, but once you taste freedom you will see what I mean. It must be achieved at all costs."

Is he referring to the plundering that's going on outside, Jason wondered.

"Only one who has served under the great Bonaparte knows the true meaning of freedom."

Logothetis watched Bournias and tried to hide the smirk that crept on his face. This man is a fool, he thought, but let him speak if it makes him happy. I'll take matters into my own hands in due time. He would find a way to get rid of this buffoon. Rallis and Ypsilantis were right in not trusting him.

Bournias ranted on, impervious to those around

him and to Logothetis' reaction.

"I told Napoleon many times that he should have come to liberate Chios. Unfortunately he did not heed me. Chios should have been free twenty years ago . . ."

Logothetis could not listen to these idiotic words any longer. He leaned over and whispered in Bournias' ear.

"Get on with it. You're wasting time . . . come to the point." He could not mask his annoyance.

Bournias was stung by his partner's comment but decided best to hide his animosity.

"Very well." He turned to his audience.

"Friends, Elders, as your general I want you to know that we have brought ashore six rolling cannons and two barrels of powder. All our men have arms and ammunition. Now this is what we want from you." He paused a moment. "Call out your fellow Chiotes. Order them to come out like the courageous Greeks they are, to bring their rifles or whatever weapons they have and meet us tomorrow when we launch the attack against the fortress. Tomorrow at Trouloti."

Fatouros let out a moan. "We've already begun the attack. You mean you didn't know that? My men are out there under your second-in-command. What kind of a Revolution are you running, Bournias?"

Bournias tried to ignore Fatouros. This clumsy villager had struck a note that hurt. The men watched Bournias, waiting for the answer. He looked at Logothetis who stared back in blank expression.

"It's not easy to keep order in this type of war, compatriot. But never mind, since you've begun the attack, we'll strengthen it tomorrow with our cannon."

Petros was whispering to Fatouros, hoping to calm him until they could get away and discuss this turn of events.

"*Signore* General," it was one of the men from the village of Kalimasia. "As you know, the Turks confiscated all our weapons last Spring. We have no rifles."

Bournias was grateful for the interruption. Fatouros might quiet down in the meantime.

"Do the best you can, friend. Find something. Fatouros' men here did very well at Kontari—and they had no rifles."

"Master Bournias, we can't use pitchforks and knives against stone walls!"

"Don't tell me what we can do and can't do! You're under Bournias now—*Signore* General Bournias—and remember that when you address me."

Jason thought he was dreaming. Things like this could not be happening. But to his amazement, they were. He spoke up now, trying to hide the tremor in his voice.

"*Signore* General, you say you have six cannon. Do you have cannon balls for them?"

"You'll find cannon balls somewhere, my boy." Bournias was annoyed. He turned to Logothetis who bit his lip and stared glumly at his partner.

Petros had remained silent through this discussion, but his anger rose with each sentence Bournias uttered. He could be still no longer.

"And where do you propose we find cannon balls, *Signore* General?"

Logothetis wondered how Bournias would get himself out of this one. He wanted to help him, for he had gone too far and was now committing them both. But he could not. Where, indeed, could they find cannon balls in a place that had been stripped of the smallest, most meager weapon?

Bournias would not be put down. Unabashed, he gave his answer. "I understand a Turkish frigate was sunk near *Tsesme* the other day. You can bring up its cannon and cannonballs."

Logothetis smiled in amazement at Bournias' audacity. Petros' anger rose.

"That ship's down too deep for us to be able to raise its cannon. You know that. And there's no use dragging up the cannonball—it would never fit your cannon."

"Are you trying to tell me about cannon, sir? *Me*, who saw service under Napoleon Bonaparte? Do as I order you!"

Petros glared angrily at him. He wanted to turn and stomp out, to let him run the show as he liked. But he knew he could not afford to do this. To desert now would be unthinkable. The villagers depended on Petros. Chios needed him more than ever now. He must meet with the village leaders and try to salvage what he could. This chaotic manner of operation would lose them the Revolution. Now, while there were few Turks on Chios, when the soldiers were inside the fortress walls, now was the time to act, to strike the final blow and raise the banner. The Turks were trapped, but Bournias was wasting time and energy.

Fatouros stood motionless beside Petros. He was pale and silent, deep in thought. Suddenly he turned and motioned to Petros, looked at Bournias and Logothetis with scorn, and walked away. The other villagers, one by one, followed suit.

"Wait!"

Logothetis decided it was time to intervene. Things were bungled enough. They could not afford to lose these men. They needed all the support they could get.

"Captain Sofronis, we wish to make you an offer."

The men stopped and turned towards the bishop's throne. Bournias looked at Logothetis enigmatically, and the Samiote whispered to his partner.

"Keep them here at all costs. Appoint the six-man governing committee you proposed earlier."

Bournias smiled. Logothetis had come up with a worthwhile idea.

"Friends, please, I have a proposal. This is no time for bickering. We must stand together to win this fight."

Petros looked at Fatouros and Jason, at the other villagers. They were silent, waiting apprehensively to hear what new plan lay ahead.

"Let's see what they have to say," Kyladitis whispered to the group.

They were in agreement, knowing full well the dangers of division. Perhaps united they might achieve victory. And yet . . .

Petros turned back, the men close behind him.

"What is your proposal, *Signore* General?"

"I hereby appoint you as a member of the new six-man governing committee."

A murmur went up among the men. They were pleased. This was more like it.

"One man from Kambos," spoke Logothetis, "and one each from the other areas."

Bournias had no idea where to begin. "Have you any suggestions, Captain Sofronis?"

"From Thymiana, I recommend Xenophon Andreadis the merchant."

Bournias nodded approval.

"Go on."

"Hadzinikolas Kyladitis from Vrondados."

What better man than the captain-shipowner who had returned to Chios to fight for his island.

Bournias waited. Sofronis had finished.

"I gave you two names, *Signore* General, the two I can vouch for. I suggest you find the others yourself."

"And if I may add," Captain Kyladitis offered, "I suggest you select at least one member from Chora and one from Kardamylla or some northern town. It is wise to have full representation of the island."

"Very well, General Logothetis and I will choose them later. Now we will go. We will meet again in a week."

"A week is too long!" Fatouros, Kyladitis and Petros cried out in unison.

"What happens in the meantime, generals?"

"What about Tourloti and the rear attack we initiated?"

"You'll hold off the attack until we find cannonball." Curse Fatouros and his rear attack on Tourloti, thought Bournias.

"I don't think we should lose a week, general," Captain Sofronis remained calm, vowing to humor this maniac. "The Turks will be preparing reinforcements from Constantinople. We can't risk that."

"Alright, give General Logothetis and me a day to lay our plans. Meanwhile take your own actions in your areas. Clear out any Turks you see, round up more villagers and arms and report to me."

The situation deteriorated with every word Bournias uttered. It was obvious these two had set out from Samos with no organized plans, without a program of action. God help us all, thought Petros.

God help us, echoed in the minds of all his men.

Only the Elders were satisfied, free to go at last, relieved of the burden of governing the island at this crucial period. Let the villagers rule themselves as they had always wished. And let these fools play Revolution. The Elders would go home now, pack their belongings and treasures, and set sail for the island of Syra where they could live in peace, in their accustomed luxury.

XI

Joanna stood on the terrace watching the outer gate anxiously. If only it would open and Jason would step into the courtyard! It had been over a week since he was in their home, eating with them, playing chess with her father. Yet it seemed years. Everything had changed since that night. Captain Petros dashed in and out, hardly speaking. Maria kept to her room with headaches. Helena stole into the house at night when it was safe, always accompanied by one of the villagers. The whole island was in a turmoil. Only Kambos, with its high walls, was safe. The atmosphere was tense, the Chiote fighters roamed the areas with any weapon they could find, searching for Turks, fighting ambushes. It was a period of disorganized warfare, of minor skirmishes, of not knowing what to do. Several of the villages which had organized in the past, as Thymiana had, were able to keep ahead. But this was only in their own areas, and they, too, were limited. Everyone waited anxiously, hopefully, for Bournias and Logothetis to stop bickering, to prepare the future moves. The Turks were still locked within the fortress, with no reinforcements in sight. How long would the Chiotes' luck last? Time was precious—but it was running out.

By now, news of the invasion had reached Constantinople. Immediately, the leading Chiotes in the Ottoman capital were rounded up to be imprisoned or hanged. Orders were issued to all governors of Asia Minor to join forces at *Tsesme* and proceed to Chios. Ships were being manned and fighters assembled. Among these troops were the fierce, fanatic Janissaries, who had been trained for just such action. They were exuberant now as they boarded the ships. They could not wait to see Christian blood flow.

"Kill!" shouted the infuriated Sultan. He would never forgive the Chiotes for this sudden betrayal. To think they would rise against their protector, the one who had offered them more than any conquered people ever hoped for, ever dreamed of having!

"Kill!" he screamed, "All males over twelve, all women over forty, all two-year-old children. Take the rest prisoners!"

He would fix these insolent wretches. The blood of the Chiotes would flow over the island in rivers. The Sultan's slave markets would bulge, his harems would be replenished. If this was the thanks he received from Chios, the favored island, then Chios would pay dearly. History would remember this year of 1822!

On the island, Captain Petros and the new governing committee busied themselves in procuring stores and arms, in conscripting men to fill the ranks, and in setting up some system of government. Bournias and Logothetis were in the background, busy fighting among themselves, arguing as to who was first in command, who would be the eventual leader. Bournias insisted it was time he promoted himself to generalissimo. Logothetis spurned him and ordered his men to ignore any orders the Chiote issued.

The Sofronis gate suddenly opened and a group of men led by Captain Petros hurried inside. Joanna rushed down the steps looking for Jason. She hugged her father, trying to hide her disappointment and turned to him questioningly.

"Jason?"

"He's in Chora loading powder. He's alright." Petros sensed her concern. He stroked her hair and kissed her forehead.

"Don't worry dear. He's fine. We don't have to worry about Jason."

He looked toward the house.

"How's your mother?"

"She's not well, father. I'm very worried. She hardly eats a thing, and she stays in her room all day. Jason's mother is with her now. I don't know what we'd do without *Kyra* Helena."

"Tell them I'll be up to see them later. I have some things to attend to first."

Before Joanna could reply, he turned to his men and motioned them to follow. They gathered in the magazine and pulled up chairs around the small table while the servants hurried about. Joanna ran after them.

"Sit down men," Petros was flustered, hurried.

They had reached a decision and were here to draw up the plans. One of them was to sail to the mainland for help. It was their only chance.

"Father," Joanna's tone was hurt, disappointed, "aren't you going up to mother? She's ill and you've been gone all these days."

Petros did not mean to be inconsiderate. But was anything more important than righting this ridiculous, hopeless situation? Chios came first, above wife and family. Even above Helena, whom he longed to see, whom he ached for every night. The thought of her now made his heart beat faster. Embarrassed by his daughter's reprimand, he turned to his men and excused himself. The servants entered with bottles of wine, plates of olives, pieces of liver, cheese, fresh bread. It had been days since the men had eaten from plates . . . on a table.

"Have something to eat until I get back, men. I won't be long." Petro ran up the steps to the main floor.

He opened the door without knocking and stood there looking at the two women. His breath caught at the picture they made—Helena sitting beside the bed where Maria lay fully dressed on top of the covers, half-asleep. The sharp contrasting beauty of the two made his heart turn. Helena with her dark eyes, her olive skin and black hair; fair-skinned Maria, the deep color of her cheeks now gone, her blonde hair falling over her shoulder, her eyes as blue as the skies over Chios. They are both so beautiful, he thought wincing, and both so far from me, now. He sighed and walked over to them, pausing at Maria's bedside.

"How are you feeling, Maria?"

His voice was grave as he noticed her wan face, her

thinning body. Nonetheless his heart ached to cry out to the other woman, to ask her how she was, to tell her he missed her. He noticed that Helena looked worried. What was wrong with Maria? Was it fear of the Turks?

"I've been scolding Maria. She refuses to eat. Please talk to her."

Helena motioned to Petros behind Maria's gaze.

"Maria, shame on you," Petros reprimanded, "why don't you try? Please stop being a child and make an effort." The doctor had found nothing physically wrong with her. Petros could not understand.

My poor Petros, Helena thought, if you only knew. If you only knew what is torturing your wife. She almost laughed at the irony of the whole situation. What a mad circle we're in, she thought, and wondered what the final conclusion to this affair would be. Only Jason and Joanna seemed to have hope for the future. At least if their children could find happiness together, Helena would ask nothing more. She suddenly thought of Joseph and decided it was futile to ask God for his return. It would be too much.

Maria smiled half-heartedly at Petros. He was telling her to eat. Where were you all these years, she asked silently, where were you when I needed you? I don't need food, I need Ali Bey and the love you never gave me. This would never have happened if you had showed more interest in me.

She had gone to Ali Bey partly out of whim and flattery, partly out of desperation from the years of loneliness. It was exciting, daring, to be loved and wanted by an attractive Turk. But after that night in his bed, she was not the same. Maria belonged to Bey, she could not live without him. His love was more than desire and passion. It was genuine, a deep, lasting feeling evident in his every breath, his every move. It reached out to her and stirred feelings she had never known before.

If I did not have Joanna, Maria thought, I would go to him now. She would give up her home gladly, even her faith for Ali Bey. But when it came to her child, a deep sense of guilt clutched her and she could not bring herself to make the final decision. Yet she knew she was bound to Bey for always. And because she could not remain with him she wanted to die.

"I'll be alright, Petros," she whispered. What else could she say to him? "I promise to eat."

In a moment of empathy, she added, "I was asking about you today. I'm sorry things are going so badly."

She pitied Petros, pitied the wasted years, his loneliness. She looked at him standing so forlorn beside her and wished that he, too, could find what she had found. But what good was it? Her ties to her child were too strong. Yet love, in time, often weakens even the strongest ties.

"Where's Jason?" Helena asked Petros. "Is he alright?"

"He's fine. I left him in Chora with Fatouros, loading rifles. The cannonball at Tourloti are too small, they don't reach the fortress. I came here to get more rifles. We're lucky the Turks are locked scared inside. They think we have many more arms and fighters than we do . . . so far God is with us."

"What's going to happen, Petros?" Maria was concerned. She wondered what Ali Bey's position would be now.

"We're sending Dr. Glarakis and Raphos to the Greek assembly at Corinth to ask for munitions and the appointment of a provisional governor. Captain Kyladitis is giving one of his ships for the voyage . . . the 'Swallow.' He's downstairs now, waiting for me."

Petros did not want to frighten the women, but he felt they should know the facts and what chances were for success.

"Once we have munitions we're safe, and the Revolution's ours."

"What about the Sultan? Won't he be sending reinforcements?" Helena would think of everything, he mused. God help us if Turkish reinforcements arrive first.

He paused, trying to think of an appropriate answer. This was what they feared. If the Turkish fleet reached them before help came from Corinth, it would be disastrous.

"We're counting on the time needed to set up the Turkish armada at Constantinople and to assemble their fighters. Then they must sail through the Dardanelles and the long distance to *Tsesme.*"

"At *Tsesme* they'll be joining the other Turkish forces, won't they?" Helena tried to hide her fear.

Petros nodded.

"And it's little over an hour's sail from *Tsesme* to here." She added with finality. She knew what that meant. They all knew.

Petros changed the subject.

"I may not be coming here for a while. Don't worry about me, I'll get word back to you whenever I can. In the meantime it would be wise, Helena, if you moved in with Maria."

In case the Turks arrived before Greek help came, it would mean fighting out in the open. Helena would have more protection in Kambos. It was the last place the Turks would strike.

"I'd like to stay in my home for a while longer. Please. There's no immediate danger."

Helena had a premonition that if she left her home she would never come back to it, never see it again. She did not know why she felt this way.

Petros tried to object, but he finally accepted her promise that if she did not hear from him in two weeks she would move in with Maria.

Maria wanted her, needed her desperately. But she understood Helena's feelings about her home. It was her security, the one thing of her own she could fall back on.

"Alright, I promise. In two weeks."

A dark cloud hung over them as Helena spoke. She was frightened.

"And Jason . . . let me know how he is. Tell him to come home for a rest when he gets the chance."

"I will, don't worry. Your son's quite a man, Helena, you should be very proud."

Their eyes met and they shared a brief moment.

"I must go . . . the men are waiting."

He kissed Maria on the forehead—she barely stirred.

"I'll be in touch with you both. Take care of yourselves."

He looked at Helena again, quickly, and the ache inside her grew. Petros closed the door behind him.

PART II

XII

"Al . . . lah Wuk . . . bar!!!"

The muezzin's call for evening prayer echoed through the city, drifted among the minarets and towers, and finally settled over the palace. Youssef rose to his feet, having paid homage to Allah, and stood at the balcony, watching the aftermath of the sunset. The purplish-red glow of the sky had a strange fascination for him. There seemed to be an invisible hand that beckoned him to the land beyond the sun—the land he was destined to fight. He stood mesmerized, oblivious to the sounds of activity from the servants inside.

He was still there when dusk crept over the city, deep in thought, pondering life and his 22 years. He looked down at his uniform, admiring the silk fabric, the elegance of its cut as he ran his hand on its shiny surface. He was proud of himself, proud to be a Janissary, a member of the most advanced fighting unit the world had seen. For nearly 200 years now the disciplined strength of the Janissaries was unmatched by any of the Sultan's enemies.

I'm a part of all this, he thought proudly, and tightened his grip on his sword.

He had come a long way from that shy child who grew up in a province where he learned the Turkish language and the Moslem religion. At 17 he was brought to the capital for instruction in military discipline and the arts of war. Now he was Youssef the Janissary, about to embark on his first major assignment. Suddenly he felt dizzy—those recurring thoughts began whirling in his head. They twisted and turned like a tornado about to sweep him off. He closed and clenched his fists, trying to fight the storm, unwilling to be carried into the past. It was happening more often these past months, but he told no one about it. And inevitably it was followed by memories of a distant time and place—translucent memories of a strange period. In trying to piece them together, later, when his mind calmed, he was even more confused by the meager information he had of his life. His group of children grew up in a province near Constantinople. In the hands of tutors and guardians, the children were well-educated and trained in the customs of their country. They were all orphans, victims of Greek atrocities, each child with its own case history. Youssef's parents were killed by the Greeks during a mild uprising in 1805. They were living near an area inhabitated mainly by Greeks when Greek rebels stormed into the town. He seemed to remember the cliffs and the sea below. From time to time he remembered other fragments, but they were no more than shadows in his mind—a child being pulled away from a woman with black hair and dark, pained eyes. At times a child's screams pierced his brain. Whenever he relived these scenes, his hatred for the Greeks increased. And then he would swear, above and beyond his oath as a Janissary, to destroy every Greek who crossed his path. It was difficult to keep this vow when they brought him Greek slave girls for his bed. Although he longed to defile them and then plunge the dagger into their bellies, the unauthorized killing of slaves was against palace law. So he did not touch them at all. Instead he took pleasure in watching them cringe with fear when he ripped off their clothing and shoved them, whimpering, in some corner of the room. He would then recline on his couch, drink *raki* and stare at the frightened forms. And his mind would whirl with confusing scenes and strange voices . . . until the *raki* took effect and he fell into a stupor. When he woke he would send the unharmed girl away in contempt. He never discussed this with his comrades, never participated in their talks of sexual prowess. Youssef was a loner, and his brooding manner kept others away.

Until the Greeks revolted on the mainland, Youssef had spent most of his time as a chosen palace guard, selected by the Sultan himself for personal duty. He was a favored one, for the Sultan owed Youssef his life. The memory of that fateful day less than a year ago, never left Mahmud. But for the quick move of the young soldier, the assassin's sword would have cut down the Sultan.

Youssef was bored with palace duty. He longed to have his share of battle action, and often suggested his feelings to the Sultan. On several occasions, the Sultan hesitantly granted permission to Youssef to join special units sent to squelch minor uprisings on the border. They were only skirmishes but nonetheless bloody and fierce. The Greeks were outnumbered but they fought, to Youssef's surprise, with amazing vigor and determination. Turkish losses were heavy, three times that of the Greeks, but Youssef felt it was worth it—the *giaours* were wiped out. He felt he made a good beginning and was satisfied that it was in the area where his own parents had been slaughtered by the Greeks. Still this was not enough for him. He yearned to sweep through the Greek villages of the mainland, shrieking the cry of victory, from town to town, killing every living thing that breathed Greek. He had a passionate hatred for these people that only bloodshed could pacify.

Twelve months had passed since Youssef completed his training. He waited anxiously to be sent to the front. His palace duties irritated him more each day. Only his devotion to the Sultan prevented him from protesting vigorously. He brought the subject up at every opportunity, though he knew Mahmud wanted him near, feeling more secure in his presence since that assassination attempt. Youssef was fond of Mahmud and tried not to add to his burdens. He knew the Sultan was having enough to cope with in the unrest of his own soldiers. He had managed to calm them since the last rebellion ten years ago. But it was obvious that the years of Janissary power were coming to an end. They were a threat to the Sultan. Dissatisfied with Mahmud's westernization of Turkey under his mother's influence, the Janissaries were in a constant state of agitation. But Youssef remained loyal to Mahmud and tried in every way to calm the dissenters within the regiment. A time of pseudo-tranquillity continued, and now they were too pre-occupied with the Greek Revolution to concentrate on internal matters.

Youssef's perseverance was finally rewarded. The Sultan had ordered new fleets to supply and reinforce Turkish garrisons on the Greek mainland. His soldiers were to advance southward through the broken coastal plains and force the narrow valleys of the Isthmus of Corinth. Then there was Roumeli. The Sultan's men needed help there. Albanian troops had come to their aid until reinforcements from Constantinople could reach them. Youssef had his choice of locations. Excitement raced through him at the thought of going to Greece. He felt a strange sensation. A mixture of emotions, some new to him, churned his insides. He could not wait.

A black eunuch stepped onto the balcony and motioned to Youssef. Ramis Pasha, the Captain of the Janissaries, wished to see him. Youssef turned and followed the tall figure silently through the ornately decorated room. Silks and draperies, carvings and tapestries filled the vastness of the marble walls and floors. The grandeur pleased Youssef. It was a welcome reward to the Janissaries. They went through the corridor and down to the east wing where Pasha waited to talk to him. The Queen Mother—the French Sultana—had taken a turn for the worse.

"Ride immediately to Pera, to the monastery of Saint Anthony and bring back Father Chrysostom."

The words jolted Youssef. He could not believe the Sultan's decision. All the way to the monastery, his blood surged in anger. To turn against Allah this way was inconceivable, not even for one's mother. But then Mahmud had often shown signs of favoring christians, a weakness that many believed would be his downfall. It had caused more than one to call him "infidel Sultan" and accuse him of destroying Islam. Youssef spurred his horse on, his loyalty torn between Sultan and Empire. And yet he knew where it should lie. Janissaries were trained to fight and die for the Sultan. Youssef must remember this and not allow Mahmud's irrational behavior—swayed by love for his christian mother—to weaken his loyalty. He felt guilty at having doubted Mahmud's intentions. Perhaps Youssef did not understand the feeling—he wondered if he would have done the same for his own mother. Somehow he felt that Allah and the empire would be above his personal feelings.

He did not realize how quickly the time passed until he saw the monastery up ahead.

* * *

Aimee Dubucq de Rivery opened her eyes. The room was dark. Dusk had settled over the palace but Mahmud had not allowed the slaves to light the lamps. He wanted nothing to disturb his mother who lay, pallid and weak, amidst the silk and satins of her bed. She turned and nodded to her son who knelt beside her. Then, groping, with trembling hand she tried to touch him. The beautiful white fingers of the girl who had changed an empire could barely move now. She tried to speak and Mahmud bent close.

"Son . . . a . . . priest . . ."

Mahmud knew his mother was dying; that now, on her deathbed, she wanted to return to the faith she left behind thirty-three years ago. And the devout Moslem ruler of a Moslem empire made a decision of love and courage. He would grant his mother's request.

"Yes mother . . . I've sent a messenger to Saint Anthony's" He placed his hand gently over hers.

She smiled and sighed. It gave her new strength. A feeling of joy swept through her. She took another deep breath. She would wait for the priest.

At the age of seventeen, Aimee was sailing home to Martinique from a French convent when she was captured by Algerian pirates. They took her to the Bey of Algiers who sent her as a gift to Abdul Hamid. The 59-year old Sultan of the Ottoman Empire was delighted with this golden-haired girl with blue eyes and a turned-up nose. She made him feel young and spirited. And Aimee adjusted quickly to her new life. Like her cousin who became Josephine Bonaparte, she was destined to become the power behind the throne of a great ruler. She was aware of this from the beginning. When she gave birth to Mahmud, the elderly Hamid who had only one other son, was overjoyed. And Aimee's position in the empire became secure. The Sultan completely forgot his other son's mother and took Aimee as his favorite. She lived in grandeur, and her French style and liberalism were a welcome change in the palace.

Aimee looked at her son now and her mind went back many years to the day they first placed him in her arms. Could she ever forget the ordeal in the harem as the midwife brought the birth-chair and helped her to the seat? She had gripped the arms and struggled to bear down while the midwife chanted "Allah is most great!" Then there was the relief and joy of birth. She could still feel the rich shawls they had wrapped about her with the onion and garlic, the Koran and blue beads underneath to guard her against the evil eye. On the sixth day they dressed her like a bride and she received her harem friends in state. And on the fortieth day she and her son took part in a ceremony where the infant was bathed to the background of music and incense. All this was strange and arduous for the Catholic Aimee, but she took it in her stride. She was well-rewarded. Hamid's happiness knew no bounds. He ordered a tulip festival to celebrate the birth of his new son. A huge kiosk made of spun sugar and decorated with palms, the emblem of fertility, was placed on the palace grounds. There were splashing fountains and cages of nightingales hanging from trees. Wrestling matches were held in the arena. The whole city was in a festive mood.

What glorious days followed Mahmud's birth. She remembered them now and thanked God and her fates. She had no regrets.

"Do not weep for me son . . . it was a good life . . . and now I go to join your father . . ."

Her voice became stronger as she looked at the grief-stricken Sultan. She must comfort him—her will spurred her on.

"We did good things, Mahmud . . . my son . . . good things for the Empire . . ."

The doctor tried to silence her but she stopped him with a nod. She wanted to talk and would not be deterred . . . now, for the last time.

"We made history together . . . son . . ." she continued, "you and I . . . think of the medical school

. . . the first in the Empire . . ." Her voice trailed off but she took a deep breath and continued. "And the newspaper . . . our first newspaper . . . the coins we minted . . . and the bridge across the Golden Horn . . . oh we did so many, good things . . ."

She paused for breath again, then smiled and nodded to Mahmud who watched her with unbearable sadness. She was a remarkable woman whom he loved and admired. She was his mainstay, his anchor. No woman in his harem had been as close to him as his mother. And though Aimee, as Abdul Hamid's favorite "wife" wielded great influence on the Empire through her ruler husband, she had even greater power as the Queen Mother.

Laughter flickered on her lips but died in the effort. "We did get into a little trouble though . . . son . . ." she managed a smile, remembering the first day the changes in dress were instigated, the turmoil and complaints and confusion that followed.

"We took their ballooning pantaloons away . . . and the sable-trimmed caftans . . . and those ridiculous two-foot-high turbans . . ."

Mahmud had needed little persuasion to accept the new modes she suggested for officials—the tight black trousers, the black frock coat and the red fez. Some of their reforms had been a bit ludicrous, and Aimee smiled again as she remembered one decree regulating the length of moustaches. She noted the sombre face of her son and with great effort, touched his face, caressing the hair over his lip. He smiled, too, and kissed her hand as a slight commotion was heard from outside the door. The messenger had returned from Pera.

Father Chrysostom donned his ceremonial robe and

made ready to administer the last rites. All eyes followed the holy man as he took the small bible and approached the Queen Mother's bedside. They spent an hour in confession. When he went to bring the chalice, Aimee's eyes wandered across the room. She wanted to remember the warmth and grandeur of it, to cherish everything and everyone in it. Her eyes suddenly rested on Youssef who stood silently near the door. Her lips moved and her eyebrows raised. She nodded to the priest.

"Wait . . . not yet . . . in a minute."

Mahmud looked at his mother with concern and question in his eyes. Then a sad smile crossed his face. He knew she was fond of the young soldier—for many reasons.

"Come here Youssef . . ."

Her voice took on an added strength again. It was as though she could will it when she so desired.

The Janissary was startled. He stood rooted there, hesitant to move. Something about the moment made him uneasy.

"Come here I say . . ." there was impatience in her tone.

The doctor motioned for Youssef to do her bidding. He went to her.

"Come closer . . ." Her hand waved feebly and he knelt beside the bed.

She touched his head, then his face.

"My blessings on you Youssef . . . you gave me my son's life . . . when I would have been a lonely, bitter woman." There was gratitude and love in her gaze.

Youssef felt embarrassed, not knowing what to do, what to say. He was not for soft words and gentle talk. But this woman stirred a feeling inside him that frightened him. It was a new, strange feeling, a yearning, an ache for something he had not known or possessed.

He nodded his head in thanks, still unable to speak. His head was bowed, for he was afraid to look into her eyes, afraid of what he might see and feel.

"Look at me . . ." She touched his jaw, just able to lift his head up.

Her eyes were pools of memory that rushed to engulf Youssef. He looked into them, startled, wondering, as though he were seeing something from long ago. They were a deep blue, he had never seen such eyes before. But the look inside them, the love and compassion seemed familiar. He felt he had seen this look of yearning, that veiled fear, before.

She coughed and the doctor came to her side. The priest and Mahmud motioned him away.

"Youssef . . . I hope . . . some day you may know how I feel . . . and how Mahmud feels for me. Someday . . . you will find your mother . . . and you will know . . ." She paused, watching his face. "Find your mother . . . son . . . and know the joy of her arms . . . around you . . ."

Mahmud motioned for the priest to hasten. He touched Youssef's shoulder, and the boy, dazed by the strange words, staggered to his feet. He looked at her as though his ears were playing tricks on him. She repeated the last words over several times and he wondered if she were ranting in her fight with death.

"*Kyrie Eleison . . . Pater Agie . . .*" The priest hurried the words of prayer.

Youssef stood by, a strange look in his eyes as he watched the sacrament. The priest took the chalice with the holy wine.

Youssef shook his head, trying to clear the confusion that enveloped him. What did she mean about finding his mother? The few times they had spoken in the palace, she had brought up the subject of his family. She had asked about his mother and he told her what he knew. These are probably rambling thoughts of a dying woman, he thought, muddled and confused. He watched her lying there, tired but content, and something stirred inside him. He felt a sadness he had never known before, as though he were about to lose one of his own. The priest was at her side now with the chalice. Aimee took the holy wine, turned to her son. Then, smiling gratefully, she gave up the soul.

Father Chrysostom folded Aimee's hands over her breast and laid a cross upon them. Youssef watched them, his eyes rooted to the spot, unable to move. He finally unhinged them to look at Mahmud who had suddenly lost his composure. He could not control the sobs that wracked his body. Youssef cringed at the sight of this weakness. It seemed ridiculous to him that a grown man, a ruler, would so condescend to emotion. He knew Mahmud was not always this way. Only last month he had ordered the hanging of twenty of the leading Greeks in Constantinople. And as further reprisal thirty other important figures of the Greek community had been imprisoned. When the revolt erupted a year ago, the Greek Patriarch Gregorios himself was hanged . . . and Mahmud had shown no emotion, no concern. This display of courage and strength won admiration from friend an foe alike within the palace. After all, Mahmud had risked the wrath of the world by allowing a spiritual leader to be murdered. Youssef had been proud of him. Now the great ruler looked at his mother's lifeless form and whimpered like a child. Youssef felt his respect for the Sultan waiver. Perhaps the others were right . . . but no, something inside warned Youssef this might be different. Perhaps this was a side of man Youssef did not, could not understand. Was it because he had not known his own mother? How would he have reacted, he wondered. He silently vowed to help Mahmud . . . he would stand at his side and help him be strong again. Youssef felt a surge of hope. He would not let the Sultan relax his hold on the Empire and its possessions. They must halt the constant rebellion of the provinces around them. They must stop losing ground, or soon there would be nothing left of the Empire . . . Youssef was furious at the thought of its dissolution. He wanted it to live forever. And he wanted a chance to help erase the Greek infidels from the earth. Yes, he would help Mahmud forget his grief, force him to turn to important matters of State. They would begin the moment the Queen Mother was buried.

A week passed and Maḥmud's loneliness became unbearable. Nothing Youssef could say, no comfort he could give him, no spurring of incentive helped. The Sultan tried to forget his loss by immersing himself in his harem. He set aside all thoughts of the Empire and searched every night, from one girl to the next, for one to satisfy him. He watched every female that came to his bed carefully, scrutinizing her, hoping to find one who would fill the needs of both his body and mind. Such women were rare, he knew, but the last stream of Sultans had been fortunate in finding them. There had been Roxelana, Sultana Nur Banu, and, of course, his own mother. All had wielded power in the Empire as well as in the bed. They had beauty, charm and intelligence. They had a sparkle in their personalities that made them stand out as rare jewels of womanhood. Mahmud sank deeper and deeper in his depression.

* * *

The news rocked Constantinople! Mahmud was speechless as he listened to the newly-arrived messenger. Chios had revolted! Chios, the Queen Mother's treasured island, the land of mastic and contented people. Chios, which had enjoyed all the advantages of freedom with none of the responsibilities. An emergency council meeting was summoned. Captain Pasha was there, and the Sultan insisted that Youssef, too, sit in attendance.

As he watched the proceedings, the young Janissary felt his blood rush to his head. Now the Sultan could not be oblivious. Now he would forget his personal grief and devote his efforts to punishing the ungrateful dogs who turned against the kindly Mahmud. He joined his voice with Pasha's, reminding Mahmud of the importance of crushing the Chiotes, of using them as an example to the other Greeks. The men pleaded with Mahmud to annihilate them at once.

"You see, Holy One," Captain Pasha offered, "these *giaours* are no different from the dogs on the mainland. You can't treat any Greek like a human—they're infidels, scum of the earth."

"We warned you many times you had over-extended your good graces to these Chiotes." The Chief Admiral had always disagreed with Mahmud's leniency towards these islanders. Now he spoke with austere propriety, his eyes blazing. He was delighted that the Chiotes had proved him right. Perhaps now this fool Sultan would let the military leaders act as they should.

Mahmud knew nothing of the year of suffering the Chiotes experienced under the new governor. His fury rose with every word his men uttered.

"Let me go, great one," Youssef pleaded, "let me lead our men to wipe Chios off the face of the earth. They don't deserve to live."

Then, knowing the effect his words would have on Mahmud, he added, "Think how the Queen Mother loved Chios—think of how good she was to them. And this is how they repay her goodness. It's an insult to her memory!"

"Kill the infidels!" Mahmud screamed in grief and rage. "Kill them all! Prepare the fleet at once!"

The command rang through the palace. "Prepare to sail immediately. And don't come back until everyone of them has been put to the sword or the fire . . . or both! I want the blood to flow like rivers. I want Chios in ashes! I want sackfuls of the dogs' heads as tribute!"

This was a Mahmud few had seen. Without the Queen Mother to guide him, to calm him and reason with the problem, he was a different man. He had no knowledge of the torture and humiliations the Chiotes suffered these last twelve months, and so he could not understand the reason for the Chiotes' action.

Pasha was pleased with the results. He looked at Youssef, and the two men smiled with satisfaction. The Janissary Captain knew of the young soldier's lust for Greek blood. The time had come to satisfy his desires. Pasha also knew that there would be beautiful slave girls to bring back. He would have first choice for his own. Chios had something for everyone.

They worked long into the nights, never stopping, hurrying to prepare the fleet for sailing. The port was a bustle of activity. Loading continued until it was too dark to see and then preparations went on inside the ships.

Pasha sat in the captain's quarters with the ship's officers reviewing charts and plans of attack. Every Janissary in the palace was summoned. The preparations would be completed in a few days. It would take another eight to ten to reach Chios. Down the Dardanelles into the Aegean Sea past the islands of Limnos and Mytilene and finally to Chios, the island of the cursed infidels. Pasha could not believe the Chiotes had actually revolted. Who would have imagined such a thing? He shook his head as he pondered the thought. He always believed, as did many others, that they were clever to accept their fate and to take advantage of the many benefits bestowed upon them, thanks to the Queen Mother and the popular mastic. Pasha motioned the cabin boy to pour him *raki*. He drank it, savoring its tasty fire. Yes, the Chiotes had contributed much with their mastic, but now all that was over. Their blood would seep into the roots of the mastic bush. They would never lift their heads again.

The sea captain watched Pasha in his thoughts.

"Eh, Captain Pasha, your mind wanders. Let's get back to the charts. What are you thinking of?"

"I'm thinking of the *giaours* and the heads that will roll. The Sultan wants tribute—sacks full of Chiote heads. I will instruct my men accordingly."

"Eh, and what about the pretty ones—the ladies

there? You plan to trim their heads too?"

"You know the orders, Captain. Kill all women over forty; the others go back home for the slave market . . ." Pasha remembered a detail. "Of course, you and I will have first choice for ourselves." The idea pleased him.

He rose from the table and began pacing the floor. "The message from Chios said our men are blockaded inside the fortress in the capital city."

"Yes, I know. They can't have much food and water. But if all goes well we should be arriving in time."

Pasha nodded in agreement. He paused near the porthole and looked at the dock below. It was overflowing with supplies. People hurried everywhere. The loaders scrambled up the gangplank at a pace accelerated by shouts from the Janissaries. Suddenly he saw a scuffle. And then a flame shot up from the crates on the dock. Shouts broke out and in a moment the small area around it was on fire. He cursed as he ran out to the deck.

Youssef pushed a man up the gangplank, twisting his arms behind him. The deck filled with men as the others below fought the blaze.

"Mohammed, you!" The ship's captain was surprised to see one of his sailors.

"I did not mean to do it, *effendi,*" the man trembled with fear. "I swear, I did not mean it. I tripped and my lamp started the fire. By Allah . . ." He fell at the sea captain's feet and gesticulated.

Youssef picked him up by the scruff of the neck and tossed him to the deck. The sailor fell with a thud and huddled against the side of the ship.

"Swine! You dare betray your Sultan!" Youssef

drew his sword.

"Wait!" Pasha was annoyed with Youssef. The idiot fool, he thought, how dare he take matters into his own hands? He noted the scowling sea captain and the cringing sailor. The others stood around, not daring to move. It was not likely the man would have attempted foul play in the open. Carelessness, no doubt. But could it be some plan for sabotage? His eyes narrowed. No, not one of the ship's crew. And no Greek in the city would dare involve himself in such plots after the recent hangings. He turned to the sea captain and spoke with a calm voice.

"Is he one of your men?"

"Yes . . . he is. A good sailor, too." He was angry at both his man and Youssef. "Been with me four years . . . very loyal." He looked reprimandingly at the culprit. "But there's no excuse for carelessness."

He turned sternly, to Pasha. "I believe I am capable of disciplining my own men." And you should be able to discipline yours, was the silent implication.

"I want you in my quarters immediately," the sea captain shouted at the cringing man, and walked away.

Pasha nodded to Youssef and the two men retreated to the cabin on the port side. The older man slammed the door and turned to his subordinate.

"How dare you interfere in the discipline of this ship?"

Youssef gritted his teeth, fighting to subdue his anger.

"The traitor . . . I don't believe him."

"Your duty was to catch him." Pasha tried to reason with Youssef. He knew this was a favorite of the Sultan and did not want to antagonize him. Still, the soldier must learn his place. "There are two men above you, here—the sea captain and I. It is up to us to handle disciplinary action."

He paused and looked at Youssef. He's a hot-headed fool, he thought, and he's going to get himself into trouble.

"You've got to learn control, Youssef. You can't go around exploding your fury on our own men. I keep telling you to save it for the Greeks. You caught the culprit—you turned him over to us. Your duty ends there. Remember that. Do you understand?"

Youssef remained silent. Pasha's tone softened.

"Do you realize your actions could bring mutiny on the ship? We have to sail with these men. Now try to control your temper until we get to Chios. Then, my friend," he smiled wickedly, "then release it in all its fury."

The tension eased. Pasha poured *raki* for himself and for Youssef.

"Here . . ." he gulped his drink and slammed the cup down. "Let's see now," he turned to the papers that lay scattered on the table. "Since you're so good at spotting dangers, why don't I appoint you officer of the night watch until we sail? You can patrol the area, Select whatever men you need." That should keep Youssef busy. "And by Allah, don't kill anyone—we can't risk trouble with our men. Bring them to me. If they're the enemy, I can handle them. If they're crewmembers, the ship's captain will handle them. Is that clear?"

Youssef did not reply. He offered his cup for refilling.

"Is that clear?"

"Yes."

Youssef was pleased with his assignment. He was certain that unknown danger lurked around the loading platforms, around the entire dock. Someone would surely try to sabotage their plans for sailing. The Greeks were sly ones. Even with the reprisals, they could not be trusted. One of them, someone, would risk his life to do them harm. Youssef would make certain he was caught. He raised his cup and with a wry smile, toasted their trip. Then, smacking his lips as the fiery liquid slid down his throat, he saluted Pasha and walked out of the cabin.

It was midnight. Youssef walked along the deserted dock, a lantern in one hand, the other gripping the dagger protruding from his sash. His sword swung at his side and from time to time he patted it with pleasure. The lights from the ship's portholes gleamed in the darkness. The moon had disappeared behind the clouds and somehow forgot to re-appear. He walked slowly, looking right and left, behind crates and planks, pausing to gaze down at the water below. He stopped, cocking his ear at the sound of something scratching from a nearby stack of crates. He waited. It came again. Then a faint cry, like that of a baby. He walked to the area and looked about. The light of his lantern fell upon a small object wedged between two crates. It cried again and the sound mingled with the lapping of the waves below.

Youssef smiled and put his lantern down. Gently he picked up the kitten. It was shivering. He covered it with his arms then placed it on one of the boxes. It looked at him, not moving. Youssef wondered why it did not run away. He stroked its fur and the animal purred.

"By Allah," he whispered, "it's almost human. It knows . . ." The thought amazed him. He sat there a few moments, watching it. He picked it up and put it on his lap, his eyes never leaving it. And slowly he felt that churning inside, that twisting of his mind. Once again thoughts began to whirl as he went back in time. He continued to stroke the kitten's back. And as it purred, his lips moved in remembrance.

"*Titika*." He said it softly, suddenly. Then louder . . . "*Titika*."

What a strange word. He wondered why it should come to him now. He said the word again . . . and closed his eyes.

A child was running through a vineyard. It stopped suddenly and looked around, listening intently to a faint whining sound. Then, gently, from behind one of the vines, it pulled out a small kitten. The animal was crying, probably lost and looking for its mother. The little boy ran with it, squealing with delight, and showed it to another child who suddenly appeared, as though out of nowhere. The two boys, as alike as two peas, hovered over their find . . . caressing the kitten, smiling, laughing . . .

The scene began to fade. Youssef opened his eyes, disturbed by the memory—or was it merely a figment of his imagination? He closed his eyes again, desperate to know more.

A woman with black hair and sad eyes appeared in the distance. She was smiling as she leaned over the children engrossed in their find.

"Titika." *The sound of her voice jolted Youssef. It was gentle yet strong. It was a voice that often came to him in dreams, when he had drunk his fill of* raki *and sank into a stupor.*

He felt a gentle scratch on his arm and awakened from the reverie. He shook his head, disturbed by his thoughts, certain they meant something, that they came from somewhere in his past. The idea that this woman might be his mother roused him . . . the thought that she was taken from him by the Greeks made him seethe with sudden rage. A deep pain turned inside and tangled with his fury. It was unbearable . . . he clenched his fists and mechanically twisted his hands around the kitten's throat.

He watched it gasp its last breath, and stared at the lifeless form. Then, still in a daze, he tossed it into the sea, picked up his lantern and slowly walked away.

XIII

Jason threw himself on the wooden bench, exhausted and out of breath. He had walked all the way from Chora to Thymiana—walked and ran, hurrying to bring news to Xenophon. He would rest awhile, here in his uncle's courtyard. Then quickly run to see his mother, wash, have a warm meal, and back to the long, gruelling battle, a battle that should have ended weeks ago. It suddenly dawned on Jason that it was weeks since he'd had a meal. But what did it matter when his whole world exploded around him?

Xenophon was pleased to see Jason, anxious to hear his report, concerned about his welfare. He made him comfortable and called to his wife to bring refreshments. Within moments she hurried in with her tray of preserves and water, thick Turkish coffee and her home-made pastry. The tired messenger leaned back, swallowed the sweet quince and began to relate the latest happenings in Chora.

The besieged Turks who had despaired inside the fort, believing the Chiotes had great forces of men and arms outside, had now learned the truth—that the Chiotes were merely bluffing, that they were disorganized and frantic, their leaders were battling among themselves, and the wealthy Elders had packed up and left the island.

"And who do you think told them?" Jason said angrily as Xenophon listened, his face clouding.

"The informers," Jason went on, "the people who gave Bechit Pasha the news of our real strength were the foreign Consuls, those men of trust and character."

Xenophon shook his head in disbelief. Was everything working against them?

The Consuls had assembled inside the fortress to speak with Pasha in hopes of ending the siege. Those friendly to the Greeks had pleaded with Pasha to surrender the fort, to save themselves and bring peace to the island. But the Consuls friendly to the Turks—Stepovitch of Austria and Gioudoukis of England—had advised the Governor otherwise.

"What's the true strength of the fighters outside?" Pasha had asked the diplomats.

"Fifteen to twenty thousand," replied the Danish Consul, stretching the truth, "and they're expecting more ships and arms from Psara and Corinth."

"That many?" Pasha was frightened.

"No, no," spoke up the Slavic Stepovitch, Pasha's drinking companion, "I doubt if there are three thousand all in all."

"I doubt it too," added England's Gioudoukis in his

small, weak voice. "But there could be ten thousand without your worrying. The fortress is safe, I assure you. These Samiotes came here to rob the island, not liberate it. They've stripped it of everything in sight. Would you believe they took the goat from my garden the first day they arrived?"

Pasha and his followers were greatly relieved. The *Kadi*, who had listened to the conversation without speaking, rose. He motioned to Pasha and took him aside.

"You hear that? I knew the Chiotes were bluffing. Those men outside are not like the *giaours* you met on the Greek mainland. Those were guerrillas up there in Gravia and the Tripolitsa mountains. Fighters, not merchants and gardeners like these people. I say hold the fort until help comes from the Sultan . . . it can't be long now."

It was an unfortunate, disastrous situation and Xenophon could think of nothing that would save them. There was only one ray of hope. That Doctor Glarakis would be successful and return in time. By now the good doctor was in Corinth where the Greek government immediately turned over to him five large siege guns. They ordered officers, phil-Hellenes, to accompany the envoys back, to direct military operations on Chios. They assembled men, fighters to alleviate the bind on the island. But the preparations would take thirteen days, and another eight would be needed to sail. One hundred twenty thousand Chiote lives hung in the balance. It was March 27th and the ships had yet to sail.

Xenophon and Jason sat together, downcast, unable to speak. It was no use, words could add nothing to an already lost cause. Chances were slim that help could reach Chios in time.

"And yet . . ." Jason tried to sound optimistic. "Who knows, uncle Xenophon? A miracle might happen."

Andreadis looked at his niece's son and smiled sadly.

"From your lips to God's ears, my son."

But in his heart he knew it was hopeless.

What a shame, he thought, what a waste. All those years we worked and planned so that boys like Jason might live free, like Greeks should. And yet our own people, in their complacency, have destroyed us.

"At least Thymiana can raise its head high." Xenophon said in conclusion, trying to ease Jason's despair, "at least we proved we're fighters. And Vrondados too, and many other villages. No one can deny that."

He paused a moment, looked away thoughtfully, then turned to Jason. His face was pale, his tone sad, ominous.

"Jason son, if anyone of us survives this . . . if our children at least, learn that all of us in Chios were not the same . . . that we fought against odds . . ."

His voice trailed off. He seemed to be talking to himself now, as though Jason were not there.

"It would be a pity if history branded us cowards. Someone must tell them . . . that for every pompous nobleman there are a hundred farmers and goatsmen and stonecutters who took up axes and pitchforks and even kitchen knives to fight off the Turks. Someone must tell them that, so they will not be ashamed."

He turned to Jason, suddenly remembering he was there.

"Remember that, Jason, if you live through this.

Remember it and mark those words somewhere for those who come after us. They must learn the truth."

It sounded so foreboding, so final. Jason was deeply moved by his uncle's words. He had always been proud of Xenophon, proud that he was of Helena's lineage. The town philosopher, a sort of oracle, Jason considered him. Yet had he not advised against joining Tombazis? And did time not prove that that was their opportunity to rise? He would not bring this up, he respected his uncle too much. Xenophon looked at him now, reading his mind in that uncanny way of his.

"I made a mistake, son, a terrible mistake of judgment." Yet they both knew it made little difference—the results would have been the same. Thymiana had voted to join Tombazis in spite of Xenophon's advice. But their voice had meant nothing.

Jason watched Xenophon in a daze, unable to speak. If he survived . . . if he lived through all this . . . but would he? He recovered when Xenophon put his arms around the boy's shoulders.

"I got carried away a bit . . . don't let me frighten you. Just remember what I said, if you can, it's important." He smiled. "Now, let's get on with it. I've made some notes on the information you brought, and I'm going to pass them on to whoever is left around here. We'll try to keep going in the village with whatever we have."

He noticed the tired look on Jason's face, the dust on his clothes. He's thinner, the older man thought, he probably hasn't had much to eat the past few weeks. He noticed the pastry was untouched. All that sacrifice, for what? He could not stand to think about it.

"Why don't you go home now? Wash up and eat something. And lie down a while."

Jason rose.

"Stop by on your way back so I can give you some food for Fatouros' men."

Fatouros was still holding the rear at Tourloti. But the Turks had destroyed most of the homes around the hill. His men were having trouble. Their cannonball were too small and could not reach the fort. There was nothing they could do.

Xenophon walked Jason to the door.

"I'll have Big Ears go back to Chora with you in the cart. Only make sure you send him back the minute you unload. He's liable to get himself killed."

At that moment a carriage sped by. Jason saw a girl beside the driver. It looked like Joanna. They were headed towards the house. Jason ran out and hurried up the incline.

He passed the courtyard and up the stairs. She was standing at the door.

"Joanna! What are you doing here?" Jason was happy to see her, happier than he imagined he could be. But he was worried for her safety. "You know it's dangerous to be out alone in the daytime."

"I had to come, Jason. One of the servants saw you running towards Thymiana." There was a pleading look in her eyes. "Don't be angry . . . I had to see you."

He wanted to put his arms around her but he hesitated.

"Where's my mother?" He looked around.

"She may be out feeding the chickens. Poor things, they've stopped laying eggs. Everything's stopped,

Jason. What's going to happen?"

Jason ran out, calling his mother. She was nowhere in sight. He turned back, Joanna close behind him.

"She's not here."

"She's probably at some neighbor's."

Helena had gone to her cousin Patra's to see if there were any fresh eggs, in case Jason stopped by. Every day she looked for him.

Jason saw tears in Joanna's eyes. She wanted him to comfort her but he did not move. She could not understand him.

"Jason, I'm afraid. Father hasn't been home in two weeks. Mother's shut in her room with those sick headaches. Where is he? Why doesn't he come home?"

"Joanna, dear Joanna." Jason took her hand and sat down with her. He tried to explain.

"Don't blame him. Captain Petros is in the middle of chaos, trying to bring order to the mess other people made. And yet he's powerless. He has to stand by helplessly and watch what's happening to our island. I can't tell you what it's like."

"All the work, all the plans gone up in smoke."

Jason looked away sadly, with disillusionment. "I never dreamed such a thing was possible."

Everywhere else in Greece the revolt was succeeding. Everywhere, on the hills and valleys of the mainland . . . and in the other islands. Yet here in Chios it was a disastrous failure.

"But why, everyone worked so hard, made so many plans."

"Why? Because those fools, Bournias and Logothetis, don't know what they're doing. They came unprepared, and then, instead of trying to salvage something from their mistakes, they're bickering over petty things, jealousies. God, it's hopeless." Jason covered his face with his hands. He was silent for a moment, then he turned to Joanna, as though he had just seen her.

"How are you Joanna? I missed you."

"I missed you too, Jason . . . terribly." She did not care that his concern came as an afterthought, as long as he cared enough to ask. "I thought about what you . . . and father . . . must be going through . . . I was frantic."

Her words brought back unpleasant scenes that came alive before him.

"I just can't believe it, Joanna. The Samiotes, our liberators," he smirked at the word and shook his head, "the Samiotes stormed through Aplotaria and stripped it of everything valuable. All the shops and houses torn apart . . . no consciences, no decency."

Joanna was shocked. What manner of Greeks were these?

"Couldn't anyone stop them?"

"No one even tried. Bournias and Logothetis were so busy with their own quarrels they let everything go to the devil."

Joanna looked at Jason and felt his despair. This Revolution had meant so much to him. It must be like the death of a loved one to see it fail. But there was still hope.

"Jason," Joanna's sudden enthusiasm reached him. "Jason, it isn't over yet. Help is coming from Corinth . . . I heard it this morning—it should be here soon. And Psara . . . they said the island sent six ships to stop any Turkish attempts to block the harbor."

"I hope so." Jason saw a light in the darkness. "If

only help reaches us in time . . . before the Turks."

He looked at Joanna's anxious face and suddenly noticed how pretty, how innocent she was. Why am I burdening this girl, he wondered. Why am I telling her all this? It was because she was a part of him . . . she belonged to him. And he wanted to share the pain and joy with her. She blushed at his gaze, and lowered her eyes, but soon raised them to meet his.

"Joanna," he took her hand, "my . . . wife."

He put his arm around her. He was shy, embarrassed, but he held her to him. They sat there together, both silent, barely breathing. Finally he let her go.

"Jason . . ."Joanna's voice was soft, hesitant. "I . . . you . . . haven't . . . we haven't spoken about . . . that evening at Prophet Elias."

Jason looked away. Did she think he had forgotten?

"You . . . you don't hate me, Jason?"

Young men often turned against girls who were easy, and that fear had haunted Joanna all these weeks. She felt she had forced herself on him that evening on the hillside, and she prayed he had not thought badly of her.

"Hate you? Oh Joanna. You brought me the only beautiful moment I can remember in my life. I just . . . I just can't bring myself . . ."

"To say you love me?" She smiled sadly. "Why Jason, is it so bad?"

"No, it's not . . . it's beautiful . . . sacred. But I always felt I was pledged to something else . . . and I feel guilty now. I swore my first duty to Chios and to finding . . ." He stopped there.

"To finding what, Jason?"

He did not answer.

"Can't you fight for Chios, and look for whatever you want to find, and still love me, Jason?"

She waited for his reply.

Helena opened the door and let out a cry of joy.

"Jason, son!" She ran and put her arms around him. "Thank God you're safe."

She stroked his hair, his cheeks, and kissed him. Then, smiling, she took Joanna's hand and sat them both on the sofa.

"Sit down. I have lentil soup. And look!" She put her hand inside her apron pocket to pull out the first fresh eggs they'd seen in weeks. She brought her hand up dripping with egg yolk. They all laughed, and the sound rang through the room, bounced off the stucco walls and vibrated through the house. What beautiful music, Helena thought, cherishing the rare sound . . . how long it's been since I heard laughter.

"And that takes care of the omelet." Jason grinned at the two women he loved. How good it was to have them standing here beside him. He wondered if they would ever be together again. What a glorious feeling it was to love and be loved. He suddenly felt happy. But there is no such thing as happiness, he reminded himself, only happy moments. Then he would cherish these moments, take them when and where they came. He drank in the scene thirstily, wanting to carry it wih him when he went back to the fighting.

"Don't worry about the omelet son. We have olives and fresh cheese. But first you must wash and rest. I'll heat some water. Sit down."

She hurried outside to get water from the well. He would relax after a warm bath.

The two young people remained silent. Joanna was embarrassed. Jason was glad for the opportunity to be alone with her . . . he wanted to ease her mind.

"You think I forgot because I didn't come to see you . . . or contact you? You think I don't care?"

He did not blame her for doubting him. She had given him the most priceless gift a girl could offer, her virginity. He knew what that meant—the risk, the disgrace. It was something cherished only for the one man a girl married. She would be nothing without it. And he had seemed indifferent, casual.

"Joanna, when this is over . . ." he took her hand and she smiled, foreseeing what he was going to say.

The sun came out in her smile. I never thought this was possible, Jason said to himself as he watched her. There used to be only pain and emptiness in our life . . . and perhaps that dream holding me up. Now I have something that makes me glad I'm alive . . . something tangible.

The thought of Joseph suddenly came to him and he felt a tinge of guilt. But he looked at Joanna again and the guilt disappeared. She was right. Joseph and Chios were separate in his heart. There was another place reserved for Joanna. I've become a man, he thought with joy and relief . . . God, I've become a man!

"When this is over," he continued, "we'll get married. A big church wedding with dancing and eating and drinking afterwards. And we'll have children Joanna. And we'll climb the hills together and look at sunsets the rest of our lives."

She laughed with joy, wanting to shout her happiness to the world. Tears streamed down her face.

Was she worried that I would leave her, he wondered. It was inconceivable to him. He loved Joanna more that moment than he thought possible. Why don't I tell her, he asked himself. Why can't I tell her? He could not say the words, but had he not said them in other ways? He spoke of marriage, of children. Surely she realized he loved her.

Jason washed and sat down to the warm lentil soup Helena put before him. He ate the brown olives heartily—the famous Chiote olives, sweet and tasty, relishing every mouthful. Joanna and Helena sat watching him.

Suddenly the voice of Big Ears came from the courtyard. He shuffled up the steps and knocked on the door. When Helena opened it he stood there grinning, his crooked teeth giving him an even more comical appearance. Shyly he handed her the fresh bread her Aunt Alexandra had baked.

"Come in Yorgo, come in."

Helena smiled and Big Ears hesitated. He always hesitated entering people's homes.

"Mister Xenophon sent me to tell Jason the supplies are ready, *Kyra* Helena."

He spoke slowly so that his words would not get jumbled the way they normally did. It didn't matter with the others, but for Helena he wanted to speak just right.

"Thank you Yorgo. Sit down, I'll get you some cold water."

He knew the water would be accompanied by her delicious fruit preserve, but what he really wanted was wine. Yet he would never ask Helena for that. He did not hesitate with the others in the village, but never *Kyra* Helena. In fact when he staggered home drunk every night, he was secretly grateful his house was on the opposite side of the village, where Helena was certain not to see him. He nodded to her shyly now.

Oh well, he thought, the preserve is not so bad . . . she made it with her own hands. He felt lucky after all.

"Oh," he suddenly remembered; how could he forget such an important thing? "*Kyra* Helena . . . oh, Mister Xenophon said for you to get ready to leave for Kambos. He said you're to go back with Miss Joanna in the carriage."

"He did? Now?" Helena was startled. Why so suddenly?

"A man came from Chora, *Kyra* Helena." The details, which had disappeared in the space between Xenophon's market and Helena's house, were coming back to Big Ears now. Words and details had a habit of disappearing from Big Ears. Ha, he thought, I caught you this time. They had all returned now. He grinned, pleased with himself.

"Captain Petros sent a man from Chora with a letter for Mr. Xenophon. A lot of words, but he didn't tell me what they were. He just said to tell you to pack your things and go with Miss Joanna . . . and that he's ready for Jason."

The letter had informed Xenophon that word had reached Chora about Turkish reinforcements on the way. The villages were to take precautions for their women and children. Petros asked Xenophon to see that Helena went to his house in Kambos. He also offered sanction to Xenophon's wife and sisters. Kambos would be safe for a while.

"Mr. Xenophon said he would explain to Master Jason." Big Ears popped the spoonful of grape preserve in his mouth and swallowed with delight. "To your health," he raised the cup of water, admiring the copper vessel he had the honor of holding.

Jason swallowed his last morsel of food. He rose

and cut off a piece of the warm bread Big Ears had brought, then another to take with him.

"Take it all," Helena urged, "here's some cheese and olives too, for later."

She put them all in a cloth napkin, tied it and stuffed it in Jason's leather pouch. "I wish you had laid down an hour or so. Surely the Revolution won't be lost in that time."

She did not fully realize the seriousness of the situation.

Jason kissed his mother hurriedly and turned to Joanna. He touched her shoulder.

"Don't worry, I'll run back the first chance I get. And we'll talk . . ." he turned to his mother, then to Joanna. "We'll talk with our parents too."

The women knew what he meant. Joanna's heart leaped. He would not wait until this was over! Helena sent up a silent prayer. Oh God, let me know one joy, at least one joy in life. She saw determination in her son's eyes. He had decided to marry Joanna.

XIV

It was Holy Thursday. Church bells tolled and the Chiotes fasted to receive communion for this Easter of 1822. The air was tense, people prayed that help would arrive from the mainland soon. They did not know how long they could keep the Turks inside the fortress. Or how long it would be before the Sultan's reinforcements arrived. But it was only three days before Easter. Perhaps Saturday night's Resurrection would bring the dawn of victory, an end to this madness.

Jason was in Vrondados, at Pasha's Fountain where Captain Kyladites was meeting his chief fighters. Since the onset of the struggle, two hundred of Vrondados' men had rallied around the captain, offering to fight if he would lead them. They knew that it was hopeless to join Bournias. Now they were satisfied that they had done their duty. They had cleared Vrondados of Turks, and were helping hold off the fort at Chora.

In the midst of these labors, the dreaded moment arrived. Admiral Kara-Ali and the Turkish fleet dropped anchor in the harbor of Chios. Three-decked ships, frigates, corvettes, transports, their cannon firing upon the town. Kyladites' men saw the ships in the distance and scattered. Jason ran to find Petros.

By the time he reached the harbor, the Turks had disembarked and were streaming along the main thoroughfare of Chora. Their screams pierced the air. Waving their sabres, they slashed whatever form of human life appeared in their way. The townspeople, barely recovered from the surprise appearance of their liberators were thrown into terrified confusion, groping in horror and helplessness. The Turkish soldiers broke into their homes and put everyone to the sword, swinging their blades in fanatic hatred. These Chiote dogs would pay for their betrayal to the Sultan. Not content to kill these people swiftly, they lingered over them, taking added pleasure in watching heads decapitated, breasts roll, ears and noses flung aside. Screaming infants were tossed in the air to descend upon sabres that pierced the tiny bodies. No one was exempted from their fury. Not old people or children or the clergy. The blood flowed in the streets and down the once busy thoroughfare, into the harbor. Soon the waters were tinted a deep red. And the winds blew . . . and the waves lapped against the ships, tossing dead bodies against the harbor walls. Within hours, the waters were filled with corpses. Others lay strewn throughout the town . . . some heaped on others . . . some still breathing, smothering under the weight of the dead. The Turkish troops continued on, through every nook and cranny of the capital city, making certain no living soul breathed before they set out for the villages. They set fire to the homes, the granneries, slaughtered the livestock. They swept into churches and tiny chapels . . . and with madness they slashed the icons, taking special care to carve out the eyes of the saints. They cut down the oil candles, ripped Holy Bibles and beheaded priests before the altars. They would not leave this wretched island until every treacherous infidel was cut to pieces or burned to ashes. Even the lepers in the lazarettos did not escape their fury. The Turks went after them, laughing at their muffled screams, their pleading, tortured eyes, their painful moans. And the young girls who were to be spared for shipment to Turkey, were caught in the onslaught of their fury. It was the first battle in Chios and the Turks wanted complete annihilation. They would take other girls along the way . . . there was time enough for that. Now, in their mania, their only desire was to see Chian blood shed to cover every area of Chora.

Logothetis' men fled in all directions. Petros and Jason watched in horror as their liberators scampered aboard their vessels and hurriedly set sail for Samos, deserting the Chiotes they had come to free. The only armed men who could fight against the Turks were leaving. Within hours Chora was in flames . . . and the streets were rivers of blood.

Petros and his handful of men gathered in the wine cellar of the Kledas home.

"It looks as though we're going to have to take to the hills," he told them. "Two of you must go to Thymiana and round up the people. And pass the word to the other villages. These men are maniacs.

They'll spare no one."

The men were silent, grim. They knew this was far more than they could handle. The shock of Logothetis' desertion had left them numb.

"Meanwhile, we'll try to get the old people into the European Consul . . . they'll be safe there. Spread the word as we go."

Petros, calm, collected, unfearing, was an example of strength to his embittered men. He inspired them . . . they would not despair.

"We're going to have to do whatever we can ourselves, men. Fatouros, you go to Thymiana and Neohori. Round up the women and children and head for Saint Menas. It'll be safe there. Take Costas with you. I'll go with another group to Nea Moni." He turned to Jason. "You come with me."

"No. Let me take another group . . . somewhere else."

But where? None of the monasteries offered the high walls and protection of St. Menas and Nea Moni, which were located high on hilltops with cliffs on three sides.

"I have it," Jason cried, remembering the village on the highest peak of northern Chios. "Anavatos! It's impenetrable. Please . . . let me."

Petros hesitated. Jason was still so young, could he risk it?

"Are you sure you can manage?"

"Please, Captain Petros, I know I can."

"Alright. Take Monios with you."

He nodded towards the man from Thymiana. Monios was thirty-five and a strong, quick-thinking man. Jason would be in good company.

They looked at each other and smiled sadly as they

shook hands, wondering if this were the last time they would be together. Then, making the sign of the cross, they ran out into the chaos.

The Turks had set fire to every building in Chora, including the churches. Bodies lay everywhere. Infants wailed . . . moans penetrated the air. Jason ran, crouching, and suddenly looked up to see the school and the library across from it, in flames. He stopped a moment, taking cover in a doorway, and watched the fire. The flames seemed to pierce his heart. Tears filled his eyes. He remembered what he must do and ran ahead.

The Turks were now in the cemeteries, digging, ripping open coffins for treasures. They piled the putrified corpses on top of still-breathing bodies of their victims—people who were running from the invaders. They roamed over the island howling like hyenas. And their cries rang out throughout Chios. Death and devastation wherever the Turk passed!

Fatouros arrived in Thymiana to find the villagers gathered in the church courtyard. Xenophon and Father Stelios had brought order to the confusion, kept the people calm as they issued instructions for the women and children. They were ready to leave now, to flee to the hills. Only a few decided to stay behind, having found hiding places in the hope that the holocaust would pass quickly and they could pick up their lives again. Doors were bolted, children rounded up, and the villagers set out, turning for one last look at their homes, one last goodbye. The human mass moved hurriedly, climbing the rocky soil of their ancestors, eager to find refuge in the sanctuary of God, miles away.

Only Perdika refused to leave the village. She decided to remain and fight in her own way, under her own roof. The Turks did not frighten her. They were only men . . . and they loved women, especially Greek women. She would save herself by her own clever ploy.

The Turks arrived in Thymiana by late afternoon. They ran through the streets, the empty houses, cursing at signs of the desertion. They searched frantically in the cellars and wells, the magazines and shrubbery. They passed Karanikolas' coffee house where the skewered lamb was still on the spit, the coals still warm. Half-filled cups of *raki* and wine sat on the small tables, as though waiting for the customers to return any moment.

The *tsaouse** looked around at the ghost town. There was nothing, no one. Curse those *giaours*! Only a few cows and goats, and some chickens roaming about unattended. Suddenly he heard a cry of joy, of discovery. It was one of his men.

The Lieutenant followed the sound to a house several blocks away. Inside the open door he saw his soldier grinning over a woman who lay on the couch in a corner of the room.

She was dark and buxom. Rounded breasts went up and down as she breathed deeply. A smile was on her face, excitement in her countenance, a bottle of *raki* in her hand. The fool, he thought, the fool whore! We'll take good care of her.

He smiled and pushed the soldier aside. Then, seeing the disappointment on the soldier's face, he muttered angrily, "After me . . . now leave us alone."

**tsaouse - Turkish army lieutenant*

The soldier closed the door behind him and hurried to find his comrade, wanting to be generous with his prize. He hoped the *tsaouse* did not take too long.

The Turkish Lieutenant went to Perdika, who looked at him enticingly, her voluptuous body heaving. He sat beside her and she poured him *raki*. He drank it in one gulp and she poured him another, filling her own cup too.

This is easy, she thought, I'm safe. She had never been with a Turk before. Perdika was a daring woman. She wanted to taste every drop of her cup. Now she put her hand on the *tsaouse's* face, touched his ear, lingering there a moment. She laughed aloud and he pulled her to him, panting, an angry lust engulfing him as he threw her on the floor. He fell on her like an animal. He was crude and brutal, but she was strong and patient. She tried to enjoy it, but he was too quick. She gritted her teeth in anger.

He rose and looked down at her with contempt. Perdika smiled and opened her arms to him invitingly. But the *tsaouse* was satisfied for the moment. He pulled out his sword and before she could scream, lashed against her bare breasts. With a second swing her head rolled on the floor.

The *tsaouse* wiped his blade and ran outside past the two soldiers who were waiting patiently for their turn. He had not kept his word. Furious with disappointment, the first soldier silently derided himself . . . I'll know better the next time . . . take my pleasure and close my mouth. He let out a scream and ran ahead to look for other victims.

* * *

The gates of Saint Menas slammed shut as the three thousand women and children huddled inside the courtyard with a handful of men from Thymiana. The nuns and priests hurried to find room to care for the weary villagers. Fatouros and his men gathered together.

"We'll be safe . . . they'll never get in."

The monastery was surrounded by cliffs on three sides. The fourth, the only accessible one was difficult to travel. A narrow footpath wound up the side of the hill. The iron gate of the monastery was unbreakable.

Two days passed. It was Easter Sunday. The people gathered in church to celebrate the Resurrection of Christ. Fatouros was in the courtyard with his men.

Suddenly they heard the noise of the screaming Turks climbing the hill. But their efforts to break down the gate were useless. The walls were stone, tall and impenetrable. They would have to find another way.

Slowly, laboriously, they dragged the cannon up the narrow path, aimed it at the wall and fired over and over. The gate remained firm. Finally, after constant barrage, the cannonball pierced the earth beneath it. There was a hole large enough for a man to crawl through. One by one the Turks slipped inside. One by one they entered the gates of Saint Menas. But there was only silence on the other side. Not a sound—not a cry. How strange, thought the Turkish lieutenant. Three hundred of my soldiers are inside—what's happened?

"Quick," he ordered one of his men, "climb that cypress and see what's going on inside."

The Turk looked down from his tree-top perch, stunned at the sight he beheld. Turkish bodies and decapitated heads were strewn in the courtyard. The three hundred soldiers who had entered the monastery had all been cut down by Fatouros who stood inside the gate swinging his sword. The Turks crawled in, one by one, felt Fatouros' blade before they knew what hit them, while his men dragged the bodies away to make way for the next entrant.

The *tsaouse* could not believe his man's report. He hastily climbed the tree and looked for himself. In rage he aimed his rifle and with one shot felled Fatouros. And as the man from Thymiana went down, he turned to an oncoming Turk, slashed him across the chest and died, smiling. He had had his revenge.

The *tsaouse's* man opened the gate and the Turks stormed inside the monastery, slashing everything before them. The blood streamed across the mosaic courtyard, inside the chapel, everywhere. Quickly, Fatouros' right-hand man gathered what women and children he could—one thousand of them—and they climbed inside the huge, deep well to the right of the courtyard. The ledges around the water filled with human beings, trembling in fear of what lay ahead. They huddled there, praying for deliverance. But the Turks saw them and set to work. They hurriedly gathered the mattresses from the nuns' cells and stuffed them down the well. When they set fire to them, they stood by and watched fiendishly, grinning as the muffled cries of women and children came from below. So the Greeks thought they could fool them! The choked sobs, the coughing, the screaming for help pierced the air that Easter Sunday on the hilltop of St. Menas. Their cries mingled with the winds that howled that noonday. And no one heard, no one listened—not man, not God—while blood flowed above that well and the triumphant cries of the Turkish jackals mingled with the wailing. For years to come this day would be remembered by all Greeks. And the world would learn of the tragedy that came to these people, and it would shudder and nod and try to squelch the pangs of guilt that mankind cannot help feeling for all atrocities that pass ignored.

Only smoke and ruins and smelling bodies remained. The conquering Turks shouted as they went onward, upward, to spill more Greek blood, to add to their victories and their revenge. They headed for Nea Moni, to finish off what was left by the army that went before them. Thousands more waited in that monastery further up the hills to the north of Chios. They waited for the fate in store for them, knowing few would live to recall this day.

* * *

Jason heard the cries from his perch inside Anavatos. He sat on the stone ledge high up on the fortress town and looked down thousands of feet below. This tiny community perched on the highest mountain of Chios, seemed to be sprouting up from the earth itself. Its stone buildings were the color of the soil, and it was a vision of nature. From afar, it rose in a peak, as though it was an extension of the mountain. And its people were content inside its thick walls all these years, tending their beehives, baking their bread, raising olives and fruit and caring for their goats and chickens. They had lived here since the ninth century when Anavatos was built as protection against pirates and corsairs. No foe had attempted the steep climb. The people of Anavatos had been safe all these centuries. But now fate had intervened, and the Turks had come. Still, it would be difficult for them. It was impossible to penetrate Anavatos. But the strongest chain can have its weak link, and after all these years of safety and contentment, Anavatos was to know disaster.

Jason listened carefully to the sound of voices. It was not the Turks. He looked closely below and spotted a group of people running up the narrow path, through the thick bushes and pines. He shouted to the men behind him.

"They're Greeks . . . make way!"

They sent out a scout who descended the steep narrow path and returned to assure them it was safe. The gates opened, and the tired, miserable, despaired Chiotes poured inside. They were more than a thousand, among them Elders who had not chosen to sail away, bringing pouches of their wealth with them. Jason watched them and smiled. What good would gold do them here? Perhaps, if they survived, they might buy their way to freedom. But the Turks were not in a bargaining mood. They wanted Greek blood, not gold.

The crowd entered and the people of Anavatos ran to make them comfortable. At last they could rest. They fell on the ground exhausted, drinking thirstily of the water the kindly Anavatians brought. Jason mingled among them, looking for a familiar face, hoping to find someone he knew.

He turned quickly when Petros' hand touched his shoulder. With a cry he hugged the man to him, laughing with joy. They could not believe their good fortune. So these people were from the monastery of Nea Moni . . . those who had escaped the slaughter that followed the one at Saint Menas.

The two men sat down together and Petros drank the wine they brought him, ate bread and olives and made the sign of the cross to thank God for his survival.

Slowly, hesitantly, Petros related the news of Saint Menas. One of the few survivors—a young boy who was with him now—had told him the details. Jason's face clouded. He lowered his head and sadness swept over him—that sadness that always dogged their footsteps. Wherever they went there would be only disaster and death. He listened carefully as Petros talked and his heart ached for his friend, Fatouros.

"He was a gallant man, Captain Petros."

"Yes, he died a hero. Thymiana has something to be proud of."

The Turks reached Anavatos the next morning. Five thousand screaming men trying to scale impenetrable cliffs, to finish off the last of the Chiotes. The island lay devastated, but they would not stop until the last man was killed. Now they had come to the last stronghold. But it was not as easy here. No one had succeeded in scaling this natural fortress.

The Turks surrounded the town from below and tried unsuccessfully to reach it. Days went by. It was impossible. When their food and patience gave out the soldiers returned to Chora with news of their defeat. Bechit Pasha refused to accept it. He ordered them back . . . success or death was his ultimatum. The soldiers re-gathered their arms and ammunition, and set out once again for Anavatos.

It was the Saturday after Easter. Dusk began to fall and the Chiotes grouped inside the church for vespers. Peace had reigned these few days, and the fear that had paralyzed them was gone. They felt safe within the protective walls. But the Turks were sly and Fate was cruel.

The soldier who stood guard beside the secret entrance was uneasy. Early that afternoon, Mandalena, the old woman of Anavatos, had begged the guard to let her step outside the walls to pick greens for her supper. Food was running low and she was hungry. After all, the Turks were gone, she pleaded, and he finally relented. But she had not returned. It was late. He leaned against the huge rock that blocked the secret entrance and wondered what could have happened to her. He should not have listened to her pleas. He was a fool to let her sweet-talk him into moving the rock. He had better report it.

As he turned to leave, the rock moved slowly. Then, before he could cry out, a sword flashed in his face and he fell into a pool of his own blood. One by one the Turks crept inside the opening, until the courtyard was filled.

"Into the church," they screamed, "kill the infidels!"

Outside the wall, Mandalena lay bleeding, her body slashed. The Turks had promised her her life if she gave them the secret to the entrance. Their promise was kept with her blood. Now they leaped upon the surprised Greeks before they could defend themselves.

The clash of hand-to-hand fighting rang in the dim light of dusk. The Turks set fires, rounded up the women and children and put them to the sword or the flame, or both. They were carrying out the Sultan's command with great pleasure.

Jason and Petros fought fiercely. Their strength seemed to double in the surprise of this sudden attack. They struggled with their opponents . . . from Turk to Turk they went, hardly breathing in relief, fighting desperately for their lives and the lives of their people. Night fell and the fighting continued . . . the Chiotes would not give up.

Jason turned from the man he had felled to see a Janissary grab a child and swing its head before the sword. He leaped from behind, knocking them both to the ground. The Janissary's silk uniform gleamed in the moonlight. His sword clanked as it hit the stone courtyard. The Turk rose, stumbled towards it and fell again. Jason stood over him now, aiming his sword, ready to pierce the young man's chest. He looked up and Jason's breath caught. He lowered his sword slowly and stood frozen to the spot.

"Joseph!" he rallied, trying to shout the words that came out in a mere whisper . . . hoarse . . . "Jo . . . seph . . . my brother."

The two men stared at each other, shocked, disbelieving, as though each was suddenly seeing his reflection in a mirror. The Turk ran his hand slowly over his beard, his nose. Then, shaking his head as though to clear it, he leaped to his feet. His startled eyes took on a fiery, mad look and he let out a cry.

"Infidel dog," he shouted and quickly picked up his sword.

Before Jason could rally, he held the blade against

his chest, edging towards the nearby building, pinning Jason against the wall.

"Wait, please!" Jason shouted to his enemy, "Joseph, I'm your brother Jason. Listen to me." There was desperation on his face, a pleading look. "We're twins, Joseph, twins! The Turks took you away when you were a child." He said the words quickly, hoping to convince him.

"You lie dog!" Hissed the other between his teeth. "I spit on you." And he did. "I'm a Turk . . . a Turk . . . you hear? A Janissary of the Sultan!"

He ground his teeth in fury . . . he would destroy this Christian dog who dared imply what he did.

He thrust his sword at Jason. The boy ducked and caught the blade on the shoulder. The blood seeped out. Youssef stood there, stunned for a moment. He did not know why he hesitated to finish the Greek off. He could not explain the feeling, the doubt that suddenly engulfed him.

He looked at Jason's face in the darkness. The moon was out and its glow lit the night. He saw the familiar features, the strong resemblance. Dark, slanted eyes, thick brows, the elongated face, the olive skin. Even though Jason had no beard, Youssef felt he was looking at his clear reflection. He caught his breath. They stood there, the two of them, alone in the darkness while the clash of swords, the cries and moans echoed in the air. They eyed each other for the first time in eighteen years. The pain from Jason's shoulder suddenly pierced Youssef's and he cringed. But Jason's pain was eased by the joy in his heart. He reached out to touch his brother.

"Please Joseph, believe me." The longing, the agony for his brother, overflowed with those words.

Youssef drew back. He turned to leave.

"Wait!" Jason was desperate. He could not lose his brother again. "Joseph, when this is over, go to the *Dzami* in Chora. I'll meet you there . . . don't forget."

Youssef looked at him, fury clouding his face. He raised his sword, let out a scream and fled into the night. He would find other Greeks to kill.

Jason collapsed. He had found Joseph at last . . . a smile came over his face as he sank into unconsciousness.

He woke as Petros and another man were dragging him to the edge of the cliff. Women and children were being lowered with ropes down the steep cliff where the Psarians waited below to take them to safety. They laid Jason in the boat and rowed out to the ship that would take them to Psara, the neighboring island that was free of Turks. Petros washed Jason's wound—it was a superficial one—and bandaged it. Jason closed his eyes and relived the scene with his brother. He could not believe it. He saw again the thick moustache and beard, the dark stormy eyes. What anger and bitterness they held. Oh God, Jason whispered, oh God, don't let me lose him again. He prayed that Joseph would be at the mosque when this was over, that his instinct would bring him to Chora. For Jason knew that the fighting would end soon. They had lost the Revolution but he had found his brother. He thought of the joy they would all know; of his mother, of Joanna. His heart felt warm and happy. The world seemed bright again and full of hope. But then he looked back at Chios, at the flames glowing in the night . . . he could almost hear the screams and clashing swords lost in the distance. And sadness swept over him again. He fell back, exhausted, on his cot and slept for the first time in weeks . . . a restless, disturbing sleep.

XV

It was two weeks after Easter. Two weeks after the landing of the Sultan's troops. The island lay in ashes—bloodied, deserted, lifeless. Only the winds blew strong and fearless, bending the few trees that survived the holocaust. The winds of the Aegean swept through Chios, trying to erase the stench of blood that lay heavy in the air. But it would not go—it was everywhere—that nauseating smell of blood and dead bodies.

The harbor of Chios was a sea of floating corpses that flapped against the sides of the ships at bay. A blanket of dead women and children, old men and young, who had tried to escape the blades that dripped Greek blood. Those who could had taken to the hills to find sanctuary in the monasteries and forests . . . most of them dead now. Those who could, had boarded ships that sailed for other Greek islands. And those who could do neither lay strewn on the land and sea of Chios, or were gathered within wired fences to be shipped to Turkey. The Turks had saved the young girls for the slave markets and harems. The younger men were taken prisoners. What chaos and confusion, what tragedy, as they shoved their human spoils into ships sailing for Turkey. Forty-thousand Greeks to serve the Sultan. Another forty-thousand to feed the soil of Chios with their bones, to quench the thirst of the soil with their blood.

The sea of slaughter flowed on, leaving Chora and the neighboring areas empty of its occupants. Even Kambos within its high walls, was no longer safe against the Turk. It, too, was deserted. The Turkish overlords were closed within the fortress and the Choran elite had sailed away to safety. Kambos, in its vastness and greenery, with its huge orchards and olive groves, its tall stately mansions, lay bare and unoccupied.

Only Ali Bey remained. He feared neither Greek nor Turk. For neither could touch him. His high position was respected by all Turkish soldiers. His friendship with the Sofronis family and his sympathies toward the Chiotes had made him a lifelong friend. Now he would repay their kindness. He stayed behind to help in any way he could. But the people of Kambos were too afraid to remain. They would not trust the mania of the Sultan's men who stormed with vengeance against the Greeks. Who could be sure that the Turks, in their fury, would respect Ali Bey and not kill him too? Yes, the people of Kambos ran for their lives, taking only their precious gold and jewels. Some buried it behind, thinking it would be a burden in their flight, hoping one day to return for it. No one, in his wildest dreams could imagine the Turks would annihilate the island.

Helena sat in her room, on the gold silken pillows amidst luxurious surroundings, quietly embroidering. She passed the days with her needle, while her thoughts roamed the island with Jason and Petros, and now, more than ever, with Joseph. Her maternal instinct told her her son was near, somewhere on the island. And her heart leaped at the thought of seeing him. Would she know him? Would she be able to speak with him? Or would his sword cut them all down before she could touch him, hold him to her, call him "son." She looked around now at the tapestries, the oriental rugs and golden cups, at the beaded curtains, all the wealth that surrounded her. She hated it here. Hated the house, Ali Bey, all the Turks. She could not bring herself to bend, not in the least. Bey had offered them refuge, saved their lives, was feeding and protecting them now. But Helena believed it was only for his own desires, out of passion for Maria and not in friendship for the Sofronis household, or the Chiotes. Sometimes she even hated Maria. She knew that her nights were spent with Bey, in his quarters, making love, sleeping in his arms, betraying Petros and the vows of her marriage. Helena could not forgive this. She knew desire now, felt it stir and twist her insides. She knew the feeling of love, of wanting to be with her loved one. But her pride, her honor rose above personal feelings, above all desires. She pondered this as she thought of Petros and the moments they had lost—moments she had thrown away. Yet she was not sorry. She could look at herself in the mirror, into her son's eyes, with dignity.

Stratis was nothing—she was ashamed of having loved him, ashamed that he had touched her, made love to her. All except that he had given her Jason, yes, and Joseph, wherever he was. For this she was grateful. Stratis was less than a man, but she had never betrayed him or the vows she took that afternoon in the chapel. But Petros would be in her heart always. She loved him deeply. And knowing he was in danger, that she might never see him again, her heart cried for him, her body yearned for his. I'm not sorry, she whispered to herself. I'm not sorry I love him. Wherever he goes a part of me goes with him.

The door opened and Maria walked in looking more beautiful, more fresh, younger than she had ever looked. Love blossomed on her face and gave her new life. For shame, thought Helena, for shame Maria. She looked at her now and smiled ruefully.

"Helena, you're thinking again," Maria scolded. "I can always tell when you're thinking." She came towards Helena and put her arms around her. "You'll never forgive me for this, will you, my dear?"

"I would rather not have come here Maria, you know that." There was bitterness in Helena's voice.

"But Petros wanted us to come. For Joanna's sake, Helena, not mine . . ." she was embarrassed. "Then for Joanna's sake, don't regret it."

"It's for Joanna's sake I'm ashamed. What if she finds out? Oh Maria, how can you go on like this? And with a Turk, a faithless one! While your husband is fighting, maybe dying, out there for you."

Maria tried to remain calm. She did not want to be angry with Helena. She loved her too much. But her attitude was irritating.

"Not for me, Helena. Petros' not fighting or dying

for me . . . it's for his precious Chios. He never cared an iota for me." Her tone softened at the look on Helena's face. She touched her shoulder. "Oh Helena, dear Helena, please try to understand. I love Bey and he loves me. If you could only know, only see his tenderness, his devotion. Look how he protects us, how he cares for us."

"For his beastly passion. No Turk has feelings, Maria."

"You're so wrong . . . and deep down you know it."

Like a flash the scene with Yusbasi Hassan appeared in Helena's mind. That night on the hilltop, the way he had caressed her face, stroked her hair, with such gentleness. Helena pushed the thought aside and looked at Maria. She knew Maria loved Bey and in Helena's heart she sympathized with her. It was only her strong sense of honor that cried against the betrayal. She could not bring herself to believe that any love, no matter how deep, was above honor.

"Oh Helena, if you could only know this fulfillment, this wonderful, warm feeling inside me. If ever you loved as I love Bey, you would not condemn. Please be happy for me. Joanna doesn't know . . . it won't hurt her."

Helena put her arms around Maria and stifled a sob that crept up, begging to be freed. They were locked in her so long, these tears, but Helena would not release them. She was complete master . . . she controlled her mind, her body, her emotions. Maria controlled nothing now—Bey had set her free.

Maria began to cry and Helena stroked her hair, pampering her as one does a spoiled child.

"Alright Maria, don't cry, it's all right."

Maria's tears always smoothed over the irritations, and Helena's reprimands.

Let her live, something inside Helena cried to her, let her live! Who knows how long it will be? And a fainter voice whispered, what about you, Helena, what will you have known in your life except pain and disillusionment? Is there a greater joy than to love and be loved, Helena? What god would deny you this happiness, shortlived as it may be? What is honor without love, Helena? What is life without someone to share it?

She was furious with the little voice.

"Stop it!" she cried aloud and jumped from her seat. She walked over to the draped window, her mind a confused muddle of thoughts.

"I won't listen to you, go away!" she whispered. Then she sighed, composed herself and turned around.

Maria watched her, startled.

"Helena, what's the matter? Who were you talking to?" She was frightened. Helena sounded irrational. Perhaps Maria had burdened her too much. Her problems had become Helena's. She felt guilty. "Helena, forgive me for adding to your own worries . . . I'm so sorry. You've been so good to us . . . like a sister . . . my dear . . ."

Helena smiled. She was fully composed now.

"It's all right Maria. Just nerves . . . nothing, really. I guess we've all had too much lately."

There was a commotion in the corridor; Joanna's voice reached them. Helena and Maria stepped out of their room and faced the messenger who had just arrived with news. Fatouros was killed at Saint Menas. Petros was at Nea Moni and Jason had accompanied the refugees to Anavatos, the last western fortress on the hill. Petros had sent word to the women to leave Kambos immediately. From all indications there would be more reinforcements from Turkey—this would mean another massacre. The women were to take the first available ship for Psara. The island was the closest sanctuary for the fleeing thousands, a temporary refuge until other ships could take them further away. The household was in an uproar. Bey appeared, looking grave.

"I've ordered my men to take you to the harbor." He saw Maria's look of fear. She was shaking her head.

"I won't go. I won't leave."

Before anyone could answer, the voices of Turkish soldiers came from the terrace. They were shouting at Bey's servants. One of them ran into the room and bowed before Bey.

"Master, they followed the Greek messenger here. The *tsaouse* wishes to speak with you."

Bey motioned for the women to hide. He walked out into the terrace.

The *tsaouse* bowed before Ali Bey.

"What do you want? What is this disturbance?" Ali asked with irritation.

"We tracked down a *giaour* fighter to your home, noble one. We understand he comes from the rebel forces on the hill."

"And what has that to do with me?" Bey was calm, his anger controlled, his fear for the women well-hidden.

"As a *tsaouse* in the Turkish army it is my duty to round up the Greeks. Now there is a Greek here and we want him, *effendi*." He hesitated a moment. "We also understand, noble one, that you have three

Greek women in your home."

"Those women are mine, *tsaouse,* they have nothing to do with your war. They are a part of my harem."

A voice came from the terrace stairs.

"Ah, but is it not a bit selfish of you to have three Greek beauties, when I have none?"

Bey looked with narrowed eyes at the figure appearing at the top of the stairs. The smiling Turk was Souleiman, a neighbor from the nearby estates, now commander of *tsaouse's* regiment. He knew Ali Bey was lying. It was general knowledge that he was hiding these women, one for himself, and the other as a favor to his mistress. Why should Ali Bey enjoy the pleasures of three Greek women? Souleiman would take one. He wanted Ali Bey's choice. He looked at Bey and his shrewd eyes caught Bey's look of steel that masked deep concern.

The soldiers stepped aside as Souleiman came forward. His silk uniform gleamed in the light. He smiled, nodded to the *tsaouse* and bowed before Ali Bey.

Ali bowed back. "Welcome to my house, Souleiman Bey." He pretended he had not heard Souleiman's comment on the women. "Will you come inside?"

"No thank you. I have much work ahead of me. We are in the midst of a great disorder here, as you well know." He, too, pretended he had not spoken of the women. He would see what Ali had in mind.

"Our men have swept the *giaours* onto the mountains and will soon rid the island of them. It grieves me Ali Bey, to see this destruction, but they were fools to have risen against the Sultan."

Ali Bey did not answer.

"Don't you agree, Ali Bey?" Souleiman pressed on.

Bey still remained silent. He looked at Souleiman, weighing his words, the look on his face. Souleiman did not care about clearing the island of *giaours*. He wanted something else.

"What can I do for you, Souleiman?"

The two men stood facing each other, both silent, both glaring.

"The *giaour*-messenger *tsaouse* wants is not here. You have my word. Someone ran past here a while ago, but he is gone."

Indeed, the Greek was gone. Ali was not lying.

"Never mind. What I really came for, Ali Bey . . . and your nobility will pardon my forthrightness. I have long admired the fair-skinned Maria Sofronis. And I request that you turn her over to me."

"Don't be a fool, Souleiman Bey! What you ask is impossible." Ali Bey could not believe his audacity.

Souleiman's eyes shot daggers. His face turned red and the veins throbbed in his neck.

"You dare to call me a fool?" He pulled out his sword. The soldiers drew back in surprise. Ali Bey was startled. He had not expected this. Surely the commander would not risk a duel here. He turned towards the door, anxious about the women. Mehmet, who was standing in the doorway, signaled behind him. Ten of Ali Bey's bodyguards rushed out. Ali stopped them.

"Step back. This is between Souleiman Bey and me."

Souleiman was eager to fight. He wanted the blonde woman and he would have her. He called to the *tsaouse*.

"Go fetch the woman. Have her ready to

come with me."

"I would not do that if I were you." Ali Bey's voice was poisonous.

Souleiman swung his sword. Ali stepped back and the duel began. The sound of the clashing swords rang in the morning stillness. Ali was in control when suddenly, from behind, he felt a hot flash penetrate him. He gasped with pain, turned swiftly and struck *tsaouse* across the face. They fell together.

"Allah praise you, *tsaouse*," shouted Souleiman.

But Ali Bey's men were upon Souleiman and his soldiers before he could enjoy the spoils of his victory. It was over in minutes.

The bodies lay one over the other, their blood mixed and flowing over the terrace floor and down the stairs. Mehmet carried his master inside and called for the *Hotza* to read the Islamic prayers while he sponged the wound and tried to stop the flow of blood. Maria stood frozen, fear and terror in her eyes, wanting to fall on Ali Bey and kiss him, hold him, pray for him. But Helena held her back. Joanna stood beside them . . . she must not see her mother in that position.

When Helena finally took Joanna to her room, she knew the time had come for them to go. But she felt—that strange premonition again—that Maria would never leave Kambos. She would remain here with the man she loved. For a moment Helena understood and sympathized with Maria. She even envied her—if only for a moment. She envied her love, her determination to have it, to live it while she could.

Helena returned to Ali Bey's room and found them together. Mehmet stood vigil by his bedside. But Mehmet was a part of Ali Bey, not another person.

Bey smiled at Helena. He was in pain.

"*Kyra* Helena," he said, "I hope you will forgive me for all this confusion. I wish no harm to befall any of you. Perhaps now you will believe that I love Maria. So much that I gladly die for her."

Maria cried out. "Please . . . don't say that." The sobs came pouring out as she placed her hand on his body and held him. Bey stroked her hair and smiled sadly. His voice was weak.

"My pretty flower . . . my life's blood . . . it was beautiful my Maria. Praise Allah. But your god, Maria . . . he did not approve . . . he is having his revenge . . ."

He paused a moment to catch his breath.

"Yet even for this little we had . . . I am grateful . . ."

"Don't die . . . please don't leave me, I can't live without you Ali . . . try . . . try to live my darling . . ."

Maria sobbed pitifully and kissed his hand, now wet with her tears.

Ali Bey looked at Maria with tenderness. He motioned Helena to come closer. The pain grew worse. Helena approached, fear and remorse gripping her. She did not want him to die. He had sheltered them and loved them all, because they were a part of Maria. But what difference did the reason make? Wasn't it enough that he loved them? What did it matter that he was a Turk? Ali Bey had the virtues of a rare human being, the nobility and generosity few Chiotes could boast of. And Helena had despised him all these months. How she regretted it.

Ali beckoned to her to lean over so she could hear him. His voice was barely audible now.

"Mehmet will help you . . . get to the harbor. There . . . you will board the ship . . . for Psara. You will . . . be safe there. Mehmet will . . . give you a package . . . jewels to help you on your way . . . to help . . . Maria . . . rebuild . . . her life . . ."

He turned to Maria and the love in his eyes said more than any words of poets. Is his love any less, wondered Helena, because he is a Turk? It was a far greater love than any Maria had known in her lifetime, from any Christian man. Helena took his hand.

"If anything . . . goes wrong . . . go to . . . the . . . Consulate . . ." He was barely able to get out the words. "The . . . Danish . . . Consulate . . . they will hide you . . ."

"Ali Bey, forgive me," Helena whispered, "forgive me, I was wrong . . . very wrong."

He squeezed her hand and she knew he had forgiven her. He could not speak now and his breath came slower, with more difficulty. Maria's head was over his heart. She listened to the faint heartbeat. Suddenly it stopped. Fear gripped her. She raised her head, looked questioningly at Helena, and turned back to Ali Bey.

His eyes were closed. He was peaceful, as though he were comfortably asleep.

Maria's screams pierced the room. Down the corridor, Joanna heard it, leaped from her bed and ran out. Helena motioned to Mehmet to stop the girl from entering the room. She turned to Maria, took her gently by the shoulders and tried to pry her away. Maria would not budge. She lay there weeping for Ali, for herself, for the lost years of the past and the promised ones of the future. There was nothing for her now.

Joanna was shouting outside the door, trying to push Mehmet away. She wanted to go to her mother. Helena ran to them, shutting the door quickly behind her.

Maria stood up slowly and stared at the man she loved so deeply.

"I can't live without you," she whispered, sobbing, "I won't."

She fumbled through the objects on the stand beside his bed. In the drawer she found his dagger. She fondled the handle, caressed the jewels that adorned it. Ali Bey loved jewels. She smiled now as she looked at him.

In the corridor, Helena had pacified Joanna.

"It's nothing dear, go back to your room. Your mother's just upset about your father . . . and now with Ali wounded . . . you understand."

"Shouldn't I be with her? Can't I help? Oh *Kyra* Helena, will Ali Bey be all right?"

"We hope so . . . You can see your mother later when she's calmed down. Go and get ready, we may have to leave soon."

"Leave? But why? How? What about Ali Bey?"

Helena led Joanna back to her room, assuring her all would be well as Mehmet returned to his master. In a few moments, Helena was back. As she entered the room a muffled cry—Mehmet's mute voice—filled the room. Helena shut the door quickly and ran to the bed. Maria lay over Ali's body, her blood seeping into his silken covers, her hair spilling over his chest. Helena stood there, her heart twisting with pain so fierce that it penetrated her whole body and left her weak. Mehmet steadied her. She fell onto the nearby couch and sat there staring at the two bodies, unable to take her eyes away.

"Perhaps you are happier now," she whispered. "Oh my dear ones, perhaps you are happier than all of us."

She covered her face with her hands, wanting desperately to cry . . . but she could not. She had suppressed her emotions so long she was unable to let go.

Mehmet was kneeling beside his master now, praying softly. He rose and stood before Helena. He saw her sadness, her turmoil, and pitied her. Tears filled his eyes and streamed down his face . . . he motioned with his hands. Cry, he tried to tell her, why don't you cry?

Helena walked over to the bed and stood over the two bodies. She kissed Ali Bey's forehead and caresed Maria's hair, her face. They lay side by side now, where Mehmet had placed them. She smiled sadly at Mehmet, touched his sleeve to show him she felt his pain.

"Thank you Mehmet . . . thank you for everything."

Her heart cried for him too. She felt sorry for this half-man. Where would he go . . . what would he do?

The sun was setting behind the hill, far out past the orchards. The winds blew fiercely, as always, and the cypress trees bowed back and forth to the wind's will. Hundreds of birds, nestled inside the branches, scattered everywhere. They would wait for evening, perhaps the wind would sleep too, and they could return to curl up within the warmth of the green branches.

Helena pulled the drapes over the windows and hurried out of the room. They must prepare to leave immediately.

XVI

The carriage sped towards Chora with the two women inside. Joanna wept in Helena's arms, unable to believe her mother was dead. Why did she do it? Her mind was filled with suspicious questions. She lay against Helena, thankful for the comfort of her arms. What would she have done without her? She thought of Jason and her heart was gripped with a new fear. What if he were dead somewhere up on those mountains? She could not bear the thought.

Helena let Joanna cry. Let it come out, she thought, she must not be like me, pent up, dying a thousand deaths inside. She tried to concentrate on their plight. What if they could not get to the ship? What if they were stopped? She suddenly remembered Ali Bey's advice. "If you have any trouble, go to the Consulate." But what consulate? She tried to remember. His voice had been so weak, barely audible. Was it the British Consulate? Yes, that was it—the British. She must remember that. She tightened her hold on the pouch containing the jewels, and smiled at the thought of the foreign consuls' concern for the refugees—but only the paying refugees. They had opened their doors, their hearts, to those who could pay for their lives. How proud their countries must be of these stalwart guardians of their honor. Buy your freedom, pay for your lives with gold. These were the terms of political friendship and brotherly love. The wealthy, powerful Great Britain was bartering in human lives.

Their carriage turned the bend to the north of the harbor and pulled abruptly to a stop. Mehmet had seen the crowd of Turkish soldiers up ahead, near the shore. He backed up the carriage hurriedly, out of sight. The ship from Psara was anchored out at sea. They would never be able to get past the Turks to the rowboat. Helena's heart sank. She squeezed Joanna's hand and smiled at the girl's fears.

"Don't worry, we'll manage," she reassured her.

Joanna believed Helena and smiled back. She felt safe with this woman. The pain of her mother's loss and the shock were still deep. But she was grateful for this shoulder to lean on, for the protection and love Helena offered. If only Jason were safe, too. God, she prayed. take care of him, bring him back. He's the dearest thing I have now. At that moment something more precious stirred within her. She put her hands over her belly and gasped.

Helena turned to Mehmet. "The British Consulate, quickly . . . do you know where it is?"

Mehmet nodded. He turned the carriage back to the

narrow streets behind Aplotaria and headed for the British sanctuary.

Consul Gioudoukis greeted them from behind his desk. He smiled, pleased to notice they were well-dressed, obviously ladies of means. He looked at the pouch Helena carried. More jewels, more gold for the British Consul. He was happy. Trade was good. If this kept up he would leave the island a wealthy man.

Helena explained their plight. She placed thirty gold pieces on his desk, watching the gleam in his eyes. He smiled, coughed, and waited, his eyes on the pouch she was holding. Too late, she realized she should have hidden it.

Tight-lipped, Helena pulled out a ruby ring, a gold and sapphire bracelet.

"Is this enough?" she asked and steel flashed in her eyes. "Does this buy our safety, your excellency?"

Gioudoukis was delighted. He chose to ignore the sting and implication in her words. What did he care what she thought of him. This was war, survival, each man for himself.

"Indeed, indeed, it is sufficient," he smiled and offered them chairs. "Sit down, dear ladies. It is more than sufficient."

He ordered coffee for them and rambled on about how difficult his task was on the island, how hard he worked, how deeply he regretted the problems between the Chiotes and the Turks.

"Personally I have never had problems with the Turks. And neither did the Chiotes for that matter." He was the epitome of dignity and diplomacy. "I can never understand, dear ladies, why a peaceful nation would suddenly rise against a friendly protector. To cause such bloodshed, such destruction . . . unforgivable."

Fear gripped Helena as she realized he was in full sympathy with the Turks. What was to stop him from turning them over now? Had Ali Bey been wrong? Could she have been mistaken? What consulate was it that Ali mentioned? Could it have been another? Her mind fought to recall the scene in the bedroom. She could not remember. She thought of previous discussions with Jason, abut the Foreign Consulates. He had told her . . . it suddenly came to her. Jason had told her the British and Austrian Consuls had revealed the true number of Chiote forces to Bechit Pasha when they met inside the fortress in an effort to bring peace. It was the Danish foreign office that supported the Greeks, that took their side in the discussions, that offered refuge without payment. Her heart sank. They were practically in the hands of the Turks, and it was her fault.

As though in answer to her thoughts, a rumble was heard outside, followed by the shuffling of feet and the slamming of a door. A clerk appeared in the Consul's office, his face flustered.

"Your excellency, there's a Turkish lieutenant outside with several janissaries. They saw the women come in."

"Nonsense. The Turks have no right here. I'll talk to them."

He rose and turned to Helena who was holding the terrified Joanna's hand.

"Please remain comfortable. I'll be rid of them and come back to you. You have nothing to fear. There are others like you here, you will soon join them."

Helena did not trust him. But could it be that the consulate would indeed protect them? Reporting the

Chiote forces was one thing and turning over human beings to the enemy was another. But she saw evil in his eyes, betrayal. She prayed she was wrong.

Gioudoukis stepped into the corridor. He looked at the *tsaouse* and nodded.

"We saw two Greek women enter here." The *tsaouse* spoke in a loud, bellowing voice.

"You have no right inside these premises, sir." shouted the Briton and smiled at the Turk. Then he extended two fingers and nodded towards the closed door. The *tsaouse* smiled. He would wait and take them all together. Well done, he said to himself, this Britisher is perfect for our work. The Danish dogs would not work with us, he thought, they even dared to threaten us at mention of our clever plan. *Tsaouse* would have slaughtered the Danish Consul on the spot if not for the strict orders issued by Bechit Pasha and the Sultan himself. "Do not dare touch a foreigner, especially a government official!"

They knew the massacre would create turmoil enough throughout the world. The traditional Turkish cruelty had exceeded its own limits and the civilized world once again would be repulsed by these heinous crimes. They could not risk killing foreign diplomats, too.

Gioudoukis returned to his office and called for his assistant to escort the ladies to the refugees' quarters.

"We are rather crowded and cannot afford to offer much comfort. Please forgive us. It will be only for a short while."

"Will we be able to sail soon?" Helena asked him hesitantly. She did not think it was possible. How would they be able to get to the ship? The Turks would leap on them the moment they stepped on

Turkish soil. Then why did Giousoukis say it would be only for a short while? Helena was frightened, suspicion gnawed at her, but she smiled to Joanna to give her courage.

They were taken to the cellar where quarters had been set up for the nearly one hundred people gathered there. It was crowded, the air was stifling. Suddenly a smile crossed her face. In the sea of women and children, she saw a familiar face.

"Aunt Alexandra!" It was her uncle Michael's wife. "How did you ever get here?"

They rushed into each others' arms. Alexandra began to cry.

"They're all gone my dear, gone from Thymiana. It's a long story."

She wiped her tears and smiled at her niece. What joy to see a loved one's face. The others here were strangers to her. There was no one from her village.

Helena was anxious to hear about Thymiana.

"They ran to the hills, at the monasteries. All gone now, every soul slaughtered." She began to cry again and Joanna whimpered.

"What about Jason? And my father? Do you know anything about them?"

"Someone said that they went different directions. Your father headed for Nea Moni . . . Jason went somewhere else with a crowd of women and children. He took them to Anavatos I think. That's impenetrable, you don't have to worry about them. No one can break into those stone walls."

How were they to know that nothing remained impenetrable to the Turks . . . there was always the certain approach—betrayal—and that the fortress was now bathed in blood, deserted of every living soul.

"Your uncle Michael was at St. Menas. They were all slaughtered there, Helena, all except the one or two who got away before the onslaught. Did you know?"

Helena held her as she sobbed, trying to comfort her.

"Fatouros was a hero. They said he fought like a madman—those that got away told a terrible story." She recounted the burning of women and children, the chaos and bloodshed that followed.

"Poor Michael, my poor husband."

Suddenly the door burst open and Turkish soldiers filled the doorway. Helena gasped.

"The beast," she whispered between her teeth, "the English beast. He betrayed us all."

They were herded together and Janissaries encircled the group, eyeing them carefully, appraising them. They would take their choice of the female prisoners first—the spoils of war. The older ones would be put to the sword, they were useless to the Turks. The middle-aged would become servants, and the young girls wuld become wives or concubines of the Janissaries. Youssef looked over the females thoughtfully. Chios was his first mission—and this was to be his first prize. He thought of the times he had rejected Greek females, and pondered the idea of taking one now for his wife, like the other Janissaries. The thought shocked him. Yet they were beauties, with wide hips so convenient for bearing children. His gaze stopped on Joanna. She did not look like the others. She's pale, he thought, a thin creature. But her skin seems soft, her eyes are large . . .

She cringed at his stare and drew closer to Helena and her Aunt Alexandra. But then she noticed something familiar about the Janissary. Hesitantly, she looked at the tall, dark soldier again. Youssef's look wandered to Helena and stopped abruptly there. His eyes fixed on hers; he was unable to turn away. She drew in her breath, closed her eyes and opened them again. Had he frightened her? She was white and looked as though she would faint any moment. She did not strike Youssef as one who frightened easily.

Helena looked familiar to Youssef, like someone he had seen before . . . perhaps in a dream. Still staring at her, he walked slowly up to the three women. Before he could speak to them, *tsaouse* called his men and motioned to Youssef.

"Choose your females later," he ordered. "We're going to clear the place now." He turned to two of his soldiers. "Take the old ones out and put them to the sword."

The men hurried to do his bidding. The *tsaouse* turned to Youssef.

"Take half the others and put them in the Kledas home, the one beside the *dzami*. Take two men with you."

He turned to another Janissary.

"Hibrahum, take the other half to the house behind the Consulate. They're expecting us, they've made all the preparations."

A buzz went over the room. The refugee women were separated into two lots. The older ones began to whimper as the soldiers escorted them out.

"There are servants in both houses," the *tsaouse* said, "they will take care of everything. Tomorrow we can choose the ones we want. We'll ship what's left to Smyrna."

* * *

Joanna stirred as the rooster crowed. She was nauseated, her head was spinning and she lay there, sick and miserable. She was frightened, but joy mixed with her fear, the secret joy that gave her courage. Now, more than ever he must come back . . . Jason . . . to learn that his child stirred within her. A week had passed since they were brought here, and the soldiers had not bothered them. They had seen the pale Joanna and left her to Helena's care. A sick female was of no use to them. But she was too young, too pretty to be destroyed. They would wait a while to see if health returned to her.

Joanna tried to get up but could not. Helena, who lay watching her from her bed, went quickly to her side. She had recognized Joanna's symptoms and her heart sank. What would they do now? If only Jason were safe, would come back. Somehow Helena would get them to a priest. The child must not be born out of wedlock.

Helena had not slept all night. She saw Jason before her constantly. And now she had seen Joseph too, in the flesh. She knew he was her son. Behind the dark beard, the thick moustache, the long hair, was Joseph, her beloved Joseph, Jason's identical twin. How would she tell him? How would he react? She wondered now how she was able to control herself at sight of him. Joy leaped within her at the thought of putting her arms around him, of calling him "son." Happiness surged through her veins. How long it had been since she felt happiness. Yet even this was tinged with sorrow, with fear. She thanked God silently for this gift, for sending her her lost boy. She would find a way to win him back.

Instinct, she thought, instinct is never wrong. Youssef had sensed something and was drawn to Helena. The surprise in his eyes, the strange look that crossed his face, did not escape Helena. She could not wait to see him again.

Another week passed. Joanna was still ill, but she seemed to be improving. Helena watched over her constantly, grateful that the soldiers had left them to their misery. The Turks passed by often, looked inside, inquired from time to time about the girl's progress, and went about their work. Youssef was not with them. But the extra milk and fruit they received were at his orders. Soon he began to stop in their room, to ask about Joanna's health, often bringing figs and nuts. Another soldier accompanied him the first few days, then two. Soon, however, he came alone. He would sit and watch Joanna and Helena, carefully, as though appraising them, measuring their words. He spoke in short phrases, often breaking the conversation abruptly and walking out. Helena waited. She understood that he was fighting a battle inside him. She longed to tell him the truth, but she felt it was not yet time.

Youssef was pleased when Joanna began to feel better. He smiled and Helena's heart leaped. She had not seen him smile before. His straight white teeth gleamed, and the light broke the darkness of her sorrow. Youssef began to stay longer, to chat with Joanna more easily. But when he spoke with Helena he was tense and leery, avoiding her eyes. As though he mistrusted her, or was ashamed. He could not understand why he felt this way. She was just another Greek woman. Yet something in her eyes drew him, held him. Perhaps it was because he had no mother, did not remember his own. He wondered about her now and the times she had come to him in his dream. He recalled the faint memory of a woman putting him to bed, bending over his covers. A dark-eyed woman with black hair caught in a bun at the nape of her neck . . . like Helena's. Perhaps this was why he was drawn to this Greek woman. Helena caught him staring at her hair. He's remembering, she thought hopefully, oh God, he's remembering.

One afternoon she finally ventured a few words, as he stared at her hair again.

"I once had a son," she said softly, carefully, "two sons . . . twins. One of them was taken by the Turks. He was five years old then." She watched for his reaction. "I never saw him again."

Youssef glared at her. Without saying a word, he turned abruptly and walked out of the room.

"I didn't know you had another son, *Kyra* Helena, Jason never mentioned having a brother."

Helena patted Joanna's hand.

"Sit down dear," and she told her the story.

When she finished, Joanna wiped her eyes.

"That explains a lot of things about Jason."

She remembered his gaps of silence, his sadness, his words about finding something.

"Oh my God, *Kyra* Helena, you've found your lost son!"

She hugged Helena and they laughed together at her good fortune. But Helena knew there were still many obstacles ahead.

* * *

Youssef hurried to finish his tasks early. He was anxious to see Joanna and Helena. Today he would tell them he had chosen them for himself. He had informed *tsaouse* that morning. His first spoils of victory were beautiful ones—human spoils—he was pleased. He wanted Joanna from the first day he saw her. He would take her for his wife. She would be the first of his harem. As for the other, he decided it was a benevolent gesture not to separate the two. He liked Helena in spite of her foolish story of the stolen son. But then, it was well-known that Greek women gloried in such tales. She could watch over the younger girl. Yes, she would be useful to them. He had made a wise choice. He had not felt so happy in years. He liked Helena. The thought of her warmed his heart. She looked obstinate and unbending, and she obviously hated the Turks. But he did not care.

The thought of taking Joanna to his bed excited him. She was gentle, soft, easy to handle . . . like a soft kitten. Suddenly the word *titika* came to his mind. How strange, that it should come to him again. It had no meaning in Turkish. He wondered if it were a Greek word.

He did not see Imamet the high priest coming down the corridor and they nearly ran into each other.

"A thousand pardons, holy one."

"I was just coming to see you Youssef. I have something to tell you." He paused. He did not like to disappoint the young soldier. He was a good Janissary and a loyal one. But Kara-Ali's pleasure and Imamet's own pocket were more important than Youssef's feelings.

"*Tsaouse* tells me you have chosen the blond girl and the older woman with her. I'm sorry, Youssef, I've decided to give them to Kara-Ali. You may select two others."

Youssef paled. "I don't want two others." Imamet had no right to refuse him. Janissaries had the privilege of choosing first, the women they wanted.

Imamet saw that Youssef was shaken.

"What's the matter with you, soldier? You're not attached to the girl already, are you?"

Youssef did not reply.

"You'll get over it." He tried to be patient. "You know that Admiral Kara-Ali's pleasure comes first. Pick two others."

"I'm sorry—I want those two."

Imanet's face flushed.

"How dare you question the decision of *kadi*? You know my word is law! The women go to Kara-Ali and I'll hear no more about it. You will take them to the Admiral tomorrow, the last night of Ramadan."

He walked away leaving Youssef standing in the corridor shaken and confused.

Imamet would be paid handsomely for his choice. These two women were prizes—the young one with her fairness, and the mature olive-skinned Helena who looked strong and still full of life. Kara-Ali might even keep them both for his harem. The thought made Youssef's blood boil. He rubbed his hands, twisted his beard in anguish. Kara-Ali must not have them. But there was nothing he could do. He decided to remain on the flagship with them until he could think of something. He was determined not to leave them out of his sight. The thought suddenly struck him that he was contemplating treason. How could he think this way? To disobey orders for the sake of two Greek women! He was annoyed with himself, shaken by the very thought, puzzled at this sudden change in him.

The next day he tried to tell Helena and Joanna. But he could not. When he saw their anxious faces, the trust they had in him, he wanted to turn and run away. He steeled himself to explain the change of plans. Their dismay and fear flustered him and he fought to keep calm, to hide his own feelings.

"Imamet did not want to separate you. Perhaps you can buy your freedom in Turkey."

His words were useless, they did not allay his fears. He knew Kara-Ali would not let them go but he was helpless to act otherwise.

Joanna began to cry. Helena held her in his arms, trying to comfort her. She looked at her son and asked quietly.

"When do we go?"

"Tomorrow night."

"The last night of Ramadan." Helena smiled bitterly. "So we are to be Kara-Ali's holiday gifts."

Ramadan would be over tomorrow . . . the Moslem's holy celebration, a time of prayer and atonement. The Turks slept all day and wallowed in food, wine and women all night. The shops and homes in the capital city, and the ships at bay were ablaze with multi-colored lanterns. Banks of musicians played by the shore. Magicians entertained the Turks and a carnival atmosphere prevailed. All thoughts of fighting were forgotten.

Joanna broke away from Helena's arms and faced Youssef. Tears streamed down her face.

"Help us," she pleaded, "help us escape, please!"

He looked at her not speaking, wanting to comply

with her wishes but bound to a higher duty.

"It grieves me that I cannot." He did not look her in the eyes.

"I beg of you . . . please!" Joanna pulled his silk shirt and wept uncontrollably against him.

Youssef turned to Helena. He was hurt, sorrowed, he explained, but he could not go against his orders. The Sultan and his country were beyond all personal feelings.

* * *

The *kadi* woke fresh from the day's sleep. It was the last evening of Ramadan. He was rested, eager to issue orders for execution of the *giaours* tomorrow, the final day of Moslem atonement. Tomorrow the heads would roll, a perfect climax to tonight's festivities.

The sun set and night fell.

XVII

The tiny island of Psara lies three hours' sail northwest of Chios, its seven thousand inhabitants nestled peacefully behind the cliffs and rocks of the coast. The people are kindly ones, and their heritage is a pure one. They are of the few Greeks whose bloodline has not been mixed by Turks or Albanians or Genoans. For they had little any conqueror could want, and no one settled there. What was there to gain from bare rocks? The Turks had no desire to utilize Psara. As long as the small island paid its taxes, sixty-thousand *grossia* a year, they were left alone. And so they breathed free and prospered with their merchant fleet that numbered fifty ships. The Turks were content as long as Chios nearby was in their hold. And they did not mind, nor bother to quell the uprising that gave the Psarians complete freedom.

The Psarians are good-natured people, and now in the disaster that befell their neighbors, they opened their homes and their hearts to the destitute refugees. They gave the Chiotes their houses, their churches, their community buildings, and soon, when money was raised, they built wooden huts in the fields and in their gardens to give the growing numbers that arrived, permanent shelter.

One of these kindly islanders, Konstantine Kanares, offered sanction to Jason and Petros. The wounded boy was nursed back to health by Kanares' good-natured wife, a girl whose beauty was as true as her goodness. The young man spent many hours talking with Petros and Jason about the Chian situation, learning details of the tragedy, wishing desperately something could be done.

Kanares was twenty-eight years old, a typical Psarian in features—round-faced, with a somewhat flat nose and a small trim moustache. He was fair-skinned, although the sun had tanned him, of medium height, with gentle features and an expression that showed determination and daring. His brown eyes were calm, they revealed enthusiasm and a peaceful nature, a look that characterized many of the Greek revolutionary heroes.

Petros watched him as he spoke and realized that Chios had a true ally in Kanares. And when the young captain's friend, George Pipinos of Hydra arrived, Petros somehow felt they were destined to make history. Kanares had not seen his comrade for a while and he was delighted that fate had brought them together again. They sat down and reminisced over a bottle of wine, discussing the present crisis in Chios with great concern. Jason and Petros watched them carefully, sensing that significant plans were in the making.

"The beasts!" Pipinos shook his head as Petros related details of the massacre, the disregard for age and infirmity, the slaughtering of women and children, the beheading of priests and nuns, the burning of churches and monasteries.

Soon the two friends were on fire. Their blood boiled for revenge against the tyrants.

"I'll be damned if I don't feel like going there myself and setting fire to the bastards."

The thirty-two year old Pipinos was the opposite of Kanares. Restless as a panther, volatile, he had an outrageous vocabulary of Albanian curses which spouted at the slightest provocation. But he was a good soul, fearless and brave, undaunted, free in his ideas, blunt in his speech, not one to speak with diplomacy or tact.

Petros watched the two men and smiled. He was glad fate had brought Jason and Petros here. They had not only found comfort but enriched their lives with two new and good friends.

"What do you say, Captain George?" Kanares slapped Pipinos on the shoulder good-naturedly, "what do you say the two of us try?"

Pipinos jumped to his feet. "Damned if we don't blow the snakes to kingdom come!"

Jason looked at Petros, then at the two sea captains. "I'm with you. Count me in."

They laughed and slapped Jason on the shoulder. "Bravo son, spoken like a Greek."

Petros did not want Jason to risk his life again. Jason noticed his concern and tried to ease his doubts.

"I feel fine, Captain Petros. The wound's healed.

Look." He opened his shirt to show the small, fresh scar that shone on the dark skin.

Petros was hesitant, but did not have the heart to crush Jason's spirit. He intended to take part in this mission himself and would have preferred Jason remain behind. He decided not to make an issue of it. He turned to Kanares and Pipinos.

"Count me in too, my friends, and on behalf of Chios, I thank you."

They poured another round of drinks.

"We'll get the fireships ready and set sail two days from now."

"We'll burn them on their Ramadan, their final hour!"

They hurried to prepare. They would need crews to man the two fireships—Jason would go with Kanares, and Petros with Pipinos—and the third back-up vessel in which they would return. Kanares would attack the Turkish flagship with Kara-Ali aboard, and Pipinos the second ship in command. If the wind was right, the whole Turkish fleet would catch fire in a chain reaction.

The next day Kanares and his group went to church, confessed their sins, took holy communion, and made ready to sail.

It was midnight. The zephyrs blew strong. The ships were ready. Thirty-four sailors and the two captains set sail. The two ships glided side by side in the calm sea, with Austrian flags, their camouflage, waving in the wind. The third vessel followed close behind. They would sail east from Psara, passing the north of Chios and south to the harbor that lay in the narrow straits between Chios and Turkey.

"It's a good wind that blows," mused Kanares as he looked up at the burgeoning sails, "God willing we'll be there on schedule."

From time to time the men waved to each other from their decks, shouting words of encouragement and daring. They were eager to blast Kara-Ali to the skies, to avenge the Greek blood that flowed through Chios.

Jason leaned on the railing and thought of many things. His heart beat fast at the adventure ahead of him. He was thankful that in his small way he had given himself to the sacred fight, disastrous as it may have been so far. He touched his wound and thought of Joseph. Would he see him again? The Turks would surely re-assemble in Chora. He might be there . . . if he were alive. Jason believed his brother was capable of protecting himself. Yes, Joseph would be there. Jason planned to remain in the harbor when their mission was over . . . he would hide somewhere and wait.

As the ship cut through the waters, a thought crossed Jason's mind. Kara-Ali's ship was the largest of the fleet.

"Captain Kanares," there was a worried expression on Jason's face, "What about the prisoners aboard Kara-Ali's ship?"

Kanares paled. They had not considered the prisoners. There would be at least two thousand Greeks aboard the flagship. He commanded his pilot to steer closer to Pipinos who stood against the rail of his ship. Kanares waved his arms frantically. The ships were soon within hearing distance.

"Captain George," shouted Kanares to Pipinos, "you know something? If, God willing, we burn the

Turkish Pasha, we're also going to burn the Christian prisoners aboard."

"Better they burn alive than end up in the slave markets," Pipinos shouted back without a second thought, "better they burn than be sold to Turks, or change their faith. Once a Christian changes faith, he isn't worth a grosse. Don't worry about it."

Kanares had complete faith in the iron-hearted Pipinos.

"You're right," he shouted back and turned to Jason.

"This is war, my lad," Kanares reassured him and placed his hand on Jason's shoulder. "Some must die so others can live in freedom."

Jason understood this, but he did not like it. He decided he hated wars and revolutions and anything that dealt in taking lives. Was it all worth it? He could not be sure. Perhaps if the revolt had been successful he would have felt differently. Now it seemed futile. The blood and the killing had not brought them freedom. His heart was heavy.

"All hands on deck . . . wake up lubbers." Kanares' shouts broke the stillness. They were nearing the straits, though still safe from hearing distance. Kanares whistled with excitement as he shouted orders. His men scurried to the deck.

"Come on men, we're nearing the doorstep of Captain Pasha!"

The sailors took their posts as the far-away rumble of cannon echoed in the night. The Turkish Navy was announcing sunset and the end of Ramadan. As the Greek ships came further south, they heard the sound of a bugle, the cry forbidding all ships, even friendly ones, to proceed, at the risk of being bombarded.

They had not been spotted, it was merely a matter of routine.

In the darkness the men made out the shore, the tall mountains of Chios behind it. There was a mist, a thickening fog as they came closer. Kanares gave Pipinos a sign—the ships were side by side, barely touching—and Pipinos swerved his ship away, sailing for his target.

As they approached the harbor they could hear music, laughter, loud noises. Closer and closer they came. Kanares took over the helm and instructed his men to get ready. They checked the gunpowder and the naptha, the sulphur and tar that lined the ship's sides, the dry weeds and resin stuffed into the planks.

"Careful now," he whispered. "I don't see Pipinos. Does anyone see his ship?"

"They're to the left of us . . . getting closer to the Turks." Jason's eye had caught them in the darkness.

"Hurry Captain Kanares," one of the sailors urged, "don't let the Hydrans beat us to it."

The men laughed. "Pipinos is a dog, and has the speed of a demon."

"Pipinos is a stalwart hero," Kanares whispered, "I don't care who gets there first, as long as we succeed. We didn't come here to compete, but to blast Kara-Ali from Chios."

Jason thought of Bournias and Logothetis, and the difference. It's men like these that make up for Bournias and the likes of him, he mused, and suddenly caught his breath. A rowboat was heading for the Turkish flagship. He watched anxiously but the night was dark and only shadows were discernible. He had no way of knowing it was Youssef taking Helena and Joanna to Kara-Ali.

Their ships glided silently towards the Turkish fleet. Kara-Ali's ship was first, behind it the second vessel and further down, one ship behind the other, the rest of the fleet . . . fifty in all. Kanares' ship came nearer. Further down, Pipinos was nearing his destination.

A storm was brewing. It would hit within the hour. If all went as planned, the winds would carry the flames to the whole Turkish fleet. They reached the side of Kara-Ali's flagship. Kanares made the sign of the cross.

"All right men, hook our boat onto the Turks'."

The men moved quickly. They threw the grappling hooks. Jason jumped after them onto the Turkish ship's side, clinging to it while he and two others worked silently, quickly in the night. Kanares lit the fuse. He and his men jumped from their ship into the waiting rowboat. The fire crept up quickly towards the gunpowder. Jason leaped into the water.

"I've got to stay behind," he shouted against the wind. "Tell Kanares I'll be all right . . . and thank him." He swam towards shore.

"Christ conquers!" Kanares' voice was heard by his men and was lost in the wind that began to blow fiercely. "This is the way we burn Turks!"

They rowed quickly towards the back-up vessel.

* * *

There was merriment aboard the flagship. The Turks would end Ramadan with glory. Kara-Ali sat on the deck with Riala Bey and the other captains around him. Dazed from the *raki* he had consumed, he turned to his men-in-command.

"In twelve days the Greeks of Roumeli and Morea

will hear the final penalty Chios paid, and they will know what to expect. Let these fool Chiotes run to Psara. We'll get them all together there. More heads to ship our Sultan. When we finish with Chios, we go on to finish off Rhodes and Crete . . . and Tinos . . . one at a time.

"By the great Mohammed, if Housit Pasha doesn't send Ypsilantis to Constantinople in pieces, he's not worthy of his title." The Turk waved his fists as he shouted.

Kara-Ali wrinkled his brow. The Greeks had run rampant through Housit Pasha's harem on the mainland, a disgrace that must be avenged by the Turks. He could not wait.

"If Housit Pasha fails," shouted another captain, "he should hang. Look at us. In this short time in Chios we sent the Sultan two thousand Greek heads, thirty sacks of ears and another thirty filled with noses." He laughed.

"Chiote ears and noses!" the others shouted, finding it comical. The roar of laughter grew, shaking the deck and blending with the merriment from the other ships.

Kara-Ali frowned. He remembered the destruction the Greeks had unleashed on the mainland. Fury overwhelmed him. His nostrils quivered, his face turned red, his eyes, bloodshot from drink and ferocity, looked ahead as though the Greek fighters were before him that very moment.

"By the great gates of paradise! By Omar and Abubakr and Ali and all the saints in the heavens," he roared and shook his fists in the air. "I cannot forget Tripolitza and the raping of Housit's harems. No, no, no!"

He jumped to his feet and paced back and forth, twisting his thick moustache with fury.

The deck was spread with tapestries and oriental rugs. Sitting cross-legged were all the wealthy Turks of Chios, before *sofrades** laden with every delicacy the Turkish cuisine offered. At Kara-Ali's words they rose in unison, folded their hands over their chests, and shouted, "Kill the faithless ones! Death to the *giaours*!"

The *giaours* would pay for their deceit. Tomorrow, the day after holy Ramadan, would be the hour of revenge.

The hold was filled with Chiote prisoners, tomorrow they would be put to death. But tonight, the Turks would drink and make merry with the female slaves they had acquired.

Imamet the *Kadi* had chosen the proper moment. He appeared before the intoxicated admiral with his prize. Now in his darker moments, Kara-Ali needed something to please him, to make him forget the miserable *giaours* and the problems they had caused. The high priest stood before him, smiling with self-assurance.

"I have a gift for you, Captain Pasha Kara-Ali."

He motioned towards the door below and Youssef appeared with the two women. Kara-Ali's eyes gleamed.

"One is for your bed, excellency, and one is for your household." Imamet pointed to Helena. "She is strong and capable."

"And she is beautiful too," added Kara-Ali, looking at Helena's dark, cold eyes.

**Sofrades - low tables*

Kara-Ali looked from one woman to the other. "One is a bud," he whispered and licked his lips, "the other a flower in full bloom."

"Never mind the household," he said to Imamet, "I will have them both for my harem."

Youssef stood by, gritting his teeth, wanting to spit on Kara-Ali and his gold pieces. But he remembered his loyalty, his prime duty, and remained still.

Suddenly the whole world began to tremble. The land, the sea, the skies exploded in a terrible blast that lighted the skies. The flagship went up in flame and smoke. There was total chaos. The men screamed, running in panic across the deck, jumping over the sides. The Turks were stunned beyond action. Kara-Ali stood on the deck, trying to shout orders to his men, when he saw the burning mast above him. It fell before he could get out of its way, knocking him into the water. Youssef ran across the deck in search of Helena and Joanna. He saw the admiral and stopped. Several of the Turks leaped into the sea after Kara-Ali.

"Praise Allah," Youssef whispered. The commander had someone to look after him . . . he could go to the women. He shouted their names as he ran from side to side, scanning the water. In the glare of the flames he glimpsed a blonde head bobbing in the waves. He leaped into the sea, now filled with screaming men and women, and swam to Joanna.

The Greek prisoners inside the hold were trapped. Several had managed to escape before the ladder burned away, but the others were doomed along with two-thousand of Kara-Ali's men. Kanares had done his job well, but at a heavy price.

In the chaos, Kanares did not notice that Pipinos' fireship had come unfastened from the Turkish ship and was drifting away. The second flagship was unharmed. Pipinos watched, heartsick, from his rowboat. The wind was moving his fireship further and further away from the Turkish fleet. He had failed in his mission. He pounded his fist in his hand and cursed aloud. He thought of rowing back and fastening the fireship to the Turks' ship again, but he knew there was no chance of reaching it and getting back in time. The fireship was ablaze and would soon explode.

His rowboat approached the back-up ship while prisoners from the unharmed vessel managed to escape in the confusion. Pipinos' heart was heavy. Disillusioned, he climbed the ladder onto the deck, turning to watch the lighted sky in the horizon.

Youssef could think of nothing but the safety of the two Greek women. He held onto the unconscious girl and looked frantically around for signs of Helena. Finally he saw her waiting in the water, by the shore, for the chance to come up without being seen. Youssef swam to her and together they climbed ashore, laying Joanna on the ground. No one paid attention to them in the chaos of screaming men and women, of fires lighting the sky, of moans and shrieks, tears and curses.

At the other end of the harbor, Kara-Ali's men dragged up their admiral's unconscious body. They worked over him anxiously, whispering hurried prayers for his recovery. He revived, but only for a moment.

"The *giaours* will pay heavily for this new treachery," hissed the Turks as they knelt beside their dead leader.

Soon the Sultan's word would ring again

throughout the east. Kill them all, even those in the precious mastic fields. They had been spared up till now, but there must be no Chiote left to breathe on the island.

Helena led Youssef, carrying Joanna in his arms, through the darkness and up the hillside to a deserted windmill. They went inside, safe at last, and laid the unconscious girl on a stack of hay. He stayed with them all night and the next day, and the night after that. Only once did he leave to bring food and water.

Outside, Chora was burning again, flowing with blood, being cleared of any remaining Chiotes. The same was happening to the neighboring areas of Kambos, Thymiana, Neohori and Vrondados. The Turks had sworn vengeance and they were taking it. They slaughtered every remaining Chiote in the city and chased after those who escaped, dogging their footsteps every inch of the way. The Greeks hid in caves, in wells, in the forests. But the Turks were close behind, searching, slaughtering, burning. On the third day, Chora was once again ashes and smoke . . . and dead bodies and dried rivers of blood. Those few Chiotes who escaped death came out at night, quietly creeping about, trying to find food to survive. They picked greens from the hills, stole fruit from orchards. Inside their caves, they built small fires and cooked what beans or dandelions they had gathered. The hostages too, were dead, their bodies dangling from ropes near the plane-trees in the town square. The Turk had taken his revenge—the great minds of Chios, one by one, had a noose around their neck.

Within the deserted windmill, another scene unfolded. Helena watched Youssef from where she sat, looking at her son with longing. She could not believe he had returned at last. She looked at his large brown eyes, the lids that slanted so like Jason's, with that sad look. How alike they are, she thought, identical in features. What about his heart, his soul? What poisons have they fed him? Yet underneath it all and in spite of it, he has emerged a compassionate human being. She yearned to run and put her arms around him but she held herself back . . . it was not the proper time.

Youssef caught Helena watching him. She is curious about me, he thought, she thinks I'm that boy she lost. She's a fool!

"I'm Youssef the Janissary," he said suddenly, angrily, "I am a Turk, woman, I am not your son."

He was afraid to admit what he feared.

"But you are not certain, are you Youssef?" Helena grasped the opportunity to speak up. She looked him in the eye, daring him to prove her wrong. "How can you be?"

They stood there facing each other.

"You are not sure, Youssef, are you?" She repeated pleadingly.

He thought a moment and his face clouded. He remembered the other woman with the dark eyes, the hair in a bun, and looked at Helena carefully. He thought of the kitten, and that strange word.

"What is *Titika*?" he asked suddenly.

She smiled . . . the world was hers. Oh my son, her heart cried, oh my beloved Joseph, you remembered!

Finally she spoke.

"*Titika* was a kitten my son Joseph found roaming in the vineyards in Zagora. He brought it home and I let him keep it." She watched Youssef as she spoke slowly, cautiously. "He and his brother Jason spent many happy hours playing with *Titika*." Then, taking courage she added, "It was a few weeks before they took you . . . away from me."

Youssef lost his composure.

"No!" he shouted, frightened and confused by her words. "Never! I'm not a Greek . . . and not your son! I'll die first."

He turned his back, wanting to leave, but unable to do so. Something kept him here, against his will.

Joanna stirred, suddenly conscious. Youssef turned to her, his anger subsided, almost as though it had never been. Helena sat, heartsick at his fury, at the hatred on her son's face when he shouted. What she had feared had come to pass. The beasts had succeeded in poisoning him against his own people, his heritage. And yet, looking at him beside Joanna, he appeared a completely different person. Hope sprang in Helena's heart.

Youssef was silent. He bent over Joanna with concern. The color had come back to her face. She smiled at him and turned to Helena. She gasped at the whiteness of her face.

"Don't worry *Kyra* Helena, I'm all right, really."

Helena said nothing. She watched them both, unsmiling, unmoving. Would it have been better not to have seen him, she wondered? She did not know the answer. She knew only that Youssef was denying his own mother.

He looked at her now with embarrassment. And yet he felt pain inside. He was furious with himself. First that fool *giaour* at Anavatos and now this silly woman. How dare they even mention such a thing. A Greek! Never! He opened his mouth to speak of

Jason but thought better of it.

It was dusk when they heard the sound of footsteps outside. Youssef crept out, grabbed the figure that hurried by, and dragged him inside. His wicker basket was filled with food, with skins of milk and water.

"Good," Youssef whispered. The last two days' hunger gnawed inside them. They could certainly use this.

"*Yorgo*, it's you! It's our friend, Youssef, let him go." Helena was happy to see the familiar face.

Big Ears dusted himself off and smiled shyly. He shifted from one foot to the other, twisted his hands and rolled his head about. Joanna wanted to laugh at the comical sight he made, but Youssef began passing out the new-found bread and cheese, and eating became more important. He lifted Joanna's head and placed the goatskin to her lips. She looked at him smiling and drank the milk gratefully.

Oh my son, Helena thought, watching his tenderness with the girl, my darling Joseph, you have Jason's kindness, his good, innocent heart. Those beasts have made you hard,.yet they have not touched the core of you. You are gentle still. She wanted to put her arms around him. She stood beside him now, and touched his shoulder. He turned, looked at her a moment, somberly, then shrugged and rose.

"Take some bread," he said gruffly, "eat!"

"You stay with them," he ordered Big Ears, "while I go out and look around."

"Wait, I just remembered," Big Ears cried, pulling Youssef back.

He turned to Helena, looked from her to Youssef, amazed at the resemblance to Jason, but unable to explain it.

"*Kyra* Helena," he went on, "I saw Jason. Jason's down there." He pointed towards Chora.

"He's hiding down there . . . with Captain Petros."

Helena gasped.

"He said he was looking for someone . . . and to go away quickly."

"Jason?" Youssef turned to Helena, puzzled.

"Jason is my son, your brother . . ." Helena said the words quietly, slowly. She was frightened again. Jason was in Chora where no Chiote was allowed to breathe. "If they find him they'll take his head."

Joanna muffled a cry. "Oh my God, what is he doing there . . . is he mad?"

Youssef spoke slowly, as though to himself.

"He said he would see me in Chora . . . in Chora." He looked at Helena intently, a question in his eyes.

She went to him, raised her hand hesitantly. Her fingers touched his face, carressed it. He took her wrist and held it a moment. They looked at each other—she, stern and waiting, all her love in her eyes. He stood there unmoving, fighting his anger and the urge to fall into her arms.

He turned to Big Ears. "You stay with them." And to Joanna, "Rest . . . don't get up. I'll be back soon."

He ran outside before they could stop him. Helena watched him from the crack in the wall as he ran down the hillside and disappeared into the valley where Jason waited.

XVIII

"We were fools to come, Jason, this is madness," Petros whispered as they crouched in the darkness of the deserted shop in Aplotaria.

From the boarded window slats, they could see the road. It was deserted. The area was in shambles. The smell of the dead still permeated the air.

"I should never have let you come."

"I had to, Captain Petros, I told my brother I would be here."

Then, feeling guilty, he added, "You shouldn't have followed me. It's not fair to risk your life for me."

"I promised your mother, Jason. You may be a man in many ways, but you're still a boy . . . my . . . my son . . ." he repeated the last two words with love.

Jason smiled.

"I told Joanna the next time I saw her we would talk with her parents."

"Then perhaps I may get to call you son in reality." Petros was overjoyed. He patted Jason's shoulder. "All right, what do we do now?"

Jason motioned him to be silent. There in the distance, a figure was running towards Aplotaria. The sun gleamed on his silken uniform . . . it was a Janissary.

"Joseph!" Jason whispered and dashed out before Petros could stop him.

"Come back," Petros noticed the three Turkish soldiers who appeared from behind. He shouted desperately, "Jason look out!"

Petros leaped from his hiding place and ran towards them, oblivious to his own danger. Jason ignored the warning and rushed onward to the approaching figure, waving his hands frantically. Youssef went for his pistol, then seeing it was Jason, raised his hand in greeting and hurried towards him. At that instant the Turkish soldiers reached Jason. Petros, close behind tried desperately to reach him. Youssef called out to the soldiers. But it was too late. In an instant, the sword had cut Jason down.

Youssef's command rang in the air. "Stop! Stop in the name of the Sultan!" An empty command . . . his cry came out choked as he looked at the sprawling figure on the ground.

The Turks froze. Petros lowered his dagger, stunned with grief. Youssef reached his brother and stood over him, the blood draining from his face. If only he had called out a moment sooner . . .

"Jason," he cried, kneeling down and touching his wound.

The blade had pierced Jason's belly. The blood seeped through his clothing and flowed in a small stream. Youssef knew that thrust, no man survived it. He looked at his brother now, frantic at his inability to help him. He touched Jason's forehead, took his head in his arms and stared, unable to speak. He wished he were in Jason's place.

The men stood silently by, amazed at this strange scene between Turk and Greek. They noticed the stark resemblance of the two boys and realized what it meant. There had been frequent cases of Janissaries finding their Greek families, but they seldom ended on so tragic a note. Although Janissaries never disavowed their Moslem faith or gave up their customs as Turks, they sometimes acknowledged their Greek families and returned to visit them. This would not happen here. The Turks stared, embarrassed.

Jason tried to talk but it was difficult. The pain was excruciating.

"Joseph . . ." he bit his lip and his pain ran through Youssef's body. Youssef cringed.

"Joseph . . . I wanted two things . . . to free Chios . . . and to find you." He tried to smile. "At . . . least . . . I got . . . my second wish."

Youssef looked at his brother with desperation, hopelessness. His heart seemed to turn over with pain and longing.

"I found your . . . mother . . ." he finally whispered, "she's safe."

"*Our* mother . . . Joseph . . . *our* mother . . ."

"*Our* mother . . ." Youssef repeated, his eyes staring blankly.

The noonday sun was warm. Its rays descended upon the small group, blunting the sharpness of the winds, caressing the men who stood despaired, in the middle of Aplotaria, the once busy thoroughfare of Chios. Jason saw only darkness now, and felt his breath slowly leave him.

"Joseph . . . there's a girl . . ." He winced with pain. "Jo . . . an . . . na . . . Go . . ." He did not complete the sentence.

Youssef looked at his brother in disbelief, tightened his arm around him, and fought the emotions that tore him inside. Tiny hammers pounded in his head and he felt sick . . . a feeling he had never felt before. Finally, he laid his brother's head on the ground, against the soil of Chios that Jason had loved, that Youssef had trampled. He rose slowly and stared down at the lifeless form.

"Jason . . . brother . . ." The words were dragged out in fury mixed with pain. He wanted to scream, to deny them. But his eyes could not leave Jason's body. A battle raged inside him. He gritted his teeth—pain twisted his gut and his mind clouded. He closed his eyes and opened them again. Jason still lay there. He stared at the body and steeled himself for what he was about to say, hoping Jason would understand and forgive.

"Jason . . . my brother . . . you are a Greek . . . you died a Greek." The softness in his voice changed to a harsh sound that fell cold and unrelenting around them. "But I am Youssef the Janissary, brother . . . I was raised a Turk . . . and I will die a Turk. Nothing can change that."

He looked to the sky and raised his arms to it.

"Praise Allah," he shouted, "may the gates of Paradise open wide for you . . . my brother . . . Jason."

Only the winds answered.

Suddenly, the stillness was broken by a distant cry.

"Lay down your arms! Put down your swords!"

The voice came clearer now. It was a Turkish messenger running towards them, waving his arms.

"The Sultan has ordered amnesty!" he shouted. "Lay down your arms! An end to the massacre!"

The men looked up. In the distance another figure appeared. It was Helena, running behind the messenger, praying the news would reach her sons in time.

The messenger approached. He saw the still body, the men around it, and realized his news came minutes too late. All eyes turned to Helena. She was no more than a hundred feet away when she stopped suddenly.

She knew . . . no one had to tell her. Her dark, penetrating eyes had embraced the scene from afar—the body on the ground, Petros kneeling beside it . . . and Youssef, standing there, staring silently. She tried to scream but nothing came out. Then she began walking slowly towards them, her head up, her eyes brimming. And swiftly, like rivers dammed up for eons, her tears came rushing out, flowing at last, unending. They streamed down her face as she walked to her sons.

The warm Aegean sun looked down upon them. And the winds blew mercilessly.

EPILOGUE

Chios . . . 1825

The narrow streets are wider now, my Jason. Almond trees bloom again and the winds sweep over the island as always. The stench of blood finally gave way to the scent of lemon blossoms, and Chios breathes again. Not free as you had hoped, my son, but cleansed of misery and despair. We picked up the threads of life—what life was left—and are building it again with renewed hope.

Once again the Turks have become our protectors, our friends. The yoke is there, but it is a loose one. Bechit Pasha is gone and we have a kindly, understanding Governor who leaves us to our own course . . . until one day others like you will rise again and make Chios free.

It is almost sunset now, Jason, and I stand on our hilltop near the chapel of Prophet Elias, where we spent many hours together—remember?—meditating, sharing unforgettable moments. You are everywhere my son, in the glow of the sky, the smell of the pines, the whisper of the cypresses. You are everywhere, my Jason, for you are the only one who is free.

The tears flowed easily now. She was no longer afraid to cry. Helena held her head up, feeling the winds, the fierce *meltemi* against her face. It was like a caress, the touch of a loved one. She looked down and saw three figures hurrying up the path. Suddenly a fourth appeared, a tiny one that broke away and ran ahead to Helena's opened arms. She raised the child up and held him tightly to her.

"Why are you crying, grandmother?" He patted her hair. "Mother and father are coming. See? And grandfather, too. Please don't cry."

"I'm crying because I'm happy darling . . . my darling Jason."

She said the name clearly, loudly. Once she had been afraid of the pain its sound would bring. But now that fear was gone.

"Jason! Jason!" She laughed and kissed the little boy through her tears.

The sun fell behind the hill. Helena and the child watched Joanna and Youssef approaching, his silken uniform shining in the dimming light. Petros was close behind. They were smiling. Time has erased their sorrow, she thought, but not mine. Never mine. She remembered the scales. Once again they had balanced—joy and despair, that strange coupling.

A flock of birds flew into the cypress trees. The winds calmed, and dusk fell.